AF596454

The Breedlow Legacy

This is a work of fiction. Names, characters, places, and incidents either are the product of the author's imagination or are used fictitiously, and any resemblance to actual persons, living or dead, business establishments, events, or locales is entirely coincidental.

ISBN: 9798368016818

Other Fiction by John M. McNamara

Iske Park in Quarantine

Renner's Reboot

Finbar Lovely at the Crossroads

Hunter's War

Failing Billy

Summers on the Nebraska Shore

The Unabridged Songwriter

Madonna

The Dreams of Teddy Schreck

Harmony House

A Final Reflection

For Robin

1.

That was a long time ago.

A refrain that ricochets within my skull like a Gregorian chant in a stone cathedral. Every rebound against those soaring walls transforms the intention. A reflection. An explanation. A dismissal. An excuse.

Despite an affirmation to avoid reminiscing about my past, I indulge, and that refrain, like an endless chorus, regardless of how often I repeat the words, seeking to neutralize so many decisions, doesn't defuse the accusations. It underlines them. Emphasizes them. But I made a career of evasion. Of deflection. Learning and teaching along the way that the easiest person to dupe is oneself, that the purest form of deception is self-deception.

My home rests on a bluff above the eastern shore of Lake Michigan; across that body of water lies Chicago, where I lived and worked for more than forty years. Sometimes on clear nights, ambient light from the city is visible in the distance. That's as close to the city as I care to be. The reasons for maintaining a distance are as varied as the interpretations of the refrain. *That was a long time ago.*

Standing at my bedroom window, an expanse of glass that spans the width of the house, I watch a black squirrel perched on the roof of the summer house at the edge of the bluff. It eyes the power lines spanning the gap between the two structures, reaching its front paws to gauge the reliability of the footing. In the city, its gray cousins scampered along power and cable lines, using them like highways, but this creature regards the wire with hesitancy. It rears onto its hind legs, raising its front paws as if debating. Then it pitches onto all four legs, jerks its furred tail, dashes to the edge of the summer house roof, and leaps onto an oak tree, scuttling up the trunk and into a high branch. It squats and squawks.

I squint, speculating about what caused the animal's behavior, when a woman enters my peripheral vision. My instinct is to step away from the window to avoid being seen, but I remain still. No one wanders onto my property, chosen for its isolation. Set back and not visible from Lake Shore Drive because of the trees and the curve of the driveway. The mailbox lists the house number. No name. Someone walking onto my property must have a purpose. An intention.

The woman walks to the crest of the bluff, pausing at the wooden steps leading to the beach and tucks a strand of hair behind her ear as she gazes over the water. Small waves roll against the shoreline, crumpling on the sand as though weary or bored. The sky is hazy but cloudless to the horizon. The two of us watch the same vista, the woman unaware she is included in my observation. She turns as though having heard my thought and stares directly up at me. Neither of us moves for a moment and then she steps away from the bluff toward the house. She wears jeans and a navy blue turtleneck beneath a gray canvas barn coat, the collar turned up. Late March in Michigan remains a cool month. I try to estimate her age, but I'm horrendous at such guessing. In her early forties? As she nears the rear of the house, I glance down from the second story and see traces of gray in the dark strands of shoulder-length hair. Early fifties, then. Why am I fixated on her age when her identity and purpose are more pressing?

I hesitate for a moment at the bottom of the stairs, narrowing my eyes, searching her face for any hint of familiarity, but dredge nothing from memory. She waves and smiles without exposing any teeth. The first floor of my house is an open living space, with the kitchen and dining area against the east wall, and the living space afforded the lake view by accordion doors that open onto the patio. I approach the door and ask what she wants.

She clutches the strap of her cloth shoulder bag and says, "You're Daniel Breedlow, aren't you?"

I sigh and nod, then shake my head. "What do you want?" I repeat.

Two years ago I published a novel whose main character, a cynical practitioner of public relations, marketed by my publisher as a "timely and biting expose of the disinformation machine infecting today's media." The puffery earned both detractors and devotees and staring at the woman on the other side of the glass, I wonder which camp she inhabits.

"If you're Daniel Breedlow, then I'm your niece," she says. "From your brother Aidan's first marriage. I'm Margaret. Maggie Breedlow."

She clasps her hands together, holding them in front of her in a patient gesture, and fixes a passive expression on her face, while I assume she studies mine for any reaction to her statement.

"My brother is dead," I say.

"I know. That's not why I'm here." She pauses and then asks if she can come inside. "I've been vaccinated and I have a mask." She retrieves a black mask from her coat pocket. It dangles from her fingers by one of the ear loops and I recognize it as a KN95, identical to those in the box on my kitchen island. "The year's most fashionable accessory, right?" she says, and chuckles.

"What are you doing here?" I ask.

"Okay, so we'll have this conversation through the door," she says and then pauses, tilting her head, making her antipathy with my hesitancy obvious. Her eyes are round and deep brown. All my siblings have blue eyes. I strain to remember my brother's first wife, but he married when I served in the Air Force during the Vietnam War and I cannot recall anything of the woman, with whom he had three children before divorcing. My mother told me he surrendered his parental rights in exchange for child support relief when the woman remarried. The new husband adopted the children. This woman must have retained Aidan's last name.

"We're not going to have a conversation," I say. "I don't want you here. You should leave."

She lowers her head and pauses. I imagine anger rising against the bluntness of my rejection, expect the customary pleadings: "It'll only take a minute." "I came such a long way." But when Maggie raises her chin, she says, "Grandma said you'd say that."

That my mother accurately predicted how I would react makes me wince at the betrayal. She and I have an understanding about my reluctance to communicate with my family. I talk with her on birthdays and anniversaries, occasionally with my sister, Laura. There's no communication between me and my remaining brother and other sister, both ardent Trump supporters. That extends to their children. They don't speak to me and I don't speak to them. On my mother's birthday years ago, she predicted that after her death, I'd cut off all contact with my remaining siblings. I didn't disagree with her.

"That's how you found me," I say.

"Grandma ratted you out, yeah." Maggie smiles.

"So she endorsed this," I say.

Maggie grins. "She said it was important that we meet."

"Important to whom?"

"Both of us, I think," Maggie says.

"No one in my family has any idea what's important to me," I say.

"I dreamed about this last night," she says. "A premonition of exactly how this conversation would unfold."

"If dreams were premonitions, I'd already be dead." I pause. "How did you convince me, in your dream, to talk to you."

"The solution wasn't in the dream," she says. "Grandma said to play up to your obsession: curiosity. Your need to know."

I stare at Maggie for a moment, then laugh and unlock the door, telling her to wait a moment. At the kitchen island, I remove a mask and fix the loops over my ears, tugging it to cover my nose, muscle memory learned during the pandemic, while I struggle to recall any contact I have ever had with this woman. Aidan married three times, and I never met any of his wives. Every crumb of information I received about him came through my mother, who remained tolerant, if not loyal, to him until his death. Prostate cancer, which she claimed could have been treated if he had seen a doctor. My sister, Laura, called me with the news, her voice tearful, and my first instinct was to comfort her for her loss, as I felt none at the news. My relationship with Aidan, soured since high school, relied on intermediaries like my mother to exist at all. Which is to say, we had no relationship. *That was a long time ago.*

The granite island top is cool beneath my hands, and I skim a palm across its surface. Maggie stands on the rug by the rear door, looking at me across the room. The dissonance of the situation wallops me, an uneasy moment of foggy consciousness, like floating away from myself for an instant to encompass the scene. A fleeting spin, momentary lightheadedness, a dizzying perspective, leaving me disoriented and untethered for a second.

I center the mask cup on my face and ask, "What do you want?" My voice is snippier than I intended.

Maggie unbuttons her coat and drapes it over the back of one of the black leather Barcelona chairs that flank the hearth on the north wall. "Should I take off my shoes?" she asks, pointing at my feet, clad in rag wool socks.

"Please," I say.

She kicks off one shoe, black Merrells, then the other, and flexes her toes in green socks emblazoned with red marijuana leaves. "The floor's warm," she says.

"Radiant floor heating," I say. "Throughout the house."

"It's amazing," Maggie says, glancing around the room. "Very minimal."

Neighbors call my home the "box." A two-story rectangle of concrete and steel. Glass spans the entire western face, offering unobstructed views of sunsets over the lake. I've photographed the wonder hundreds of times and have attempted to write a song that encompasses the fullness of the astonishment I feel as the sun sinks below the horizon. I strummed major seventh chords on my guitar, trying to capture the sense of tranquility the sunset instills, but the lyrics remained incomplete signifiers of what so far defies description.

I nod to Maggie, who seems satisfied with my response. "Let's get back to why you're here," I say, motioning for her to sit.

She presses her lips into a straight line, narrows her eyes. I recognize the expression from years of working with clients who could not decide how to begin their story, who hesitated before explaining why they sought the services of my public relations firm. Often the cause of the delay was embarrassment. A confession of a mistake or a flaw. They could not be rushed into their revelation, but I'm impatient with Maggie.

"It's going to sound a little broad, I'm afraid," she says. "But I want to know about my father."

I wag my head and chuckle. "I'm not the person to tell you."

"And also about you," she adds. "Grandma has told me some things, but they don't match what my mother says."

"I don't even remember your mother," I say, sitting on the sofa across from her. I extend my legs, cross them at the ankles, and fold my arms across my chest. This pose is defensive. A protective posture. By contrast, she sits upright in her chair, hands on her thighs.

"I know. She said she couldn't remember ever meeting you. But my father told her stories about you and most of them seem to have been lies. Bullshit he spewed to paint you in a pretty unfavorable light. He did it to make himself some kind of victim."

"That's funny, but mostly sad."

"I've pieced together a picture of a very troubled man," she says. "He was seventeen when I was born."

I remember speaking to my mother on the barracks telephone during Air Force language school in El Paso, hearing the news that Aidan had gotten married to his pregnant girlfriend. He dropped out of high school and found work as a construction laborer. The two of them lived with her parents until Maggie, was born. During my enlistment, my parents moved from St. Louis to Tucson, but Aidan and his wife stayed in Missouri, so when I visited family on leave in Arizona, he was absent, which I think each of us enjoyed. Our relationship was always contentious. Exacerbated in high school, where I excelled, he floundered, and teachers flung the contrast in his face.

"You're not asking me to crack open a nut," I say. "This is a giant onion with more layers than I want to unpeel."

"Oh, I know," she says.

"And just showing up here uninvited…"

"I understand," she says, holding up a hand, palm facing me. "But please hear me out."

I pause and shake my head. "I have no desire to satisfy your curiosity. That was a long time ago and I don't even know if you're who you say you are." But I know I'm lying about that last assertion. I can see Aidan's and my mother's chin in Maggie's face. The high forehead we all seemed to have inherited from my maternal grandfather's family. Casting doubt on her identity is an avoidance of telling her I am not interested in anything to do with my dead brother.

"I cut off contact with your father more than fifty years ago. I know it's hard to believe, but after that he rarely entered my thoughts. No one in my family does. I keep my distance and all I ask is that they do the same." I stand, to signal that we're finished, but Maggie remains seated.

"Grandma told me as much," she says. "And I know it may be a lot to ask, but…" She pauses. "His other children won't talk to us. To me or my sisters. They either act like we don't exist or that we're radioactive. My picture of him is incomplete."

"But I'm not the person to complete that puzzle. Don't you see that?" I lower myself to the edge of the sofa cushion and raise my hands in frustration.

"I'm not looking for an annotated biography," she says. "But within what little I know, you're the mystery. Before my mother died, she told stories about you and dad, your feud. She said he hated you, blamed you for everything that went wrong in his life."

"Losers need scapegoats," I say, then raise a hand before she speaks. "*Flawed* people need scapegoats. No one is a hundred percent anything. My mother said Aidan changed in the last years of his life. Became more responsible."

"And found Jesus," Maggie says, her sarcastic tone unmistakable. "A lay preacher in West Texas. Evangelical. Anti-gay. Anti-abortion. Anti-immigrant. Anti-Semitic. Anti-intellectual. If the cancer hadn't killed him, I'm sure he'd be anti-vaccine and that COVID would have. You can view his funeral on *YouTube*. It's three hours long. Prayers and songs and testaments to his goodness. Videotaped in the mega-church where he preached. My half-siblings sat in the front pews, guns in holsters strapped to their waists." She pauses. "Fucking Texas."

I wonder if Maggie believes what she's saying or, having been coached about my beliefs, is aligning herself with my sympathies to lower my defenses. Skepticism often marches in lockstep with curiosity. "Seems you already know more about him than I do."

"Not from the early days. See," she leans forward, gripping her knees, the tendons on the back of her hands stiffening. "There are gaps. From when he was married to my mother. I never pushed her until she was diagnosed, and then she didn't want to talk about him. So much of what I know is sketchy. Incomplete." Her voice grows more hurried as she speaks.

"Why's it so important to you?" I remember a young associate at the firm who joked she wanted a switch installed in her brain that would allow her to turn off emotions when dealing with troublesome clients. Maggie needs that switch.

"It's my family," she says. "I know we have differing views about that."

I nod, softening, I realize, toward her, my *niece*, a novel experience for me. My mother speaks about grandchildren, cousins, nephews, and nieces, and also about their children. There are more extensions of those connections than I know. Or care. Families were the first tribes. And tribes, as our current situation teaches us, are dangerous. Destructive.

"Not to sound egotistical, but did you read my book?"

Maggie nods.

"Then you know that I'm a cynical bastard who doesn't care about my family. What could you hope to glean from me?"

"Truth. That isn't varnished or tarnished," she says. "Something caused a rift between you and my father and I'm curious about it. I think it changed him into what he was when he was married to my mother."

"If you're looking for someone to blame, you're talking to the wrong person," I say. "I'm not interested in polishing a turd for you."

"That's not what I'm after." Maggie raises her hands and wipes her eyes with her fingers. I'm intentionally frustrating her.

"I don't want to rehash a part of my life I've…" I pause. "Forsaken." I dislike the biblical nature of the word, but it's appropriate. "Wait, though. That's not entirely fair. It's not a part of my life that I've forsaken, it's Aidan I've rejected. I wasted years dwelling on the animosity I felt toward him, but I reached a point where I moved on. I cut him out of my life. I understand you can't do that, but I have." I paused. "I can't help you."

"Can't is just won't with sugar on it," Maggie says.

"Jesus Christ! You sound like my mother."

"Actually, it's something Dad used to say."

"Well, he learned it from my mother, who learned it form *her* mother. Time to retire it."

"It irks you because it's true," Maggie says, smiling.

"Like dry ice on bare skin," I say, recalling a saying my former partner in the firm used to describe how the truth burned.

"What a horrifying image," she says. "Time to retire that?"

"Whatever," I say, wagging my head at the digression from my point: I don't want to discuss Maggie's father with her. *Maggie's father*. I realize how

I referenced Aidan in my thought. Not as my brother. How do I explain to her that frame of mind? That distinction in my regard of him.

"I wasn't intending for us to sit down now and have a long, prying conversation," she says. "Think of this as an overture."

"A very unwelcome overture," I say.

"Grandma said you indulged in intentional forgetting."

I haven't forgotten anything but I don't tell Maggie that. "She's wrong. I just don't practice intentional remembering. There's a difference of intention between the two."

"I'm well aware," Maggie says. "My father perfected it, too. With my sisters and me. He cut us off like diseased limbs."

Her voice betrays an undercurrent of bitterness, and I suddenly recognize how our distinct curiosities in Aidan intersect. She seeks the key to abandonment by her father from someone who abandoned him. For the first time since opening the door to Maggie, I feel sympathy for her quest. *Quest*, I reflect. More passionate than a mere search. A noble pursuit. This woman, my niece, seeks her Holy Grail. She's on a mission to investigate a void. Maggie's responding to a calling that cannot be unheard. The fervent pilgrim that too often morphs into a treacherous martyr.

"I'm not sure I can help you," I say, rising again.

"There's no one else," she says. Her eyes water at the edges. I know if I refuse her request, I'll receive a telephone call from my mother this evening, berating me, and while I've grown adept at rebuffing her criticism, I'm not eager for the conversation.

"Have you spoken with Laura?"

She nods.

This peculiar encounter with my niece has already disturbed my morning routines, has interrupted the rituals upon which I rely to provide structure to the endless stream of days with little dissimilarity. But the disruption of my rituals will be less costly than the price she asks of me.

"What makes you think my memories of your father are any less sketchy than your own?"

"Grandma thinks they are."

"You keep invoking my mother as though that's somehow going to change my mind."

Maggie chuckles, shaking her head. "She also said you'd say that." She pauses. "Does it irritate you that she knows you so well, considering how you try to keep such a distance between the two of you?"

Something my old partner used to say, that the child determines the man, echoes through my brain like the old refrain. My mother knew me as a child and now believes she knows me as a man.

"She must have told you what she thought I'd do," I say. "What did she predict?"

Maggie huffs a short breath. "She said you were a lost cause."

I mull her words. *I* was a lost cause. Not the approach or the request. No...*I* was the lost cause. Am I being manipulated? Handled? Guided toward Maggie's desired outcome? Such an ironic application of my own professional skills.

"Oh," I say. "I am a lost cause. Which makes your coming here all the more bizarre. And believe me, you've made this a very bizarre morning. If you didn't think you had any chance of getting me to cooperate, why are you here?"

"I disagree with Grandma," she said.

"That's it? That's all you have to say? You disagree? You don't know me. How could you make such a judgment?"

"Mom always said I had a hopeful nature," she says. "And since Dad was such a liar, a cheat, she eventually decided that she couldn't believe what he said about you."

"That's nice of her, but not relevant," I say.

"Maybe not to you. But truly relevant to me. Important to me."

The conversation threatens to slip into a loop from which neither of us will escape. It's time to weigh my inclination against Maggie's temptation and decide. But as I consider how I framed the moment, that what she offers me is tempting, it hits me: I've lost a measure of resolve. Inched toward acquiescing. My earlier obstinance seems like *a long time ago*.

"Where do you live?" I ask.

"Iowa City. I teach at the university."

"Psychology by any chance?"

She laughs, raising a hand to her mouth. "No. American history."

"I studied journalism and political science," I say. "After Watergate, I wanted to be the next Bob Woodward or Carl Bernstein."

"But you wound up in public relations, right?"

I nod. "If I agree to help you," I say, trying to steer her away from any immediate inquiry, "It'll be on my terms. Understand?"

"Of course. I'm on spring break right now and I'll return to Iowa tomorrow."

"Flying?"

"Driving. I hate flying."

I smile, amused by how after logging hundreds of hours as a Vietnamese linguist in the Air Force, intercepting enemy radio communications while orbiting in the Gulf of Tonkin or over Laos, I also shy away from flying. My avoidance is irrational, but I have thought when considering the odds of dying in a plane crash that probability is sneaking up on me. That I sidestepped the inevitability of a crash when I was younger and that continuing to fly would tease fate unnecessarily. Now with the pandemic, flying is out of the question.

"Are you staying in town?"

She shakes her head. "I didn't see the need. If I couldn't convince you in a short visit, I probably wasn't going to."

"Good instinct. But never underestimate the power of a dripping tap."

Maggie laughs. "So you'll help me?"

"I'll talk with you, but how helpful it'll be is out of my control."

"Thank you," she says. "All I ask is that you be honest with me."

"That's fair," I say. "But it'll be confidential, every word of it. Understood?"

She nods.

"I need to hear you say it."

"Understood," she says. "Do you want me to sign a nondisclosure agreement?" She smiles.

"I'll think about that," I say, returning her smile.

We both fall silent for a moment before she rises and steps forward, as though to hug me, then checks herself. "The pandemic," she says. "Sorry. But I'm so grateful."

I walk her to the front door, where she slips on her coat and shoes, turns, and smiles at me, shaking her head. "I truly didn't know what to expect. Meeting you. I see Dad's face in yours."

"We were Irish twins. Do you know that expression?"

She nods her head. "Close in age. What, eleven months apart?"

"Yeah. My father joked that he waited the bare minimum after I was born to start fucking my mother again." I pause and watch Maggie's brow furrow and mouth twist into a scowl. "That's the kind of crude family you come from," I say. "You're asking for honesty, so be prepared to get it."

2.

Moments after Maggie steers her silver Audi down the driveway, I stand at the kitchen counter, brewing a pot of green tea while biting into a banana, trying to reclaim my normality. We arranged to chat online until the end of the semester, when she'll return for in-person interviews, a procedure reminiscent of the promotions organized when my novel came out: author tours, media interviews, book signings and readings, including one at a bookshop in Iowa City. Had Maggie been in attendance? If so, why hadn't she come forward and introduced herself?

Gazing across the yard to the lake, a mug of tea warming my hands, I appraise the view. A grayscale version of a color photo. Everything overcast. No whisper yet on the tree limbs or in the garden beds of spring's greening. I begin my habit of assessing the aftermath of making impetuous judgments. Like a debriefing after an initial client meeting. I wonder when my mother will call, claiming credit for putting Maggie and me on this path. She yearns to remain relevant in my life; when I send signals that she isn't, she says my isolation is vanity, a sin of pride. But I've aged out of any sense of vanity.

My old partner, Grayson, never understood my disdain for family. We were opposites in that regard. His wife, Iris, and his two children comprised his world. My disentanglements baffled and amused him, but he prized detachment when I dealt with clients; I never emoted, and Grayson either ignored for convenience or dismissed from indifference how those instincts drove both situations. Joked that I was a one-sided coin. I preferred he regard my consistency as integrity.

The squirrel reappears on the summer house roof and I beam my thoughts toward it: I won't cushion Maggie from how I feel. I won't intentionally be mean or harmful, but I won't refrain from being factual, even if it hurts her feelings. The summer house remains the lone holdover from the original cottage on the property, an antiquated and unlikely embryo for the new house. I've repaired the screens and roof shingles, repainted the clapboards, and replaced the musty rattan furniture left by the previous owners. I say "I," but my handyman, George Van de Berg, does all the work. His father maintained the struture that stood on the lot for decades. George, continuing the family business, stood beside me, itemizing the additions to the original one-room structure from the 1920s, as the demolition crew collapsed the roof and crumpled the walls. I asked if he resented me for razing the old house but he insisted that maintaining it was becoming a frustrating task. That he looked forward to caring for the new building, especially since I planned to reside in it year-round, not rent it out to summer vacationers. George removes snow in winter, rakes leaves in fall, spreads mulch on the garden beds in spring, and mows the lawn in summer. An affable, part-time companion, who accommodated my precautions during the outbreak of the pandemic, masking, skipping our customary sit-downs during which he kept me current with all the goings-on among my neighbors; some still regard me as an outsider, an interloper, though others appreciate that I keep to myself. While he doesn't say he believes the virus is a hoax, he cares little about safeguards. Tells me he's vaccinated but I never ask for proof. That would violate our friendship.

Before the pandemic, George commented on my solitude. "You're lucky," he said. "To afford being alone." So many are alone now who didn't choose solitude.

If he were here right now, I'd tell him that when I saw Maggie, it crossed my mind in the moment she spoke my name outside the door that she might be a long lost daughter come in search of her father. Not too far from her actual purpose.

After I retired and moved here, I worried that my conversational skills would deteriorate from disuse, and days pass now when I only speak when I talk to myself. Or call out a thank you to the Instacart deliverywoman who deposits the plastic bags of groceries by the front door every few days. What passes for conversation are online chats. With my old partner, who lives in a Chicago suburb. With men with whom I served in the Air Force. With a select coterie of Twitter friends. Typing on a keyboard affords me the freedom to edit the words before I hit the Send button. It's the habit of a cautious man. A former PR professional who regulated his speech with exactitude that my peers frequently regarded as callous, although they valued my meticulousness. The nature of the relationship with many of my colleagues: hate-love. Despising what's good for you. Like making a child swallow awful-tasting medicine. I recall my mother trying to dispense cough syrup to Aidan when we were young, chasing him around the house, yelling at him to stand still. He sprinted for the back door, where my father enveloped him in a bear hug, and pried open his mouth for the spoonful of cherry-flavored syrup. "It's not a goddamned needle, you little shit," my father said. That statement encapsulated his approach to parenting. "Shut up and calm the fuck down. There's always something worse." Had Maggie had any contact with my father before he died? Hearing those conversations unfold would entertain me.

There's one trait the Breedlow men have in common: we're serial philanderers. My parents divorced because of infidelity. Aidan divorced because of infidelity, *twice,* as has our youngest brother, Sean. I've never divorced but only because I never married. I saved myself, and a woman or women, from the discomfort and shame of divorce. I would never have been faithful to a wife. An important epiphany in my life, one that led to the realization that God was a human invention meant to perpetuate power, was that I could have sex without first marrying the woman. My Catholic upbringing set up the two acts like dominoes, but Maureen Finnegan shattered the notion. In my father's Buick station wagon, when we were juniors at separate high schools, (Catholics understood the hazards of teaching hormonal teenaged girls and boys in the same classrooms), she instructed me in *female anatomy and tactile responses.* PR jargon for "how to find my clit." An excellent and experienced teacher, Maureen guided my fingers and reaped the benefits of her coaching, murmuring how much more enjoyable it was to have someone other than herself get her off. She repaid the favor with unhurried, almost lethargic, hand jobs that had me squirming on the Buick's back seat waiting to climax, growing addicted to the smile on her face when I came on her freckled breasts. My first orgasms that weren't self-induced. Fucking was off limits but I didn't care. I'd absorbed the lesson. Marriage was not a prerequisite to sex and, more importantly, girls craved sex as much as, or more than, boys, and the Church's directive of sex only for procreation was the religion's survival tactic: create more Catholics. I can't overestimate how shocking an epiphany it was for me. Little Danny Breedlow, an indoctrinated grade school altar boy, who under his mother's tutelage knelt in prayer beside his bed each night, professing unquestioned love for God and his son, Jesus Christ, who sacrificed his life for our sins, yet we all wound up born into sin anyway. Maureen topped the sundae of my misgivings with an amazing cherry, but as I encountered Catholicism's myriad inconsistencies and contradictions, I drifted a little farther from the faith each time my father tossed me the keys to the Buick and winked leeringly at me. Knowing how to find Maureen's clit also opened breathtaking doors for me in the future. That was a long time ago.

I sip my tea and begin the dissection of my encounter with Maggie, beginning with her smile. The right side of her mouth rose higher than the left in a lopsided grin. Inferring a satirical sense of humor, I imagine our conversations, pausing after each question about Aidan before answering. Carefully choosing words to convey the erosion of the bond we shared as brothers. A lesson akin to my father's, whose experience as the older of two brothers of a single mother shaded his view of family in a way I was only later to understand. He accepted the inescapable responsibility for his mother and brother. Cast himself at an immature age, (unwillingly, I later learned), as the head of the family, working after school to augment his mother's income, but battling internally against the imposed obligation. During World War II, at seventeen, he enlisted in the Navy to escape his family, serving on a destroyer, surviving when a kamikaze pilot hit it off the coast of Okinawa.

Maggie's eyes regarded me with intensity that troubles me now. Intelligence lurks behind her gaze and I'm revisited by a longstanding insecurity that someone smarter than myself is judging me.

Like most children in my school, I assumed everyone lived in intact families: a mom and dad with their children. My father's father, we 'd been told, had died before any of us were born, but when I was a teenager, Grandpa Breedlow returned from the dead. My father explained he'd deserted the family for another woman and that Grandma Breedlow had preferred the consolation given a widow to being branded and shamed as an abandoned woman who couldn't keep a husband. Since that revelation, I've always found victims boring. Prior to the man's first visit after reconciling with Grandma, my father gathered all of us and cautioned that Grandpa Breedlow might try to buy our affection with gifts. Grandma worked as a receptionist for a company that printed comic books, and whenever she visited, Aidan and I always loitered at the front door, impatient for her to distribute the coveted issues of our favorite superhero exploits, so my father's warning caused our imaginations to skyrocket, marveling about what kinds of presents Grandpa

Breedlow might shower on us. I wanted a chemistry set or a microscope. My father, however, overestimated Grandpa Breedlow's desire for our love; he appeared empty handed for his first visit.

I don't remember which superhero Aidan idolized, but I coveted the speed of the *Flash*. My mother linked my passion to being impatient about all things, especially growing up and leaving home. Growing older cured me of impatience, although I'm anxious to begin my conversations with Maggie.

What approach to take? Chronological? Beginning with my earliest memories of Aidan and myself before Laura was born? Recollections as incomplete as Maggie's of her father when she was young, I imagine. Memories forged by stories told by my parents more than my own recall. Revisionist history. My mother recited tales of the devoted attachment between me and Aidan as boys to reconstruct it between us as adults. A belief in miracles persists in Catholic families, I suppose, even a family as splintered as ours. My father, shaped by his father's abandonment, adopted the same reviled behavior by repeatedly cheating on my mother. "Sins of the father" my mother told me years later, as though my father lacked free will. Or Aidan. Or Sean. Or me. She sought allegiance with me when they divorced, not with Aidan, since his second divorce coincided with hers. On a late night call, she vented her bitterness against the Breedlow men. "None of you can stay married," she sobbed, and I refrained from telling her not to worry about me. I had sprung a step further: I cannot love. The lowest, most depressing point in her life and I felt no inclination to lessen her heartache, but I listened. Listening is a skill and underrated as a practice. A lazy man's method for mollifying aggrieved people. Letting them stream their grievances until emotional exhaustion provides a temporary antidote to their frustration. Eruption of words as catharsis. Interrupting with questions that reassure the speaker you're paying heed to what they've said. In the case of listening to my mother, it gained me credit for supporting her without having to provide actual comfort or a solution.

Maggie may be more interested in what provoked the rift between Aidan and me. The short answer is that he tired of living in my shadow and strove to differentiate himself from me, regardless of the consequences of being my opposite. Though eleven months apart in age, we were two years apart in school because of the juxtaposition of our birthdays, and he resented that difference. I achieved the honors class in school; he earned poor grades with pride in a lower section. I loved reading books; he mocked reading as a waste of time. I played wide receiver on the high school football team; he shunned sports. These visible differences swam above dozens of less noticeable divisions between us. Until I left for the University of Missouri, we shared a bedroom and inevitable instances of confrontation angered my father. When I enlisted in the Air Force after my freshman year, (freed from the Catholic parental yoke, I partied irresponsibly and earned low grades in Columbia, making me vulnerable to the draft), he scoffed, and threatened to join the Marines. An insincere threat. Follow-through was not his strength.

Pinpointing an incident that provoked our schism is problematic. I honestly can't remember a specific event. I long ago accepted the separation as an evolution, not a sudden rupture, at least on my part. I can't remember Aidan waking one morning, gazing at me in the upper bunk bed, and concluding he hated me, and although the straw that broke his camel's back may have existed, searching for that straw may frustrate Maggie more than not knowing what it was.

Was agreeing to help her a mistake? Will I find myself in the position of a client? Seeking assistance in remedying an error, when instead I should have sought counsel before leaping to a decision?

Lawyers should never represent themselves. Doctors should never treat themselves.

Do people only ignore proverbs that arise from common sense?

As predicted, the telephone rings and I see MOM on the screen.

"Mom," I say, depressing the green Answer button. "Don't gloat or I'll hang up."

"I'm not going to gloat," she says; her voice retains the raspy hoarseness of a lifelong smoker, although she quit twenty years ago and the assisted care facility where she now lives forbids it. It's difficult to remember when she didn't sound like her voice had to scratch its way out of her throat. "I wanted to thank you for speaking with Margaret."

"You're welcome since this is all your doing. And please don't waste my time trying to deny it."

My mother inhales audibly and I wait for a caustic reply. She does not manage criticism with grace. Has said that she has earned the luxury to be surly if she chooses. A reward for longevity. "Why would I deny it?" she asks. "I want to help that girl. She's my granddaughter and she has a right to know about her father."

"Then you talk to her, Mom. I don't know what I can add." My temper flares more than I expected and it's evident in the tone of my voice.

"I have spoken with her. We talk all the time, for your information. More than I talk with you."

I wince at the longstanding barb.

She continues. "You could have some sympathy for her situation, Daniel. Her father rejected her mother, her sisters, and her. Allowed Lisa's new husband to adopt them because he didn't want to have to pay child support any more. Traded his responsibilities for debt relief. That's how she sees it. She's never known him, really."

"And now you want me to convince her how lucky she is?"

"Stop being difficult!"

"How are you feeling?" I ask, a question I hope diverts her attention. Even she jokes that the consistent fallback topics of conversation in her facility are health and food. Guaranteed to elicit complaints.

"I'm fine," she says. "And don't change the subject. Margaret is both family and an adoptee who's searching for information about her family. I don't envy her that burden."

My mother flips the lesson of listening on its head for me. I relied on it to nudge others into realizations about themselves through their recitations, but she's made me, the listener, grasp an aspect of Maggie's entreaty I overlooked: a duality of identity that certainly nagged at her during and after her childhood. How old was she when Aidan walked out and then when he severed his financial obligations? The double rejection by Aidan surely damaged her in ways that even her step-father's love couldn't completely repair. The best case scenario now is that those wounds have untwisted into simple curiosity.

"I understand," I say. My mug is cool. "Gotta go, Mom," I say.

"Sure," she says, in a tone that makes me know she feels dismissed, acknowledging that I control the frequency and duration of our contact. "Love you," she adds.

"Me, too."

She used to end every conversation asking when I was going to visit but doesn't anymore.

As I refill my mug, my mind glides into the familiar pattern following every call with my mother. Low-grade anger directed both at her and me. Self-anger that a frisson of guilt lingers about cutting off my family, and anger at my mother because I suspect she made me this way.

The mantle of discipline fell to my mother. My father was the hammer with which we were threatened, his hand or his belt, if any of us dared disobey her. As the first tower of authority in my life, she captured my first resentment. Others joined the queue, (the Catholic Church, the Air Force), but my mother started it all. All indignation flows from her. Is that how Maggie feels about Aidan?

I carry my mug upstairs to my study and boot my desktop. The log-in image of a sunset over the lake appears. The gray water reflecting stacked, puffy clouds washed pumpkin orange and amber, a scarlet slash defining the horizon, purplish sky above the leafy treetops. I took several photos that evening, on the patio, the bluff, and on the beach. I prefer this image, the trees on either side of my property framing the sunset.

Following a ritual, I first check email, scanning both the Inbox and Spam folders, amazed at how swiftly ads for items similar to what I purchase through Instacart or Amazon appear, as though I might buy a dozen beard trimmers, air purifiers, or cordless vacuums. I catch Maggie's name in the Sender column and click it open. From her iPhone, a short message, thanking me and suggesting we chat online when she returns to Iowa City. Asks if there is a time more convenient than any other. I admire her efficiency, her prompt follow-through and mark the message as Read but delay answering, not wishing to suggest that she's my only priority, although it makes me appear petty, that hostility at her intrusion persists. I will control this back-and-forth. The price Maggie will pay for disruption.

Happenstances rooted in improbability, hypocrisy, or arrogance intrigue me. Fulcrum moments Grayson called them, outcomes that influenced the pursuit of balance. Of equilibrium or symmetry. He preached give-and-take like an algebraic equation: subtract from one side only if one added to the other. What are Maggie's needs and desires and what will I add and subtract from them? Convincing clients that solutions were not always binary comprised an important aspect of our practice; nothing about dealing with Maggie can be black and white.

Enough questioning. I scan my news feeds, glossing over headlines, distracted by the morning's events. Mixed economic news. Political divisiveness. A third of the country poised for civil war in service of a grifting demi-god with neither morals nor ideological principles beyond making a profit. So much sameness in *news*. I'm not bored as much as leadened by the morning's events. Once, in trying to explain to Grayson my lack of a relationship with my family, I attempted to make him understand that neither my parents nor my siblings occupied any of my day-to-day thoughts, a notion alien to him. His wife Iris, his son Kevin and daughter Carrie, never strayed from his consciousness for long. When we related stories of younger days, I told raucous tales from my military service or the more successful, second round at college. Grayson ignored his own tempestuous student history, describing instead children's first words and steps, birthday parties, school plays, summer vacations at their cabin in Wisconsin. The conspicuous contrast sparked humor between us. When speculating about switching lives, he admitted we'd each revolt against the other's existence.

I should reply to Maggie with a story about Aidan. Something to whet her appetite. But which one? I neglected to tell her that I'd already viewed the YouTube video of his funeral. Laura sent me the link. The church's minister emceed the ceremony, introducing speakers, announcing the choir's hymns, praising God at every interval. One of Aidan's sons from his second marriage delivered the longest eulogy and at the conclusion, invited those gathered in the pews to rise and approach microphones located in the church aisles to add their own reminiscences of my brother. I huffed my revulsion at that moment, disgusted at how the spectacle shriveled into a low rent talk show. Maggie was correct: Aidan's last crop of children sat in the front pew, holstered pistols visible on their waists when they rose to chime "Amen" after each testimonial. One of the two daughters from that final marriage declared to the congregation that one of the most emotional moments in her life was when Aidan gifted her the Glock she proudly wore wherever she went. A loud pompous "Praise Jesus" underscored her self-righteous arrogance, embraced by the mob with applause and cheers of "Amen!" I understand Maggie's need to discover something unrelated to the Aidan portrayed in that video. I'm simply not sure I can provide a portrait that doesn't presage what he became: my deliberate opposite, although my mother insists I overestimate how much Aidan considered me in establishing his identity. Perhaps the belief he performed as my opposite is integral to *my* needs.

What Maggie needs to realize before we talk about her father: the absence of a relationship with Aidan after high school had no effect on my life. Escaping him was a byproduct, not the purpose, of escaping my parents. Aidan was an annoyance within the greater turbulence I faced with my mother and father, during a time of political, social, and generational upheaval. In 1960, my father supported and voted for Nixon. I advocated for Kennedy at every opportunity. My mother failed as a mediator between us. The Kennedy assassination in my freshman year of high school cemented the division between us. My father only begrudgingly allowed us to watch The Beatles on the Ed Sullivan Show and regularly monitored my sideburns to insure they didn't creep below my ears. His intransigence encouraged me to exacerbate my diminutive rebellion until we achieved a Lilliputian version of our own Cold War: sullen avoidance of one another. Mine was a waiting game. High school graduation and a getaway to college. I worked summers and banked my earnings, took out a student loan, and boarded a Greyhound from St. Louis rather than ask my parents to drive me to Columbia. I carried a portable typewriter and one suitcase and the elation I felt on that bus ride convinced me I would never again live at home. As the current meme goes: "Sure, sex is great, but have you ever…claimed a window seat on a Greyhound bus knowing you're leaving home and will never live there again?" In the Air Force, I experimented with pot, LSD, uppers and downers, psilocybin, hash, and opium, but I never approximated the exact euphoria of spirit of that bus ride. Like Maureen Finnegan's hand jobs, the first time remains special. But that was a long time ago.

I'm struck by how yesterday, having a niece was an abstract. But now Maggie is a real person with a life that touches mine, and I wonder what, aside from my mother's meddling, brought her to me. Fate or destiny? I find such concepts wasteful exercises, but when younger believed my fortunes lay apart from my family. Our values should evolve as we mature. Aidan's certainly changed, veering from mine with what I assumed was intent. Determined to remain my opposite. My mother, the conduit, relayed news of us to one another. My father seemed not to care. I recall one of the only meaningful conversations my father and I had, during a visit to Tucson on leave before being stationed in Thailand. We contrasted the profound differences in the realities of our individual experiences on Okinawa, twenty-five years apart. He and his crewmates who survived the sinking of their ship, the USS Bush, transferred to other vessels, and continued fighting. He described floating in a lifejacket off the coast of the main island, as kamikazes relentlessly attacked the fleet. Hundreds of ships damaged. Twelve destroyers sunk. The stench, he recalled, of the oil slick that clung to everything in the water. Screams and moaning of the wounded. After the infantry secured the island, he visited friends in a hospital in Naha. I told him I rarely ventured beyond Koza, the town outside Kadena Air Base, where I enjoyed the carnal and musical diversions available on both Gate Two and BC Streets, frequenting bars, massage parlors, and strip clubs. My father complained he'd never gotten laid on Okinawa and I reminisced about the lessons in his Buick with Maureen. Sex during my time in the Air Force was transactional. Cash business and none of the providers cared about their own pleasure. The quicker the customer came, the more lucrative an evening's earnings. Some of my friends found girlfriends, rented apartments in town, but theirs was simply a longer-term transaction. The women knew the relationship would end when the man's tour ended and they'd begin searching for a new companion.

"Lot of men died on that island," my father said. "If Truman hadn't dropped the bombs, a lot more would have died in Japan." A lifelong Republican, my father retained a soft spot for President Harry Truman, certain the man had saved the lives of hundreds of thousands, if not a million GIs.

What bearing does this have on Aidan? Maggie better prepare for these digressions. Tugging on the tendrils of memory inflames surprising departures from purpose.

3.

In a gas station west of Michigan City, Indiana, Maggie checks for a reply from her uncle. It's brief. He prefers afternoons for their conversations. Email exchanges are fine, as are online chats or FaceTiming. Did she expect more than a terse reply? Counts herself fortunate that he agreed to speak with her. Grandma Breedlow doubted he would cooperate. Reasoned that since he spurned interaction with immediate family, Maggie would never convince him to collaborate with her, that she lacked the capital to resort to extortion, but Grandma's advice to entice Daniel's curiosity, his obsession with *knowing*, paid off, even though she was certain he saw through the gambit, assuming he relented as a reward for the effort. A tip of his hat for the doggedness driving from Iowa to Michigan demonstrated. Grandma Breedlow's idea. "He won't even answer the phone if you call," she'd said. "Deal with him in person. Let him see you." She'd been right.

When Maggie asked what to expect of her uncle, her grandmother deflected. "I don't want to influence you ahead of time," she said. "I'll just say that your father and your uncle remained brothers in many ways."

"What does that mean, Grandma?"

"We all know apples don't fall far, Margaret," the woman said, "but overlook that they're apples from the same tree."

Maggie appreciates that her grandmother refrained from prejudicing her conception of Daniel but providing expectations of what she might encounter would have been helpful. When she walked around the side of her uncle's house, the gray concrete box, and paused on the bluff, she gasped beholding the splendor of the lake vista, even on such an overcast day. Turning toward the house she imagined living there, the model retreat for an introverted academic. Then she spotted him in the upstairs window. Black sweatpants and gray t-shirt. An unruly beard. Close-cropped hair. Arms at his sides, staring at her, unsmiling. Obviously antagonistic toward uninvited visitors. She steeled herself and approached the house, admiring the design: a two-story frontage of glass, taking advantage of the view. Striding on the matted grass, she imagined the lake in changing seasons. Dreamed of gazing out upon a squall. No such vision existed in Iowa City.

When he paused at the base of the metal stairs, she waved and smiled, then glanced quickly around the room. Spacious, high-ceilinged, and minimal, as though he'd pared down every aspect of his life to necessities and nothing more. But there was artwork on the walls: watercolors and Asian-themed woodblock prints punctuating the monochromatic space with washes of muted color; huge, framed photographs of a city neighborhood and of the lake view. On the mantle above the fireplace a thick log of bleached driftwood, adorned with carved symbols, like glyphs or runes. Maggie absorbed this in the brief time it took for her uncle to approach the door to the patio.

Their conversation proceeded as she expected. Initial resistance. A softening of his unfriendliness. His acquiescence startled her. Grandma Breedlow thought she'd fail. "He dislikes that I stay in contact and tell him about the family," she said. "He'll guess that I told you where to find him and it'll be a strike against you. He's a master at holding a grudge."

She had prepared herself for failure and celebrated victory in the car once she turned from Daniel's driveway onto Lake Shore Drive. A mile down the road, she pulled over and called Grandma Breedlow to tell her the news.

"Well, color me stupid," the woman said. "Good for you, Margaret."

On the route south to Holland, the tree limbs arched over the roadway and Maggie envisioned them in full leaf, a shadowy tunnel looming over the blacktop. She resisted the temptation to stop at the outlet mall and glanced at Google Maps on her phone, noting the drive time to Iowa City. Five and a half hours. More than enough time to settle on the tactics for a future interrogation of her uncle. Unlike her grandmother or her Aunt Laura, he presented the thorniest problem. They witnessed the enmity between the brothers; they weren't the principals and it tainted their reliability as sources. She resolved to address this conundrum with an historian's discipline.

She sends Daniel a thumbs-up emoji in response to his email, following his lead to keep communication brief, for now. Climbing the ramp to I-196, she dismisses the hunger she feels and wonders what her uncle did when she left. What is his daily routine living alone in that boxy house? His novel was well reviewed and she wonders if he's writing another, a sequel. Does he sit before a keyboard each day, logging a quota of words before allowing himself a respite, as she had when drafting her dissertation? Such different forms of writing. She taps the Notes app, activates the microphone function, and dictates into the device. "What's the earliest he remembers the two of them drifting apart? Was it a sudden realization or did he watch it happening over time?" She pauses. "Did it bother him or did he welcome the separation?"

She closes the app, places both hands on the steering wheel, and reflects that her inquiries can't seem overly focused on Daniel, instead of her father. Grandma says the history of one links to that of the other, but Maggie withholds judgment for the moment. It's too early in the process to evaluate the extent of the linkage. She needs more information, more evidence to support any conclusion, and imagines Samuel, her partner, chuckling at her thought.

A chortling he unleashes when she descends into the vernacular of inquiry. It's flirtatious and no longer scratches her self-consciousness and insecurity because she knows it stems from affection. Understands his intention. Samuel is a kind, supportive man, fond of weekend lounging with her to watch BBC mysteries or South Korean horror films, a genre confession at which she laughed after they'd been seeing one another for several weeks. He admitted delaying the revelation until he'd established a beachhead in their relationship.

"Like an invasion?" she said.

He hesitated and then nodded. "Just like that," he said, releasing the chortle he now reserves for mocking her vernacular. "Love is war."

She nodded her agreement, the statement evoking past disappointments and the reprieve from them her hiring at the university represented. Change the scenery and you'll change your life, she mused. Perhaps. But she also accepted that she could never change her nature, regardless of how much she wanted to muzzle it.

She tells her phone to call Samuel. He answers on the second ring.

"How'd it go?" he asks.

Maggie smiles at the sound of his voice. "Better than I expected. He agreed to talk with me."

"Congratulations, Mags," Samuel says, using the nickname she allows him and no one else to use. To her sisters, she's always been Maggie, although Jessie once called her Maggot during a childhood argument, and she and Hailey, her other sister, tease her with "OK, Maggot" during family gatherings when Maggie becomes bossy. "I may be a maggot," she responds, "but I'm the chief maggot, so back off!" Their sisterly bond weathers this mild thrumming; like Samuel's chortling, it emerges from love.

"Are you still in Michigan?"

"No," she says, "Indiana. Coming home. He agreed to talk by phone or chat online. Then I'll come back at the end of the semester and spend some time with him."

"Sounds like it went much better than you hoped," Samuel says. "What's he like?"

"Hmm, tall. Six foot one. Slim. Short gray hair and bushy beard, to hide the weak chin he inherited from his mother. Has her analytical blue eyes. His face remained unexpressive. He's guarded about revealing anything when he speaks."

"Sounds a lot like someone I know," Samuel says. Maggie hears traffic noises in the background.

"Where are you?" she asks.

"Walking to work."

They met when she requested access to the rare documents section of the library for a research project. Samuel, a senior reference librarian, guided her to the basement room that housed those collections. At subsequent visits, he escorted her, remaining to chat. She found his transparent lingering endearing and during the fourth instance of forced small talk, asked if he'd like to join her for coffee when she finished her work. He accepted with relief that caused them both to laugh. They uncovered compatibility in many shared beliefs, foremost that meeting at a point in both their lives when they accepted the absence of any desire for children as serendipitous. Neither had been married, joked they'd been too nerdy to attract a significant other, and professed awkward inexperience with the other sex. Samuel told her he lost his virginity in graduate school when he was twenty-three. Maggie countered that she lost hers at twenty-five, a one-night stand during a conference in Seattle with a colleague from USC, with whom she never again had any contact. Seven weeks after she returned to work, with her period overdue, she bought a pregnancy test at Walgreens, sat on the store's toilet seat, and sighed when it indicated a positive result. She scheduled an abortion and never told her sisters, for fear her Catholic mother would disown her. Maggie maintained the secret well after her mother died.

She and Samuel made these disclosures, some whispered, while lying in bed the third time they slept together, each trusting they'd endorsed an unspoken agreement, that their relationship might endure.

"I should be home before you," Maggie says. "I'll drive straight through."

"Don't push yourself," Samuel says. "Pull over if you get tired."

"Actually, Sweetie, I feel energized."

"New project," Samuel says. "It's how you get. Optimistic and eager."

He knows me well, she thinks. "I've already started jotting down what to discuss with him. I don't know how patient he'll be. How much time he'll give me."

"Will you ease into the tough subjects or spring them on him?"

Her uncle impresses Maggie as a person who appreciates directness but wonders whether a more graduated approach would be more effective. "Still undecided," she says. "I'll prep for both and decide as we go along."

"Does he remind you of your father?"

The two discussed this before she left for Michigan, whether meeting Daniel would spawn memories of her father, and if so, whether they would be reliable or corrupted by her mother's chronic histrionics about the man. Later in her life, Maggie's mother gifted her daughters with silence about their father.

"He resembles the child in the old photos of the two of them Grandma Breedlow gave me," she says, "But they were incredibly young then. In the recent ones, they don't much look like one another." She considers the photo of her father his final wife sent Grandma: wearing a red western shirt over a bulbous belly, a black bolo tie with a silver and turquoise slide, a gray goatee and mustache, hair slicked back from his high forehead, deep set eyes she felt looked piggish in his face. Projection, she thought when she viewed the image on her iPad, conditioned as she had been all her life to despise the man.

"It's a tossup if people seeing them side-by-side would think they were brothers."

"They spent a lifetime trying to be different from one another," Samuel says. "Can dissimilar behavior manifest itself in appearance?"

"I don't think Daniel cared enough about my father to look different from him," Maggie says, checking the left lane in her side mirror, preparing to pass a semi. The thrill of getting her uncle to agree to speak with her makes her buoyant; she suppresses an urge to accelerate the Audi far beyond the legal limit. "I see more of Grandma in my father's face. My uncle looks more like his father."

Years ago, after Maggie reached out to her grandmother, UPS delivered a package, a shoe box of photographs. The enclosed note explained that Grandma had copied them from the Breedlow family album. By contrast, her mother destroyed every photo of Maggie's father. Portrayals of her and her sisters' childhood pictured her mother but not her father. Sometimes she scissored him out of photos, creating oddly-shaped prints, some with his face excised from the photo, which exemplified their family disarray more accurately than her mother intended. Other times she burned a photo in the kitchen sink, the prickle of smoke lingering for hours, but she never divulged a rationale for which option she chose. Maggie's anxiety during those years manifested as a performance of aloofness and composure, but she had not anticipated some men finding mysteriousness attractive. In her teen years, she regarded boys with reticence, her mother's warnings twittering in her brain. "Don't trust men," an admonition alternating between vocal and subtle expressions. When her mother drank too much wine, the woman who fell pregnant too early in life emerged, on occasion aiming an accusatory finger at Maggie, railing about what the girl had cost her. Other times, her mother insisted her children were precious gifts from a loving God that she cherished above all things in her life, but her daughters shouldn't repeat her mistake of reckless sex and premature motherhood.

By the time Aidan signed away his rights, the muddle of her mother's entrenched mindset and Catholic scare tactics weighed on Maggie, an impending punishment. Even after her mother married Scott, the vein of distrusting men throbbed in Maggie's subconsciousness. On dates in high school, when a boy tried to unbutton her blouse or snake a hand up her skirt, she recoiled with unconcealed loathing. As the boys recounted these incidents to one another, Maggie gained a bitchy, prudish reputation, classmates at her all-girl school badgered her openly, and invitations for dates dried up. She received no offers to attend the senior prom and deemed it a melancholy reprieve. In college, she concentrated on scholarship, masturbating when desire distracted her from classwork. The pattern she established, cycling through academic pursuit and sexual self-release, persisted through graduate school. She considered abstention from a relationship a benefit to her studies, but each time she sought relief with her fingers, she fantasized about a man. No one specific. An everyman who'd go down on her, bracing her knees apart, reaching up to cup her breasts, massaging her asshole with a wet finger. Her fingers became a serpent's tongue, grazing her clit, and when she came, tensing the muscles in her legs, she envisioned this everyman enveloping her vulva with his mouth until she screamed through clenched teeth. She relied on this fantasy for so long that she feared she'd never seek out a real lover. She dated fellow students in graduate school, but they intuited her platonic inclinations early in the relationship, and none bothered to explore if those preconditions arose from stringent morality or fearful uncertainty. The encounter with her USC colleague was an unpremeditated submission to curiosity, an experiment in comparing the enchantment of her fantasy with the potential satisfaction of reality. The man, older and married, was attentive, but not the everyman of Maggie's imagination, and although he failed to equal her ideal, Maggie understood what her masturbatory fantasies lacked: tactility. The afternoon of her abortion procedure, while resting on her sofa, wincing at the mild cramping, she hovered above depression, admonishing her fabrication of the everyman ideal, recognizing it as an obstruction to intimacy. She slept with other men, disappointing episodes, and reverted to self-pleasuring fantasies. Until she met Samuel, it never occurred to her that the intimacy of sharing her fantasies with a man might inflame both their passions. The first time they made love, he lay beside her and asked what she liked; the guilelessness of the question emboldened her, so with a hand on the back of his head, she guided him, grasping his hair, coaching him in how to flick his tongue across her clit, murmuring approval when he settled into an impassioned rhythm, and instead of everyman's face, when Maggie closed her eyes, she envisioned Samuel's pale gray eyes and walrus mustache. Her orgasm shuddered along her spine and she pushed against Samuel's head as the pleasure approached pain, but he persisted until she wrenched, twisting her body away from him, coiling into a fetal curl.

"Holy shit," she hissed into the bedsheet clutched in her fist, shivering as Samuel slid along the mattress and spooned her. She gripped his arm and wrapped it around her. "We are definitely going to do that again," she said. They laughed and his breath on her neck triggered another full body shudder.

Months later, on the anniversary of that occasion, they mused about how each's inexperience, rather than inhibit lovemaking, encouraged sexual experimentation, and they shattered boundaries like a pair of outlaws. Making up for lost time like horny teenagers, they agreed, at a stage in their lives when most would be swapping the boredom of long term attraction for tenderness. "We'll skip that step," Samuel said, "and die before we get bored." Her relationship with Samuel, occurring when it has, parallels her mother's second marriage to Scott. An attraction between two people who discovered their entrenched habits and routines were compatible with one another's.

"I won't be late," Samuel says, jolting Maggie back to their conversation. She lurches back and forth between the Audi's mirrors, momentarily frightened by how outside of herself she feels at the moment, with no memory of passing the semi.

"I'll open a bottle of wine," Maggie says.

"You've earned it," Samuel says. "Love you."

"You, too. I mean *me*, too," Maggie says, giggling as the connection ends.

An hour later, she approaches the left fork onto I-80, glancing at the traffic turning onto I-294 north to Chicago, where the hazy, indistinct silhouettes of the city's skyscrapers are visible. Daniel lived there for decades and she flirts with visiting his old neighborhood, driving by his former home and the building that still houses the firm bearing his and his partner's names. But she takes the fork, impatient to return home, equating her arrival at their Victorian house with the beginning of the process, like typing the title and first words of a paper.

Another question occurs to her, one she will not ask Daniel but which he might ask her: why are you doing this now? A necessary question in any historical investigation: what factors affected the timing of an event? Maggie squandered an opportunity in the interval between her mother's and her father's deaths. For years she refrained from contacting her father, out of consideration for how it would have wounded her mother. After her death, when Maggie and her sisters sorted through her belongings, they discovered legal documents authorizing their adoption, the relinquishment of their father's parental rights and child support obligations, and a letter to their mother expressing his desire for none of them ever to contact him again. Hailey, the youngest, wept reading the letter, wondering aloud why their mother kept it, hiding it for so many years, and then crumpled against Jessie when she draped a comforting arm across the woman's shoulders. Maggie felt in the moment a tremor of suppressed hatred toward the man for the resurrected pain he inflicted on their family. Not the first time she speculated about the disgraceful character of a parent who could abandon a child, although she had developed a scabby crust that depersonalized their father's history, to regard it with detachment, not involvement.

Her mother's death opened a window to exploring her father's motivations. To connecting with him. She wondered if time impacted him as it had her: had the years dulled the barbs of examining his decision to abandon them? Would he discuss it with her? Why did she want, or *need*, to understand his decision? Did he regret it? Would he do anything differently if given the opportunity? She'd listen to revisionist history if given the chance to speak with him, certain of her ability to sift through lies and recognize the truth. But she hesitated. Dallied. Consumed time debating far too long with herself about whether and how to contact him without provoking antagonization. Then her father died, shuttering that window, and she resolved not to repeat the mistake with Daniel. Lesson learned.

Grandma Breedlow immediately sympathized when Maggie said she wanted to speak with Daniel, would she pave the way for Maggie to contact him? Grandma advised the cold call. An unannounced visit. "Ambush him," she said. "Hanging up on someone is easier than closing a door in her face."

Her grandmother grew mirthful as they conspired and Maggie understood the woman hoped her son, when confronted by his niece, might reconsider the embargo of his family. Farfetched. Grandma judged her chances of success as "slim to none." But it gave Maggie insight into how her uncle's exclusion of family pained his mother. Cooperating with Maggie provided Grandma Breedlow with a piggybacking incentive, and the awareness of being used didn't offend her, rather, the mutual benefits of her grandmother's intention, those potentially advantageous byproducts, intrigued her. The lost opportunities with her parents engendered Maggie's empathy for her grandmother's anxiety about reconciling with her son.

It is a reconciliation she seeks, Maggie senses. Something in the Breedlow history provoked Daniel's uncoupling not only from his brother, but from the entirety of his family, and the pretext for the schism arouses Maggie's curiosity. She doubts her uncle's rejection of family connections is as clean-cut as Grandma asserts. Not a result merely of extreme sibling rivalry. She knows from experience there is always more to the story than first appears. Another conflict or disagreement, perhaps a trauma, caused Daniel's renunciation, and she revisits the assumption that Grandma Breedlow, Aunt Laura, and her other aunt and uncle were only spectators to the combat between brothers. She resigns to unearth and expose that primary issue.

The muted droning of her tires on the concrete roadway calms her. The suburbs fall away and she passes through swaths of farmland on either side of the flat interstate. Red barns amid plowed acres. Tall silver silos. A landscape so similar to that surrounding Iowa City, it taunts her, makes her feel she could be home in minutes, not hours, and she again resists the temptation to depress the accelerator. Whenever she and Samuel return from St. Louis after visiting her sisters, she tenses as they near Iowa City, wanting to speed the final miles, to reach home as swiftly as possible. She wonders, when she feels that urge, if homing pigeons fly faster the closer they near their coop. Her home with Samuel is special. It provides a reassuring sense of belonging. Nothing like the displacement she felt in childhood, in college, or in the years after graduate school. When she arrived in Iowa City for her initial round of interviews for the tenure-track position, the city's scale seemed tailored to her moods. The unthreatening Iowa River, not as brown or formidable as the Mississippi, meandered through the college town. Iowa City seemed the fulfillment of her aspiration for an idyllic home and she strove to control her excitement during the interviews. When the chairperson called her with the selection news, she barely restrained her joyfulness. A notion akin to inevitability overcame her. As though she had found her place, where time, purpose, and location intersected in serendipity. Then she met Samuel, snapping any tendril of lingering doubt about the providence of her fortunate happenstance. He finds it fascinating when she dissects the timing of their relationship, picking through the influences about men engrained by her mother that Maggie had to outgrow or discard before she was primed to meet Samuel. A year either side of her life's timeline and she might have rejected him as she had others. She associated it with the concurrence of coming to the university, of publishing her first book, of fast-tracking tenure, scoring flattering student reviews. He called her a "rising star." "In a tiny galaxy," she countered, but she loved his description. Samuel appreciated her, not a trait her mother had prepared her to expect. Love was a begrudging obligation. Not a gift. Maggie understood this intellectually but her rational and emotional dispositions grappled constantly, and mistrust usually suppressed its opposite. She told Samuel she could not pinpoint what quality in him convinced her he was trustworthy. Something conscientious about his candor. An absence of subterfuge she'd experienced with men focused more on fucking her than knowing her. The words her mother reiterated excessively: "Men want one thing." Never considering that women might want the same thing and could find it with a loving, harmonious man. Maggie suspected her mother viewed marrying Scott as capitulation. A necessary, if acceptable, acquiescence to provide her and her daughters with security. She and Scott rarely argued and Maggie wondered if her mother refrained from conflict because she feared a repetition of what unfolded with Aidan. The terror of desertion remained a powerful influence in her mother's life, and Maggie understood why the woman bowed to that fear. How that anxiety manifested itself in Maggie's life nagged at her for years and in the aftershock of every discarded relationship, she analyzed the abandonment, attentive to how her mother's influence affected the outcome. Surprised by the triumph she achieved with Samuel, Maggie clarified a significant difference between her and her mother: Maggie didn't *need* a man; her mother never stopped seeking one.

4.

Maggie unpacks the overnight bag, a contingency Samuel hoped she wouldn't need. They each expressed uncertainty about what she would encounter in Michigan and agreed the possibility of staying overnight if her uncle behaved...well, how would he behave? They grew weary of guessing how he would react to her materializing on his doorstep, their speculation encompassing the extremes of aggravated hostility or solicitous acceptance, and they belabored points on that spectrum until their discussion devolved into silliness.

This morning before dawn, Samuel leaned into the window of the Audi to kiss her goodbye and growled, "Into the great unknown."

"It's just Michigan" she said, smiling, softening her eyes.

"They plotted to kidnap and assassinate their governor," Samuel said, standing and folding his arms over his chest.

Maggie snorted, assuring him she would be careful, then backed out of the driveway.

As she replaces clothes in her dresser drawers, marveling again at the fortunate outcome of her trip, she tempers a self-congratulatory impulse. Access doesn't guarantee success. Disappointment remains a possibility.

Her uncle might never divulge anything intimate or useful. What if she accomplished nothing more than prying open the door to an empty room or another bolted door? "Step two," she envisions Samuel saying tonight, leaning in to clink his wine glass against hers. She appreciates his optimism and his benevolence when confronting pessimism. No woman, she thinks, should ever have to deal with a man until he has reached the age of fifty. Conversely, young men should only interact with fifty-year-old women. Extend the role of teacher not merely to academics, but to life learning. Sensitivity. Compassion. Trust. Sex. And love. But she understands the flaw in her stratagem: the maturity required to teach these values must be coupled with the maturity of willingness to learn them. She fears the chaos that exemplifies both grand and miniscule human history will persist, will prevail over order.

In the kitchen she pours a glass of water from the pitcher in the refrigerator, reviewing the breadth of the day's events, how much transpired since she left this morning. She promised her sisters an update and debates sending an email to them both or speaking with each individually. They do not disapprove of her quest to learn more about their father but disagree on whether it's helpful or appropriate. Jessica expressed more support than Hailey and Maggie attributes that to their relative memories. Their mother's stories shaped young Hailey's recollections of their father and she remains the most adamant detractor among them. Jessica remembers enough about their father to tame their mother's loathing, attempting balance, but also wonders what Maggie's point is in reaching out to an uncle who never expressed any interest in them.

"Aren't you curious about him?" Maggie asked them during a conference call the weekend before she drove to Michigan.

"Not in the least," Hailey said, her tone insistent. "I think you're crazy."

"That's not helpful, Hailey," Jessica said.

"Did I say I was trying to be helpful?" Maggie heard her younger sister snort.

"Stop being bitchy, we all know how you feel."

"I'll hang up," Hailey said and Maggie urged them both to calm down.

"I'm not doing this to pit you two against one another," she said. "This is something I need to do."

"Fine, Maggot," Hailey said, snickering. "But don't expect me to be a cheerleader for this. He's never given any indication that he cared about our family."

"Or his," Maggie said. "He hasn't singled us out for that treatment."

"I am curious about that," Jessica said. "Why he cut everyone off."

"I'll let you know what happens," Maggie said. "Love you both."

"Yeah, yeah," Hailey said. "Love you both, too. Just don't get your hopes up."

Maggie's hopes, she realizes, never rose to the prospect of achieving the concession she secured from Daniel. For years, the lies told by her father formed the image of her uncle; her mother could not recall ever meeting him, but accepted that if Aidan hated him, she would practice the ancient Sanskrit proverb: the enemy of her bastard, cheating husband was her friend.

Hailey's phone goes to voicemail and Maggie leaves a brief message that she is home and for her sister to call. She wonders if Hailey has abandoned the quarantine she enforced at the outset of the pandemic, recalling her sister grumbling about her sons' colleges shifting to distance learning. Their frenzied presence stretched her maternal forbearance to its limits. She'd grown contented in her intermittent empty nest. Her nephews, born fourteen months apart, reminiscent of Maggie's father and uncle, chose separate universities and majors. Thomas, the older, studies art history at Vanderbilt and Benjamin studies business administration at Missouri, staying closer to home. Siblings, she muses, on diverging paths. Must all brothers drift from one another? Another question for her uncle.

When Maggie calls, Jessica answers immediately. "Well?"

"Better than I hoped," Maggie says. "He'll talk to me."

"Well, goddamn," her sister says.

"Yeah. Surprised me, too, Jess. Not what I expected," she says.

"Hailey is gonna freak," Jessica says.

"I tried calling but got voicemail." Maggie sips her water, wondering what she'll fix for dinner.

"Might be intentional," Jessica says.

"Stop," Maggie says. "She's not that petty."

"You don't know her like I do, Maggie," Jessica says. "She blames Dad for abandoning *her* more than for leaving Mom. She can be self-centered as hell."

Maggie pauses. "What does she think I'm going to learn that'll upset her so much?"

"Anything that contradicts what she believes, I suppose," Jessica says.

Maggie envisions Hailey's face, the fair skin framed by expertly colored blonde hair, eyes deep and dark brown like her own, and wonders how profoundly Hailey's confidence in those beliefs underpins her relationship with her husband and sons. The sisters rarely explore the powerful fixations that influenced their lives. Hailey, when describing her husband Paul, labels him reliable, reinforcing, Maggie believes, dependability as her primary benchmark. Unsurprising that the three of them so prize trustworthiness. Expect it. Demand it. And yet are reluctant to accept it. Maggie imagines if any of them discovered their partners cheating, their fury would outstrip their mother's. The fool-me-twice proverb provoking guilty rage.

"That's sad," Maggie says, wondering if her sister constantly skates close to the edge of disappointment or if Maggie's visit to Daniel resurrects emotions Hailey keeps buried. "I don't want to be the cause of her reliving all the bitterness Mom fed her."

"There's not much you can do to avoid it," Jessica says. "Just stay sensitive to how she's coming at this. For her, you're not picking at a scab, you're cutting into a scar."

"I know you're right, Jess, but I can't let her feelings keep me from this." Maggie pauses. "He doesn't look much like Dad."

"Really? There's no family resemblance?" Jessica asks.

"Some. But it's not like they're identical dolls wearing different clothes. I wondered if I'd see him and flash back to a vision of Dad, but it wasn't like that." Maggie realizes she's been standing at the open refrigerator and like earlier in the Audi, has misplaced moments, cannot remember scanning the shelves. "Daniel is fit. Slim. Not like Dad in those photos Grandma sent me. He's got an unruly beard and short hair, but not in a redneck way. His eyes are sharp. He seems very private and analytical."

"That's what Grandma Breedlow said, right?" Jessica says.

"Exactly," Maggie says. "But hearing it and seeing it. Two different animals."

"What're you going to do now?"

"We'll chat online. FaceTime. He invited me to visit at the end of the semester, assuming he's still talking to me by then."

"Wow," Jessica says. "That's impressive. How'd you convince him?"

"Grandma's advice," Maggie says. "Arouse his curiosity."

"Men can't help themselves when you pose a problem. They'll try to solve it without being asked."

"I think there's some of that," Maggie says. "But he's also incurably inquisitive. Approaching him at this point in his life is propitious. Grandma doubted he'd cooperate but that there'd also never be a time when he'd be more open-minded."

"Prophetic," Jessica says.

"Optimistic," Maggie says. "How are the girls?" Hearing about Jessica's three daughters delights Maggie. They're strong-willed, independent, clever. Values Jessica instilled early in their childhoods.

"They're good. Coping with the pandemic. Being smart and staying safe."

"I'm glad to hear it. You stay safe, too."

"We will, Maggie. Give my love to Samuel."

"And mine to David. Love you. Bye bye."

"Back at you. And well done, Maggie."

Maggie thinks about the misplaced consciousness in front of the refrigerator and the spacing out in the car, wondering if the events in Michigan induced these leakages in concentration. No, she muses, they're not leakages, they're realignments. Usually she welcomes such refocusing, envies it in others, especially students, who if they've never before experienced such intense absorption, celebrate them as an epiphanies. As milestones.

Her phone pings the arrival of a text message. She glances at the screen. Hailey. Okay, she thinks. You don't want to talk about it, but you're curious.

How'd it go?

Good. He'll talk to me.

Congrats.

Call me later?

When I've got time. Love you. She adds a heart emoji.

She smiles at Hailey's tactic for learning what happened while avoiding Maggie prattling on about it. She was six years old when their father left. Maggie twelve. Jessica ten. Maggie has stressed to Hailey that her memories are regurgitation of their mother's indoctrination, propaganda, but Hailey bristles at such suggestions, remaining the most strident defender of their mother among the sisters. Jessica and Maggie remember instances of their father's loving side. Him playing with them when he came home from work, even if only at his wife's insistence that the girls had been underfoot all day and she needed a break. Reading to them at night before retreating to the living room to their mother's criticisms and accusations. Their mother claimed Aidan left her, but Maggie remembers her father's banishment from the house. The woman needn't embellish the story to confirm herself as the victim; their father slept around and the night their mother threw him out, he moved in with the current girlfriend. Their mother stacked resentment at the ease of his transition from his family onto the pile of aggression she amassed for his unfaithfulness. Maggie and Jessica feared for their mother's emotional and physical well-being during the weeks after their father's departure, frightened by eruptions of tearful bitterness followed by smiling reassurances that everything would be all right. Hailey asking in her pint-sized voice when Daddy would come home and their mother repeating each time, "Oh, Pumpkin, I don't know." Some nights, Maggie snuck into her mother's bedroom to insure she still breathed, as a mother might in an infant's room, fearful of crib death.

It was a precarious, vulnerable time, underscored when their maternal grandmother, Grandma Howlett, arrived for a "short" visit that lasted two months, providing their mother with an outlet for nightly outpourings once the children had been sent to bed, but which Maggie and Jessica heard while lying in their beds. Years later, Maggie recounted the process by which her mother replaced the incessant philanderer version of her husband with a horrifying abuser. "Nothing physical," her mother always stressed to her daughters, "but the emotional trauma that man inflicted left me a damaged woman." She insisted that meeting and marrying a man as virtuous and faithful as Scott was a blessing.

Maggie appreciated Scott, who recognized his tenuous position within this new family and accepted the role of substitute parent with restraint, expressing to the girls that trying to be their father's successor made him uncomfortable, but if any of them ever wanted to talk to him, about anything, they shouldn't hesitate. Poor man, Maggie remembers thinking. She and Jessica sniggered about the uneasiness he'd feel if they asked him how to deal with their mother's insanity. Ironic, she muses, that the two of them felt, despite having two fathers, that they'd grown up in a home without any. Aidan was absent and Scott didn't count. Hailey, however, clutched their mother's second husband as a fatherly replacement and the girl's seamless transference of affections to Scott irritated Maggie, because it abetted their mother's determination to completely erase their father, an effort their adoption cemented: the elimination of Aidan from their lives.

Even Jessica agreed, in later discussions with Maggie, that nothing would ever have satisfied their mother in her quest to defame Aidan, and Maggie imagines the ferocity of her mother's bitterness on her deathbed knowing he would outlive her. To have lived a life of such constant anger saddens Maggie and she wonders if her mother could have chosen another path if her uncle had been a presence in their lives. Could he have provided an example of how to release that hatred? But then Maggie realizes she doesn't know that he has, that she wants to hear that from him. Not from Grandma Breedlow or Aunt Laura.

She doesn't want to cook tonight. She wants a bath and food delivery. Chinese or Indian. She texts Samuel, asking his preference, but he predictably defers to her.

What time should I expect you?

Eightish.

Kisses.

She knows they could make a meal of just papadums and minty yoghurt dipping sauce from their favorite Indian restaurant but scans the menu for entrees as she turns the clawfoot tub taps, inhaling through her nose the rising steam from the hot water, closing her eyes as it condenses on her face. She strips, sighing as she unclasps her bra, enjoying the release, massaging the tendons above her collar bones. She should have removed it when she stopped to call Grandma Breedlow. In the mirror she turns, glaring at the red impressions her bra left under her breasts and those around her waist by her belt. I deserve a good soak, she thinks, stepping into the water, wincing at the heat, then tenderly lowers herself, resting her head against a folded washcloth on the tub's edge, listening to the resonances of their old house, ambient sounds that soothe her.

Samuel's words come back to her: "optimistic and eager." An observation but also a caution against Pollyanna-ish hopes, prudent, but she's certain her discipline will moderate her enthusiasm, even in a situation as fraught with personal attachment as this. Will help her maintain objectivity and accept what her uncle has to offer with the impartiality required of an historian. She closes her eyes and imagines Hailey chanting "Good luck with that, Maggot!" Maggie fears Hailey, far more than Jessica, because of her inflexibility, will react destructively to Daniel's revelations if they contradict her allegiance to their mother. What Daniel will reveal, she thinks. Like Grandma Breedlow, he may possess his own reasons for relenting, for presenting his version of the family alienation. Grandma Breedlow said Daniel never challenged his brother's account of their estrangement. Why should he care that his siblings believed what Aidan said about him, when he didn't care about any of them? Maggie heard the sadness in her grandmother's voice when she laid out Daniel's rationale. Yet, as the woman hoped Maggie might facilitate Daniel's reconciliation with his mother, what did her uncle hope to gain from the exchange? If he did not care what his siblings believed about him, why cooperate? Why choose now, this moment, to contradict years of family lore? Could it be as simple as the fact that no one had ever before asked him? She knows sometimes it is that simple, but she'll remain alert to her uncle's possible underlying motives. No one is totally selfless. Believing there are always two sides to a story is too linear. Each person's story contains elements of both truth and falsehood. She hopes by interviewing her uncle to braid the truths from each version into whole cloth.

As the warm water relaxes her, Maggie supposes the task ahead will stress her. Will untangling the enmity between the two brothers, dissecting how each determined how he distanced himself from the other, engender tension, not only in her uncle, but in herself, her sisters, Grandma Breedlow? A price will be paid; how dear it is unknown to her now. She stretches her legs the length of the tub, grazes her toes against the far edge of the tub; her arms float at her sides and she waggles her fingers. *Her fingers.* Her reliable tempters. In two hours, Samuel will be home, more than primed to replace them with his mouth, with his tongue, in a practiced and familiar rhythm, to banish her anxiousness, but she drifts her fingers to her clit, rationalizing that individual accomplishments warrant individual rewards. It's not unfair to Samuel, whose face she envisions; after dinner, she'll double-dip as part of their celebration and that's fucking fine.

Later, Maggie leans into the mirror above the sinks and stares at her eyes from a distance of mere inches. When she did this as a child, she prayed for an epiphany, having read about the eyes being a window to the soul. Back when she believed in the existence of her soul and feared its damnation not merely for her actions, but for her thoughts. The imprinting of such fear onto a child's psyche disgusts her. In that respect, Hailey's sons parallel Daniel and Aidan. Thomas, the future art historian, like Daniel, rebuffs his religious upbringing, but Benjamin, the future MBA, remains unswervingly Catholic. Might Hailey fear a justification of brotherly alienation? Maggie's mission shakes the limbs throughout her family tree and she intuits that the encumbrance of knowing might fracture some boughs. "Is it worth it?" too often becomes the question: "Was it worth it?"

When Samuel arrives home, he finds Maggie at the kitchen farmhouse table, containers spread before her in a semi-circle, the bouquet of curry spices flooding the room, and he smiles before hurrying to envelope her in a hug from behind, nestling his nose in her hair.

"I missed you," he says.

"I've haven't been gone any longer than any other day," she says, twisting in her chair to face him.

"It was distance, not time, that I felt," Samuel says. "I'm so happy you're home." He steps back as Maggie rises and then pulls her into an unyielding hug, rubbing her back as she rests her cheek against his chest. During intimate moments like this, Maggie swears she can feel Samuel's voice.

Maggie closes her eyes as Samuel's touch releases emotions that underpin her appreciation of the improbability of their pairing. History, she knows, owes more to luck than to destiny.

As they eat, Samuel asks questions about Daniel and listens to Maggie's answers, prompting her for impressions, predictions based on what she gleaned from her trip.

"How cooperative do you think he'll be if what you're asking paints him in a bad light?" he asks.

"I'm not going to blame anyone for the events that drove them apart," she says, tearing a piece of naan and dipping it into a bowl of saag, steeling herself for the spiciness of the green curry.

"That may be your intention," Samuel says, "but I wouldn't rely on him knowing that."

"I'll make it clear," Maggie says. "Besides, everything we know about him is that bad light isn't something he cares about."

Samuel sips from his glass of beer that Maggie thought paired better with their food than wine. "Have you spoken with your sisters?"

"With Jess. Hailey texted when I left her a voicemail."

Nodding, Samuel spoons rice and jalfrezi onto his plate. That and the vindaloo are too spicy for her, but Samuel craves their heat, so she orders it for him, laughs when he holds a forkful of either dish for her to try, waving him away each time, possessive of the endearing, longstanding ritual. One of countless enchantments they enjoy as a couple. Maggie wonders if her parents enjoyed such moments or were the seeds of their loathing sown in the early years of being together. Likewise, has Daniel ever had relationships last long enough to nurture such endearments?

"I've been thinking about my lines of inquiry," she says, and Samuel emits his chortle. "Yeah yeah, I know," she says. "But as curious as I am about what caused Daniel and my father to isolate from one another, I'm also interested in how that separation influenced them throughout their lives.

From what my grandmother says, Dad asked about Daniel far more than Daniel ever asked about him. It follows that my father was more reactive to his brother than the other way around. My uncle never seemed interested in what Dad was doing."

"So it may be a more one-way street than you imagine," Samuel says.

"On its face," she says. "That's what I want to explore. My experience, where family remains important, makes me question how Daniel was able to sever ties so completely. How could he never wonder about what his parents and siblings were doing? About their lives?"

"Do you think it's just been a performance for him? All these years?"

"I do and don't want to believe that," Maggie says, lifting a napkin. "But the speed of his compliance is suspicious. It doesn't square with Grandma Breedlow's narrative, with the impression she gave."

"Like he wants something from this, too?"

"I've considered that," Maggie says. "I told you my grandmother hopes this will draw Daniel back into the fold, and it's possible he has a purpose beyond correcting what he thinks is a flawed record."

"I know you know what you're doing," Samuel says, placing a hand over hers.

"Thank you, Sweetie," Maggie says, gazing at his gray eyes, noting how when he smiles, his cheeks rise, elongating his mustache, flattening its customary droopiness into a straight line above his mouth like a whisk broom, and Maggie anticipates gripping the back of his head later in bed, feeling that mustache against her vulva as his tongue replicates what her fingers did in the tub.

"It's been one hell of a day," she says.

"Are you worried about your sisters?"

"Jess is fine. Hailey doesn't want to validate what I'm doing but she's too curious to ignore it. She'll call at some point. We don't ordinarily deal with this and I know she doesn't appreciate what I'm doing. It does puzzle me why she wants to adhere so vehemently to Mom's party line. Any time Jess and I point out the gap between the date of their wedding and my birthday, it's like a fog falls over her. Six months. Hailey acts as though Dad forced the marriage, not Mom's family."

"You think that's where your father's cynicism originated? With a shotgun marriage?"

"Oh, that's interesting," Maggie says. "I never thought of it in that way before. Cynicism."

"It seems like a logical way to look at being railroaded into a marriage," Samuel says, lifting their plates from the table. "Like the stages of grief."

"Except he was deeply religious when they got married, according to Grandma Breedlow. She says he stepped up to his responsibility without much prodding," Maggie says.

"More performance from the Breedlow boys?" Samuel rinses the plates and stacks them in the dishwasher. "Another beer?"

Maggie nods, considering whether her father's habits of subterfuge and deception were in play when he agreed to marry her mother. Had he chosen stoicism when confronted with a forced marriage? Was that the germ of his later feelings? Being trapped? Had he suspected her mother of intentionally becoming pregnant? Indeed, had she?

"I waited too long," she says, shaking her head. "So many questions only the two of them could answer."

"Your father and your uncle?" Samuel asks, twisting the cap off a bottle of beer, pouring it into Maggie's glass, the foam rising to the rim.

"No, my mother and father."

"But that's not what you're looking for with Daniel," Samuel says.

"It's a mélange," she says. "All these offshoots branching out from one another. Separate but connected. Daniel knows why my parents got married and doesn't care how that affected their relationship, but I think my father held it against him. Being forced to do something his brother didn't."

"Always measuring himself in his older brother's shadow?"

"Or having others do it for him," Maggie says.

"Did your mother do that with you and your sisters?"

"Some," Maggie says. "But she never had high enough expectations for any of us to use one as an example to the other two. Does that make sense?"

"Sadly, yes." Samuel sits across from her. "I know she wasn't a model parent."

"Never laid claim to that title," Maggie says, tracing a fingernail along a vein in the table's surface.

"One way of looking at it," Samuel says, "is that she taught you self-motivation." He chuckles, a gentle snicker different from his teasing chortle.

"Thank you, Mom," Maggie says, raising her beer glass. "For instilling in me the virtues of self-reliance, self-sufficiency, but also self-doubt and a smattering of self-loathing."

"You forgot cynicism," Samuel says.

"That, too," Maggie says. "It makes me a good historian."

"Maybe that comes from your father's side of the family."

"Wish we all had a dose of it. Hailey refuses to hear a word against Mom. But Jess said something interesting today." Maggie pauses. "She spends more time with Hailey than I do and said our little sister is angrier with Dad for abandoning her than for leaving Mom or us."

"Isn't that natural?" Samuel asks.

"As Jess told it, Hailey's fixation is nearly pathological. She's totally self-absorbed by it. Unsurprising since she's such a parrot when it comes to Mom's version of what happened."

"Maybe you need to include your sisters in your interview list," Samuel says, chuckling again, but Maggie dismisses his droll intent. When the three sisters debate the facts of their family situation, they quickly devolve into settling for agreeing to disagree. Hailey internalizes a vastly different view when comparted to hers or Jessica's and Maggie stirs with curiosity about whether and how Hailey's sons absorb their mother's prejudices when relating to her and to one another. The notion of her father's impression on his children determining not just his but their legacies fascinates her, as well as the observation that she and her uncle each shunned the passing on to any unfortune offspring of such detrimental traits. Common ground, Maggie muses, logging it as a lever to use if necessary in her discussions with Daniel.

"Are you tired?" Samuel asks.

"No, "Maggie says, grinning. "But I'm ready for bed."

He laughs as they rise, placing his hands on the swell of her hips as they hurry toward the stairs.

5.

My mother's fingerprints are plastered all over my niece's ambush and I doubt she cares about the transparency of the ploy. Points for perseverance, Mom. I'm more sympathetic to your impatience as I grow older. Never thought I'd be this old, especially in my twenties, after the war, after I'd cheated fate. In San Angelo, Texas, before leaving for Okinawa, a woman I'd been sleeping with read my Tarot cards. The final card was Death, a skeleton in black armor riding a white horse, just what I wanted to see before heading into a war zone. She cautioned me to avoid a literal interpretation of the card. Death signified endings and beginnings, change and transformation. "Death is inherent in finding the beauty in being alive," she said. I seized upon that interpretation and nothing cemented the truth of its premonition more than when I visited my parents after my discharge. I'd never lived in Tucson so it didn't feel like home and I doubted that after the war, any place ever would. My mother treated me as though I should cast off the years I'd been away and slip back into her notion of a dedicated first son. She never understood that enlisting was a consequence of the depressing, claustrophobic atmosphere of the family into which she now expected me to reintegrate. Childhood had seemed to me a trap, one I escaped, and I knew within days of my discharge that I'd leave everything, every place, and everyone behind. A birth and rebirth signified by the Death card. My future didn't lay in Tucson, Arizona. I bought a used car and left for Chicago, an acceptance to Northwestern, (I'd applied for admission during the last weeks of my service), and a smattering of savings in my pocket. But as I drove north and east, what elevated my expectations was the certainty that the desert landscape and any connection to my family were the literal and figurative images in my rearview mirror.

My disenchantment bordered on vitriol, and as I examine it now, I'm struck by its inevitability. The men toward whom I gravitated during those years, educated and liberal, were contemptuous of the system that coerced them to enlist in the Air Force rather than take their chances with the draft. We caught the tail-end of the Sixties, its fervor, its passion, inferring within one another as we smoked dope and dropped acid an emergence of a new awareness. We applauded the Age of Aquarius and spun dreams about what we'd do when we returned to the "world," forgiving one another when a buzz of desperation entered our narratives. Several buddies proposed settling in San Francisco after discharge, a hapless impulse to capture a magic that had long since abandoned the place. Haight Ashbury was gone. While on leave between reassignment from Okinawa to Thailand, I'd sought out the legendary neighborhood, roamed the streets like an anthropologist, and felt nothing but disillusionment. There was no magic in the panhandlers, the prostitutes, and the waifish runaways shuffling as though in a stupor. The counterculture we envied and coveted had moved on but I had no idea where.

I'd never visited Chicago. My perceptions of the city stemmed from an appreciation of blues music and the demonstrations and police riot during the 1968 Democratic Convention, so I had no expectations of what Evanston held for me, other than a journalism school with an excellent reputation, and a determination to avoid being ensnared by my past.

For decades I had no contact with any Air Force friends. At Travis Air Force Base north of San Francisco, on the day of my discharge I waited with two buddies, both of whom had studied at the Air Force language school in Monterrey, who tried to convince me to rent a car and join them for a few days along the coast, "You gotta see Carmel, man." I demurred. Claimed I was anxious to visit my family, promising we'd stay connected. In addition to reinforcing my disgust with the war, the Air Force, and the government, in truth, I was weary of their company, a habit Grayson often pointed out to me, mostly in the context of relationships with women, but which he swore I exercised with others as well.

"Sometimes I think I'm your only friend, Dan," he said. "You extract what you need or want from people and then you turn them loose."

Grayson's not my only friend, but he's the closest to a confidant I've ever had in a male friend since my days in the Air Force. I see a parallel between my time in the service and my family, how I turned my back on those to whom I grew close. My mother accused me of trying to escape where I came from. I don't disagree but she misunderstands my motives. I'm not doing it only because I'm ashamed of those origins, not solely because they're embarrassing. Who'd want to be associated with an ass like Aidan? Or the youngest two, Luke and Elizabeth, Trump loyalists I imagine waking every morning, salivating at their keyboards, logging online to discover the latest Qanon conspiracy. No. I absolutely don't want people lumping me with that squalid gene pool and I'll make that clear to Maggie from the outset, but I'll tell her obliquely.

I descended the steps to the beach last night to photograph the sunset, fiery orange and red in a sky studded with puffy cumulus clouds, the blistering reflections shimmering on the waves. The weather was chilly with a mild wind that tossed the foam across the sand when the waves broke against the shore. I switched the camera to video mode for ten seconds, panning to capture both the sights and the sounds, yielding to a sense of nostalgia; status has changed with Maggie's visit. A sense that nothing about my sanctuary will remain as it was before she arrived. Will it be that invasive, I wondered. I'll remain in control. The arbiter of what we discuss. Besides, Maggie will soon learn that my memories of Aidan are sparse. Deliberately so.

Jettisoning memories of when the two of us got along as famously as Mom says we did is subconscious, not intentional. I had other matters to occupy my attention, to supplant memories, but I never viewed them as replacements for family reminiscences. Proximity determines priority. As does absence. The longer the absence, the fainter the glimmering. Or so I discovered. Dismissal of my upbringing involved much more than severing the tethers with family: mindless adherence to religion; rejection of my father's conservative politics; determination of who deserves trust and loyalty. In the years after the war, with Watergate fueling my passion for studying journalism, I knee-jerked my reflexes, adopting any stance if it represented the opposite of what I had been taught. It took years for me to tame that compulsion, to recognize mindless obstinacy as an impediment. Rebellion needs a clear head to succeed.

Forgetting Aidan never taxed me because it wasn't a conscious decision; I just allowed those memories to fade but convincing my mother and now my niece of that will be challenging. I know Mom believes putting so great a distance between us was a spiteful decision and despite trying to dissuade her of that belief, she adheres to her opinion. She needs that conviction for selfish reasons. If she abandons it, her entire family construct tumbles. My role as the vindictive, malicious outcast fortifies vital aspects of a persona she has promoted for decades. People need enemies in their lives to justify their prejudices and besides, I find victims boring.

My niece's appearance upsets me. After photographing the sunset last night, a practice that usually calms me, I reviewed the images, playing the ten-second recording of the evening beach panorama, but instead of enjoying its serenity, I dwelled on what Maggie wants. Impressions of my brother. My mind wandered, like fingertips flipping through an old library card catalog drawer, but the cards are blank. Recalling childhood memories of the two of us is a dredging operation. But then I remember an incident when the two us were preteens. Aidan slouching at the kitchen table, chrome legs and a gray and pink patterned Formica surface, as my parents lectured him for another stupid thing he'd done. I listened from our bedroom but couldn't make out the words. For a change, my father didn't raise his voice or threaten Aidan with his belt. The upbraiding ended as it always did: my parents, usually my father when the offense was serious enough to warrant his involvement, securing from Aidan an assurance the offending behavior wouldn't be repeated. Then securing that assurance again, making Aidan, I knew, even more angry at the punishment he'd receive following the reprimand: suspending his allowance for a week, limiting his TV time, or banishing him from the dinner table without dessert. Aidan once confessed he'd rather suffer our father's belt than the deprivation punishments. The pain was fleeting, less demeaning than having Dad flicking his wrist dismissively and telling Aidan to push away from the table, as Mom scooped ice cream, or sliced cake or pie wedges for everyone but him.

That night he returned to our bedroom, fuming, and his contorted expression as he flopped onto the lower bunk tugged at my sympathy. We were imperfect brothers but siblings should be allies in the struggle against their parents.

"You okay?" I asked, sitting at the student's desk, a science textbook open.

"Just leave me alone."

"What'd you do?" While our alienation was incomplete, its groundwork had been established. Talking to him like this was out of the ordinary. I'm sure he expected me to gloat that our parents had reprimanded him. That I'd enjoy his humiliation.

"Nothing," he said, his anger then bursting into a familiar tantrum: clenching his jaw and grinding his teeth, pounding the mattress with his fists, kicking the bottom of the upper bunk, rattling the wooden slats that supported it in the frame. The bed was honey-colored pine and it didn't take much force to bang it against the wall, which always elicited a warning from our parents.

"Musta been something," I said.

"I said to leave me alone," he shouted, then fell quiet, listening for footsteps in the hallway, fearful one of our parents would investigate yet another annoying argument between us. When breaking up our shouting matches, Mom's final request was always a forlorn appeal that we get along. I don't think she ever understood how early Aidan and I elevated ordinary sibling rivalry into detesting one another.

"I was trying to sympathize with you, jackass," I said. "Your loss."

"The last thing I want is your sympathy."

"I guess that's about when you'll get it then," I said.

Then we hurled more insults at each other. Scoring the last word allowed one of us to claim victory in the squabble, but when the victor crowed his triumph, another round of futile sparring ensued, and we'd hear the hurried footfalls that signaled an impending scolding. I remember that exchange as one of the last times I ever tried to empathize with Aidan, to make him see what common ground we shared. From that moment, I got under his skin through silence, through ignoring him.

Maggie will want me to pinpoint the start of my alienation from her father, and the recollection of that squabble makes me doubt suggesting that it didn't begin with one incident, that I can't nail one quarrel as the point of origin. Will more memories come back to me? In Zoom sessions when I reminisce with buddies from the Air Force, they refer to incidents I've forgotten but begin recalling as they describe them. Will something similar happen as Maggie and I talk? Perhaps. And how will I feel about those memories? Will what I remember change my outlook?

I know Mom hopes they will. Her purpose, as I said, is so transparent.

Did she tell Maggie I was lonely? Bored? When I retired from the firm, colleagues wondered how I'd fill my time. An energetic, successful man in a frenetic, competitive career field alone in an isolated house. How would I occupy myself? Adapt to such radical changes? Only Grayson knew I wanted to write and I'd sworn him to secrecy. My transition upon leaving the office on a Friday and beginning the draft of my novel on Monday was emotionally seamless, but still required adjustment. That first morning, as I sat at my computer, challenged by a blank screen, I wrote feverishly. For *hours*. Paused for a sandwich at noon and then resumed, completing more than five-thousand words of the draft. I printed out the pages and stacked them in a neat pile on my desk, pleased with my accomplishment, but guarded against smugness. I knew the difficulties of writing, but in other orbits, journalism and press releases, not fiction. Reviewing those pages the following morning shattered any expectation of an easy transition from one orbit to the other. The work couldn't have passed muster as a disjointed stream of consciousness. Haste, as they say. I deleted the bulk of what I drafted, understanding the foolishness of sprinting at the start of a marathon, of allowing my enthusiasm to charge unchecked, but soon fell into a practice of writing during the morning, with a goal at least five hundred words but no more than a thousand, before stepping away from the keyboard, (reminds me now of Aidan pushing back from the kitchen table as he's denied dessert). I recalled a professor at Northwestern expounding like a preacher that all successful writing stems from meticulous editing. I'd earned a reputation at the firm as a first-class nitpicker of copy and chastened myself that Tuesday morning for abandoning that discipline. Fiction was my undiscovered country, but I was not a novice and should have known better.

I drafted the manuscript in seven months, working on all but a handful of days. And I read. Every afternoon. Walked along the beach, making notes on my phone about the work. The pattern of those months paralleled my time at Northwestern, where I demonstrated an ability to focus on academics that earned praise from my faculty advisor. Dean's List every semester. I confessed the laxity of my first year at Missouri and he nodded and grinned as though he'd heard my story hundreds of times and told me he appreciated teaching veterans who reentered college, that they approached their studies with a sense of purpose often lacking in traditional students.

It's illuminating that what I latched onto in our discussions was the inference that I was untraditional, a portrayal that thrilled me. Still the rebel.

I now regard writing not as a labor of love, but as a clinical practice. Perhaps because of my age. Younger writers approach the task with fiery enthusiasm, with hot-blooded vehemence, driven by what they assume is a vocation, a calling they can't ignore. I was sixty-seven years old. Patient. Experienced and thus steadier of purpose. Those inevitable moments of mental blankness, when staring at the monitor yields nothing, never threw me into turbulent reevaluation of my decision to write. I accepted those uninhabited spaces as opportunities to step back and observe the workings of my imagination, as I often had in client meetings, when it became apparent that the man sitting across the conference table from me, encumbered by advice from an attorney, wanted a formulaic solution to his problem, and I'd sit quietly, guessing his motive, usually self-preservation, longing for a client willing to consider a creative solution, one that bordered on honesty. That rare client who would see a crisis as an opportunity for self-improvement, not a client who only sought to wrap a lie in a more palatable lie. Still. We serviced the client, even if the product lacked originality and left me feeling leadened. I disliked Grayson's portrayal of my attitude as stoicism; I loathed being so adept at deceiving others and began dreading unconscious self-deception, was scared of losing perspective and forgetting that what I presented the client was a persona, not my reality. When a client wanted to hide his secret, correct his mistakes and gaffes, I gleefully told him the size of his problem would always exceed the size of any box in which he tried to conceal it. Revelation was inevitable and we could exert limited influence over how to manage that revelation. Watching him wince and grimace when I said, "Understand that you're not in control. Our best case scenario is persuasion, and if that fails, misdirection." I counseled them against forced pomposity as I accosted them with a pretentious performance. The hesitations during those disappointing meetings, like the pauses in my writing, rewarded me with fanciful rootlessness. Liberating my itinerant imagination. These days I channel that nomadic contemplation into photography and guitar playing.

So, no, Maggie, I'm neither lonely nor bored. Those first months of retirement, as I slipped into comforting habits, I imagined a presence, a wisp in my peripheral vision, a spirit haunting the house. But I was the house's first inhabitant. Why would a phantom infiltrate my home? A holdover from the old cottage disgruntled by its demolition? George Van de Berg never mentioned such a phenomenon, but would he have? I wondered if the shadowy apparition represented a subliminal desire for companionship, something I'd outgrow. I did.

Loneliness is a spectrum, encompassing the dispassionate blue of contentedness and the overheated scarlet of longing. Solitude is rudimentary for some, unbearable for others, and I've not struggled with it in decades. Grayson wondered if my misanthropy caused the separation from my family or was a result of it. I said, "the egg was always the chicken" and he laughed, accusing me of sidetracking the question with dismissive folly, which I had because I learned early in life that everyone in this world is alone, regardless of how many people surround them. Aloneness, like boredom, its counterpart, emerges from within. Loneliness is an attitude, not a condition, and if Maggie pokes about in why I'm not lonely, she'll come face-to-face with the history of my relationships, an area I won't disclose to her. Her choice: satisfying her curiosity with stories of Aidan or finding our communication unsatisfying brief.

I descended to the beach this morning after refilling my bird feeders. A stubborn fog obscured the views of the bluff north and south, each horizon fading into misty anonymity. I like the contradictions of the lake, ever-present and ever-changing. From the haziness, two figures gradually emerged, like ghosts, an unfamiliar couple pacing along the shore, pausing occasionally, leaning over and pointing at the patterns in the sand left by the waves. They weren't wearing masks, so I waved and turned to climb the stairs, pausing at the top as a bevy of sparrows flitted from the feeders at my intrusion. I sank two poles in the turf at the edge of the patio, supporting half a dozen feeders that I keep filled with a mixture of sunflower, safflower, millet, cracked corn, peanut pieces, raisins, and nyler seeds, tailored to attract songbirds. The feed store where I buy my bulk seed stocks guides and I bought a foldout chart of Michigan birds: waterbirds, nearshore birds, birds of prey, perching birds, and the zones of the state they populate. I've identified a variety of species at the feeders: northern cardinals, black-capped chickadees, hooded warblers, house wrens, American goldfinches, blue-gray gnatcatchers, white-breasted nuthatches, tufted titmice, red-headed woodpeckers, rose-breasted grosbeaks, scarlet tanagers, but most commonly, sparrows. Song sparrows. Chipping sparrows. House and field sparrows. They consume the bulk of my provisions. The seeds they spill as they feed attract mourning doves and squirrels. At the outset of the pandemic, George shopped for me, applauding my "bird obsession," unloading a twenty pound sack of seed at the garage door each week. Despite the sparrows scattering when I climbed the steps this morning, my birds accommodate my presence. When I haul a galvanized bucket of seed to the feeders, (mice and chipmunks chewed through the plastic buckets I formerly used for storage) they retreat to the tree branches at the edge of the lawn, perching, cocking their heads as I scoop their food. When I glance up and see them watching me, I feel they're judging me, chattering among themselves about whether to descend upon me in a Hitchcockian flock, and as I replace the lid on the bucket and back away from the poles, they flap down and begin pecking their beaks through the feeder mesh, plucking seeds. At first George found my obsession with feeding birds comical. We sat on the patio drinking beer one afternoon after he mowed the lawn, when a gnatcatcher landed on a feeder. When I identified it, he knitted his brow, and I tossed him the pocket bird guide. I'd circled the species I'd seen at the feeders and he said, "I'll be damned, all of these?" I nodded. "Well, ain't that something. I never really paid attention." George is not yet a "twitching" convert but neither am I a fanatic. It's a distracting avocation, a pastime that helps keep me attentive, keeps my mind active.

If pressed about living alone, I'll tell Maggie its greatest benefit is privacy.

When Mom decided she should move into assisted living, my sister Laura called, asking if I'd fly to Tucson to help them find an appropriate facility, to sort through the memorabilia, the heirlooms, the accumulated family treasures. I declined, of course, as she expected me to, and she admitted Luke and Elizabeth argued since I wanted nothing to do with the family, I should have no input about Mom's welfare, and had no right to anything in the house. "They're adamant, Dan," Laura said. "It's funny that they think they're punishing me," I said, musing that the responsibility of parenting a parent should fall to those children who have had children. "But they're actually giving me what I want." I laughed and Laura sighed, then asked if there was anything I wanted in the house, that she'd put it aside for me without telling Luke and Elizabeth. I thought for a moment, mentally tracking through the Tucson house, and remembered a sepia print of the great-grandfather for whom I was named. Laura promised to ship it to me. It now hangs in the upstairs hallway, and each night when I climb the stairs to my bedroom, I grin passing it. Daniel Ezekiel Breedlow wearing a dark suit with a high-collared shirt and black tie, seated stiffly in a wing-back chair in front of a dun-colored wall, unsmiling, his black beard groomed to a point below his chin, deep-set eyes staring at the camera. More a mugshot than portrait, but I value it. My grandmother described her father as an outcast within the family, who in the late nineteenth century, announced his decision to journey west, leaving New York, where he felt stifled by a lack of opportunities. He stepped from the train in St. Louis and began work as a tailor's apprentice. I strain at times to find a resemblance between his face and mine, but never see any similarities. My attachment to the photo stems from our parallel natures, not any family likeness. I often wondered if as he journeyed west from New York, his train stopped in Chicago, and when I walked through the Loop or on North Michigan Avenue, I imagined retracing his steps. When I pause before his portrait, I sometimes tell him his legacy of exploration, of discontent with his circumstances, is alive, but will end with me. None of my siblings, *surviving* siblings, exhibit the insubordination we possessed.

I wonder if Maggie is the pariah in her family. There were three children from Aidan's first marriage. What's the status of her relationship with her sisters? Is there any contact with the children from the second and third marriages? Will she enjoy my curiosity about her dealings with her family? Consider any interest as a victory of sorts?

If you throw multiple stones into a pond, the ripples from splashes roll out and collide. This exchange with her will not be straightforward but she'll learn that cynicism trumps naivete.

When she left, I resolved to let at least three days pass before contacting her. It's been four, so I dial her number and wait for the connection. She answers immediately.

"Uncle Dan!"

Her excitement is palpable. "Just Dan, how's that?" I lower myself onto the sofa and swing my legs onto the seat cushions.

"Dan. Fine. How are you?" I imagine Maggie's nervousness, her uncertainty about how our conversation might unfold.

"I'm good. You?" The sofa faces the west wall and I watch more than a dozen sparrows marshalled at the feeders. There's plenty of food for them all, but they squawk and peck at one another, one bird forcing another from a perch, then that bird being forced away by another, all of them vying for dominance when cooperation would benefit the entire flock. They're just like people.

"Busy. Classes. Student meetings. Thinking about what I want to ask you about my father," she says.

"I'm sure it's overwhelming but remember what I said. I'm not sure how helpful I can be. I didn't talk to my brother after he married your mother." A squirrel hops around the base of a feeder and tries to climb the metal pole, grips the edge of the conical baffle I fixed to the staff to confound such forays and falls to the ground. A second assault ends the same way and the animal relents, pawing through the spilled seed on the turf.

I wonder if Maggie watches some similar tableau while talking to me. She's probably much more focused on her purpose than I am in fulfilling it.

"Then let me ask you about the times you might remember," she says, and I envision her consulting a printed list of bullet-pointed questions. "Grandma says you two didn't argue all the time. That for years you really got along."

"I suppose when we were very young, we did," I say. "Before we got to know each other well." I laugh, hoping she appreciates the humor.

There's silence and I fear I've overstepped, belittled the seriousness of her purpose.

"Mom and Dad both worked and they expected me as the oldest to take charge of the little ones," I say. "Aidan never saw himself as one of the little ones and cringed at the suggestion he had to obey me. But that was when we were teens. The resentment set in long before that."

"Do you remember what caused it?" I imagine Maggie holding a pen, poised to make notes.

"Are you finding this as unsatisfying as I am?" I ask. "I mean, not being able to see one another."

"Um..."

"Let's Zoom. I'll email you the details." I shift my legs off the sofa, stretching my toes on the rug, enjoying the heat rising from the concrete.

"Okay," Maggie says and I smile, thinking I've caught her off-guard.

"Great. See you in a few minutes."

6.

Maggie appears on my monitor, her hair pinned away from her face with yellow plastic clips. She wears a pale blue button-down shirt, a man's Oxford, and I realize I don't know if she is married or has a partner. Is she offended or amused by my lack of curiosity?

I scan the scene behind her. Built-in shelves stacked with hundreds of books.

"Have you read all those?" I ask, tipping my chin up to indicate her background.

She turns and then smiles, facing back to the camera. "Yes. The to-be-read piles are downstairs. I'll never get through all of them, but it never stops me from buying more."

"There are worse obsessions," I say, wondering if she'll consider the statement a jibe.

"I may have one or two of them as well," she says, chuckling.

I'm pleased by her unpretentiousness. "Well, maybe we'll delve into those when we know one another a little better." This differs from Zooming with my Air Force language school classmates; Maggie occupies the entire screen and it amplifies her expressions more than the smaller windows occupied by my buddies, when fifteen or twenty log in to the session. "Getting back to what I was saying…" I pause, pressing my lips together, an affectation perfected during my PR career. It convinces clients you're an engaged professional deep in thought about their issues. "Don't take at face value what my mother says about me and Aidan always getting along when we were young. We didn't hide it from her all the time but weren't forthcoming about it either."

"I'm accustomed to taking everything with a grain of salt," Maggie says. The skin around her eyes crinkles as she smiles. "Occupational hazard."

I rub my fingertips below my eyes, a vanity about sagging pouches. "I think the animosity we developed for one another blotted out any memories I have of the two of us getting along."

"But you can't rule it out?" She sips from a mug emblazoned with the University of Iowa mascot, a black and yellow Hawkeye profile. I attended football games as an undergraduate, when Northwestern was the laughingstock of the Big Ten, guaranteed to pad a school's win-loss record with a lopsided victory, and imagined myself in pads, running pass routes through the opponent's backfield.

"I'm not a purist that way," I say. "I'm sure there's some truth in what Mom says, that we played together, shared secrets. I don't remember that."

"Or you've made an effort to forget it," Maggie says, her expression neutral. She wrote her dissertation on the decline of churches during the Great Depression and I imagine her interviewing subjects with this deadpan expression, awaiting their memories, and then sifting through the contradictions and inconsistencies in their recollections.

"That's also possible," I say. "But since you left I've been considering what causes an absence of memories. In my case, I think it's unintentional but I won't rule out a subconscious compulsion. Other things in my life became more important and they replaced those earlier…" I pause. "Unfortunate memories."

"Unfortunate?" Maggie asks, narrowing her eyes, almost squinting.

Tics and tendencies, Grayson and I called them. Clues we gleaned from the gestures clients exhibited when he or I questioned them.

"Unwelcome? That's nearer the truth," I say.

She looks down and makes a note.

"I don't mind if you record these sessions," I say. "Then you'll have an accurate record of what we say. An oral history."

"That would be very helpful," she says, lowering her pen. "Thank you."

I click on the icon giving her permission to record the session. "One of the causes of my alienation from Aidan was his mindless alliance with my mother against me. You have to understand the backdrop when we were teenagers. The Sixties. Protests. Unrest about civil rights, the war. Such a groundswell of change and my parents resisted all of it. Dad issued proclamations about our behavior then expected Mom to enforce them. There were skirmishes about how long I could wear my sideburns. Dad tried to prohibit us from watching The Beatles on the Ed Sullivan Show but lost that battle when even Mom aligned against him. At my Catholic high school, at a time when the Church in general was rigidly conservative, a cadre of liberal brothers indoctrinated us with their impassioned beliefs about social justice. When I brought that influence home and talked about it at dinner, disgust washed over my father's face."

Maggie laughs, shielding her mouth with a hand, a gesture I've never understood in people whose teeth, like hers, are even and bright white. Why would anyone hide their amusement that way?

"Did you ever meet him, my father?"

"Twice," she says. "He died too soon."

"Don't we all," I say. I wonder if she thinks I'm referring to Aidan or confessing a worry about my own longevity. I'm inordinately healthy for a seventy-three year old man. At times, the Zoom sessions with my Air Force buddies devolve into a recitation of medical complaints: failing joints that either have been or will be replaced; Type-2 diabetes blamed on the Agent Orange sprayed along the perimeter of our base in Thailand; various cancers, arthritis, and depression attributed to PTSD. When the one-upmanship of cataloguing maladies reaches the point of absurdity, someone starts laughing and the infection spreads until my screen fills with guffawing old men. It's a surreal sight.

"You probably think that's why I've reached out when I have," Maggie says, grinning. "Prodding and poking before you're dead."

"Hey," I say, widening my eyes and raising my hands, palms toward the camera, in what I hope she sees as a comical expression. "I don't blame you. But I'm hoping I inherited my mother's longevity genes. She'll outlive us all."

Maggie compresses her lips again and dips her chin.

"What?" I ask. "Is something wrong with her?" Speaking with my mother irritates me, but the idea that she is not forthright about her health maddens me, and I know I'm a hypocrite for embracing both reactions. If I don't play the game, I don't make the rules.

"Nothing she'll admit," Maggie says. "She's old and getting frailer each day. The doctors are worried about her heart. She had a scare last year with an irregular heartbeat. They considered putting in a pacemaker, but the condition corrected itself. If there's a repeat, then they'll insert one."

This news triggers anger at my mother and my sister for failing to tell me of the incident. Mom, I wager, swore Laura to secrecy, or my sister would have informed me.

"No one told me," I say.

Maggie mutters, "Oh," and shakes her head. "Please don't let on I told you."

"Secret's safe," I say. "I'll worm it out of her, or never let her know I know."

"That's Machiavellian," Maggie says, shifting her head toward a voice in her background, calling her name. "That's Samuel," she says, turning back toward the camera. "My partner."

The voice grows louder. "What are you working on?" it says, and then a headless body appears in the right side of the screen. "Oh, sorry, Mags. I didn't know you were talking with someone." Maggie tugs the man into the frame, his face dominated by a bristly mustache.

"Dan, this is Samuel." He smiles and ripples his fingers in a wave. "This is my Uncle Daniel."

"Hello, Samuel," I say, nodding.

"Fantastic to meet you," Samuel says in a loud voice; Maggie grins and blinks her eyes in response to the volume. "Sorry to interrupt." He kisses Maggie's cheek. "Carry on," he tells me. "I'll be downstairs," he then whispers to her and hurries out of view.

"That's my Samuel," she says in a sing-song voice, turning her face toward his off-screen exit.

I tamp down my curiosity about the two of them, thinking instead about whether to call my mother or Laura when Maggie and I finish this session. "We can finish now, if you have to go." I say.

Maggie faces the screen and shakes her head. "I'd rather continue for a while if that's okay with you."

"Sure."

She glances down at the desk surface and then asks when I last saw her father.

"During my father's final hospital stay," I say. "Laura said his condition was terminal and if I wanted to see him, it would be my last chance."

"That was just before they put him in hospice, right?"

I recall the night I spent at the ICU. Ten minutes by his side every hour, the other fifty in a waiting room where the families of other patients treated the space as a campground. Sleeping bags on the floor. Cafeteria trays stacked on end tables. Greasy chip bags overflowing the garbage cans. Children squabbling over the remote control for the small TV mounted in the corner of the ceiling. Finding an empty chair was a constant problem. My parents were divorced by then; Dad's current wife and her kids never stayed overnight. Neither did my mom, Laura, Luke or Elizabeth. Aidan walked into Dad's curtained space at three in the morning as I sat bedside, my legs extended, an elbow on the chair's arm, my chin resting in my palm. I didn't even look up when he stopped beside me. I assumed it was a nurse making rounds, checking his IV, noting the numbers on the bevy of monitors wired to him. In the morning, he would be transported to the hospice facility. That night was my last chance to be alone with him before he died, but nothing about the scene resembled what I had imagined. The ICU is a bustling place, even at three o'clock in the morning. The dying and critically ill don't regard time in the way the rest of us do. Before Aidan joined me at Dad's bedside, one patient had coded. The tumult as nurses and doctors converged on the nearby bed cautioned me. I didn't want Dad to die in that place. It wasn't a matter of him deserving or having earned a quieter, more serene atmosphere in which to die. As a teenager, I'd envisioned horrible ways for him to die. Fiery car crashes. Fatal muggings. Even Mom stabbing him in the heart with a kitchen knife. Had I mellowed? Matured. I hoped that in his unconsciousness, my father regretted those aspects of his life that caused others pain. The times he hurt people. My mother and his children. The ICU was not the place to do that.

"That's the last time I saw your father," I say. "Before mine was moved to hospice. Aidan came to the hospital when I was the only one there with Dad."

Maggie's face goes blank and she tilts her head up slightly. An unambiguous sign for me to continue.

"I was sitting beside Dad's bed in the ICU. Three in the morning. He startled me by saying 'Hey, Danny.' Not even Mom called me by that name anymore." I pause, remembering that my brother tried to lay a hand on my shoulder, but I stood so that it sloughed off. "He folded his arms across his chest and said, 'The old man doesn't look so tough now, does he?' and

I wondered about the resentment he held onto, whether it resembled my own. But then I dismissed the thought. The opportunity for us to compare the ways we hated our father had long since passed."

"What did you talk about?" Maggie asks.

"Nothing special," I say. "We were like strangers. If you want to the truth, he was an annoyance, like the people in the waiting room. I walked out after a few minutes and left him with Dad. The rest of the time I was in Tucson, we were never alone again. A day after Dad was transferred to hospice, I flew back to Chicago. Laura called two days later to say he'd passed away and I told her I wasn't coming down for the funeral."

"How did your mother react to that?" Maggie knitted her brow. I wonder if she knew I hadn't attended the service.

"Pissed," I say, wagging my head as I recall Mom's telephone call. "There was fire in her voice as she berated and cursed me, screamed and sobbed. I told myself I was doing her a favor, a service, by absorbing her grief. Part of me hoped it might be the final straw, that she'd never call me again." I pause, watching for Maggie's reaction to my statement, but her face registers no shock or surprise. "But no such luck," I say, chuckling. "A month after Dad's funeral, she telephoned to say she was still angry with me, had not yet forgiven me. But she'd called."

"Back to my father," Maggie says. "Do you remember anything specific about the two of you talking?"

I sense Maggie wants something, a tidbit or morsel she can chew about how Aidan and I interacted that night beside Dad's bed, or in the days before I returned to Chicago. Inventing a story would be wicked, so I strain to recall anything about those minutes we stood beside Dad, watching his chest rise and fall, wincing at the slackness of the skin on his face, the stubbly whiskers on his sallow cheeks and chin, appraising the smallness of a man I'd always feared as larger than life, but I draw a blank.

"I'm sorry, Maggie, I just don't remember. I know it's unsettling to hear but seeing him again wasn't an important moment for me. I didn't know it was the last time we'd ever be together." I pause. "When did you last see your dad?"

It's obvious the question catches Maggie off guard. She flinches, sits more upright and parts her lips slightly. Not in a smile. "Huh," she says. "The last time I talked to him was my sixteenth birthday," she says. "He called, drunk and sloppy, and I thought he was going to apologize for leaving us when Mom snatched the phone from me and told him not to call us ever again."

"That must have hurt," I say, drumming the fingertips of the left side of my desk, listening to the ticking of guitar-playing callouses on wood, imagining Aidan drunk-dialing Maggie, wondering what would prompt such an impulse. My memory of his succession of girlfriends at that time is beyond indistinct. I imagine a scene: the woman suffering the inevitable epiphany about Aidan's nature, crying and cursing her own naivete, throwing him out of her home, (he would have been free-loading off her), my brother checking into a cheap motel or begging a night on a friend's sofa, and then halfway through a case of beer, calling Maggie on her birthday, his voice muddied and slurred, spewing self-pity, until his ex-wife told him off. I Imagine her scorning him: "You have no right."

"Sixteen wasn't so sweet, that's for sure," Maggie says.

"You never spoke to him after that?"

"Never," Maggie says.

"That's rough," I say, studying her face, her wistful expression, fixing her eyes not on me, but on an unseen point that I'm certain is a memory or an expectation. "It explains your curiosity." I pause and stare at her. "You need this, don't you?"

"Busted," she says, smiling, glancing down from the camera.

I imagine her mind reeling, striving for words and expressions to make light of her admission. "That's okay," I say. "It's cathartic and healthy to express your needs."

"The picture of my father is still so incomplete," she says, her voice faint, and the cynic in me wonders if she modulates it for effect. "Even with everything Grandma and Aunt Laura have told me, there are so many puzzle pieces missing."

"Maybe you're trying to build a picture that isn't real," I say. "What if what you know of him is all there is to him?" I pause. "I don't remember my brother as being an extremely complex person. If anything, he was pretty fucking simple."

"That's *your* perspective," Maggie says, her voice acerbic.

I remain silent, until the stubbornness of her clamped jaw relaxes. I scratched a sore spot. "Absolutely," I say. "We're definitely of two minds. You want to know more about your father, even if there's nothing more to be learned, and I already feel I know too much about him. Cross purposes."

"Is this the point in the conversation where I say, 'don't go away mad, just go away?'" She grins and I'm happy I haven't irretrievably angered her. She still needs something from me. Memories to flesh out an emptiness she may never accept isn't really an absence.

"I don't think you want me to invent stories that make you feel better or worse about my brother," I say. "I'll tell you the truth, even when it hurts. Isn't that what you want? What you need?"

"Absolutely," she says quickly.

"Because if you want me to spin tales, then this," I flip an index finger back and forth between our images, "won't work."

"No," she says, shaking her head. "Honesty. Please." She sits stilly, unmoving and staring straight at me. "And I'll be honest with you as well."

"Fair," I say, sensing this might be an opportune moment to end the conversation, but then reconsider. "I'll say this…I'm happier now that you showed up at my door than when you knocked on it."

"Would I be pushing my luck by asking you to rate that on a scale of one to ten?" She laughs, a bell-like tone and I sense we'll end this conversation on amiable terms.

"You would," I say. "But it'd be on the good side of five."

"Should I wait for you to call?" she asks.

"Yeah, that's fine." I pause, glancing at the photograph of Oak Street Beach in Chicago on the wall above my monitor, taken at sunrise, the glare of the sun bleaching every aspect of the shore with its glare. "Let's Zoom again in a few days. I'll send you the info and you let me know if it works for you."

She nods, says, "Thank you," and then her image disappears.

Downstairs I review our conversation, imagining Grayson sitting across from me, consulting his iPad, where he jotted client statements and requests, as well as his impressions of their temperaments and the tactics we would need to manage their expectations and disappointments. We conducted these debriefings in his office, associates arranged around us on the sofa and armchairs, gathering their perceptions of the client, of his goals. Our clients were overwhelmingly male. Grayson used to joke that we were crisis managers and only men could fuck up enough to need our help. Our job, he joked, was to salvage their work. "They're painters who can't draw hands and just paint mittens on their subjects."

"What do you think, Grayson?" I say aloud. My first question after we cleared the room of associates, dispatched to their desks with instructions for further research and preparation of possible approaches for satisfying the client. That was the secret: not solving the client's problem, because the client often didn't want a solution. *Satisfying* the client. Making him feel attended. Grayson and I often proposed and achieved solutions for the problem, but we always appreciated and fulfilled the client's purpose: attention. Attention often involved absolution. Clients came to us as sinners seeking exoneration and Grayson and I bestowed upon them the forgiveness they sought: PR as a religious substitute depressed me. I preferred amoral clients who shrugged off their blunders and demanded a whitewashing of the blowback, sinners to hypocrites.

"Maggie tries to disguise her need," I say, "but it's still apparent. No pun intended."

I imagine Grayson's laugh, a burst of "ha-ha" from his wide mouth, his chin dipping.

"I wonder if the morning we met will fix in both our minds as an important moment," I say. "A watershed."

I recall Grayson pursing his lips, nodding agreement to an assertion, how eliciting such a reaction buoyed associates who feared offering suggestions we dismissed. "No bad ideas," Grayson stressed when he noticed someone's reticence in speaking. "We're more unsympathetic to silence than unworkable suggestions. Don't censor yourselves." He valued mentoring colleagues, as we had been at the firm where we met as young associates.

"Will it be determinative for Maggie? A watershed moment? One of those instances you look back on as the instant your view radically shifted?

"The timbre of her voice is flat, uniform. So that when she adds inflection, it's noticeable. Noteworthy. Like she's telling you to pay particular attention to those words. And she appreciates pauses. A default setting for encouraging a self-conscious person to fill the unnerving silence. Remember the voice training for clients? It's like she mastered that class."

The firm hired a voice coach for clients who would appear in the public as part of their media training, emphasizing the importance of controlling both the message and the tone of the voice delivering the message. In truth, it only worked occasionally. Most people in stressful situations forget their training and revert to their normal speech patterns, and in people who feel guilt, the reversion can be amazingly quick. Good sinners are scarce. Great sinners even scarcer.

"I tried to keep a distance, Grayson," I say. "There's no good reason to be cooperating. It goes against my grain, as you know."

He'd wag his head at me for foolish self-delusion. "Lie to yourself if you must, but not to me, Dan. This partnership is the perfect marriage. It demands absolute honesty."

"Hmm. Maggie's going to insist on the same and expect me to own up to any mistakes I've made."

Have I made any missteps with regard to Aidan? I answer "no" to that with contemptuous certainty; the question itself antagonizes me. What does my reluctance to recall my history with Aidan say about my sense of culpability in our alienation? I accept my responsibility for it. I wanted it and I don't care how people judge me for that.

"Still the indifferent manager, Dan? In your professional life just like your love life."

I'm voicing Grayson in this give-and-take, so introducing my love life puzzles me. He inferred a disturbing correspondence of detachment in my professional and personal demeanors, which for ego-stroking purposes, I labeled consistency and predictability. But what I appreciated about Grayson was the absence of judgment in his observations. His moral code never demanded a verdict of my behavior, as long as it didn't harm the firm. I know he found my lifestyle disappointing, because it didn't allow me to experience what he found in his family, while I sometimes smirked at the extent to which he idealized his marriage, a perfect union of soulmates tethered to one another by unshakeable devotion. At a Christmas party at his home in Iske Park the week before the expected Y2K crisis, I waited outside the door to a bathroom on the second floor. When it opened, his wife Iris grinned when she saw me, leaned in for a kiss to my cheek, but I clutched her chin and kissed her on the lips, staring into her eyes for the brief duration, as did she. In the moment when we backed away from one another, I sensed Iris pondering the temptation, deliberating and assessing, before she smirked, shook her head, and muttered my name.

I dislike myself for that encounter. Not drunk but nearing that state. I never drank at work functions and usually moderated my consumption in personal situations. Dates. Friday evenings with our staff. My father, while not a classic alcoholic, drank in excess and it affected his behavior, manifesting itself as clumsy ebullience; he was a sloppy, happy drunk, never violent, prone to tearful bouts of lamenting his shortcomings as husband and father. Accosting Iris that night, when my father's example governed my drinking, bothered me. Why had I tested her? The morning after, when I reviewed the event, I considered that I hadn't sought the pleasure of kissing her, I'd kissed Iris to erode Grayson's faith in the flawlessness of his life, to whittle a splinter from that bastion of perfection. Reinforced by a hangover, I spent the day mired in remorse, resisting the compulsion to call Iris and apologize. We never spoke of it and no other such encounter ever happened.

"Yeah, Grayson," I say. "Still coldblooded and indifferent."

7.

Maggie tilts Daniel's novel off the shelf and reads the promotional snippets about him, then opens the back cover and examines her uncle's black and white author photo. The beard was shorter and less gray, neatly trimmed to a uniform length, and her attention is drawn to the sharply-focused intensity of his eyes, reinforced by an unsmiling gaze. Had he shown her a genuine smile when they visited or when they Zoomed? She still senses reticence. It's not complete uncooperativeness, but for all his bluster about not censoring the truth, he seems unprepared for all-inclusive candor. She told Samuel that if she touches on out-of-bounds areas, her uncle will deflect or refuse.

"There are walls," she said.

"Climb them, go around them?" Samuel asked.

Maggie shook her head. "Wait for him to open a gate. He's created no trespassing areas of his life."

"Deserves his privacy, doesn't he?" Samuel reclined in his favorite wingback chair, feet propped on a matching ottoman. He cupped a tumbler of vodka and ice in his lap, swirling the cubes in the glass after each sip.

Maggie nodded. "But I want in," she said.

"If you can't go over or around, you'll have to be patient."

"I'm afraid his adamance will outlast my patience."

"Vigorous patience then, Mags," Samuel said.

She chuckled at the resourcefulness of his non-sequiturs.

"Passive aggression," he said. "Camouflage your intentions."

"He's not a stupid man," Maggie said. "He'll recognize the ploy."

"When a farmer mounts a scarecrow in his field, the crows know it's not a real person, but as a token of respect for the farmer's effort, they leave the corn alone."

"I think you've lived in Iowa too long," Maggie said, wagging her head in laughter.

"Show your uncle respect for his boundaries, but keep pressing. Show him your intentions aren't a threat to him."

Maggie fell silent, considering Samuel's advice. Moments like these made her wonder why he'd never aspired to a different career; she believed him skilled enough to excel in academia, law, or psychology, but the first, and only time she broached the subject with him, Samuel's eyes deadened, his smile withered, Maggie recognized her blunder, and swore never to repeat it. "Information is worthless if you can't find it," he told her. "I'm its curator. A steward. I funnel people from knowledge to wisdom." Maggie valued this prideful streak in Samuel's otherwise easy-going and affable personality.

"Drip-drip rather than a tidal wave," she said.

"Exactly," Samuel said. "He needs time to shift his stance, not be bowled over."

"Time is not my friend."

"I suspect he doesn't think it's his either," Samuel said. "If he's determined to take secrets to his grave, then nothing you do will force him to open the gate. But if his reticence is an artifice, he might appreciate your persistence and invite you in."

"He's not anxious for his story to be told," Maggie said. "And there may not be any amount of cajoling to convince him."

"Then you get what you can and congratulate yourself for trying."

Maggie replaces Daniel's novel on the shelf, deciding not to bring it for an inscription when she travels to Michigan next month at the end of the semester. She keeps a file of reviews for the book and imagines Daniel doing the same. A duality of his nature: generally unconcerned with other's opinion of him except in certain areas. Like those secrets about himself she'd love to uncover and examine. Grandma Breedlow told her no one understands a man like his brother, prompting Maggie to think of how she related to her sisters, how growing up with them afforded her insight that their husbands and friends would never know. Spouses, partners like Samuel, form the most intimate bonds in a person's life, but a sibling connection remains unique. Secrets about who you are aren't held as dear as secrets of how you became that person, and your siblings are the witnesses to that process. They're causes as well, she thinks. Daniel shared a childhood with her father, had watched the boy adapt, resist, accede, and harden into the man who married and divorced her mother, who abandoned and shunned his family as Daniel had. Non-communication isn't distance, she thinks. Her father never detached from his mother or Daniel's other siblings. Although contact was infrequent, they talked, they visited, and her father reinforced distance from them by rejecting any commonality of belief. Especially of religion. Only Daniel dropped the curtain on all association with his brother.

Samuel called examining their relationship a fascinating opportunity, considering how Daniel had arrested it at such an early age. "Tracing the paths each led after the break will be intriguing," he said. "I assume there will be unintentional parallels, even though the disconnect was purposeful."

"I'd love to know the ratio of intent to reflex," Maggie says.

"Which one do you think made the greater effort?"

"My father was more reflexive," she said. "His reactions may have started as choices to do the opposite of what Daniel did, but then they became habits.

Intrinsic to his personality. Daniel distancing himself not from my father, but the entire family, was intentional from the beginning and remains that way."

"And you want to know why," Samuel said.

"About my father's influence on why, yes."

"Your curiosity isn't that circumspect, Mags."

She tilted her head and widened her eyes. "If in the course of exploring my father's relationship with his brother, I happen to learn something about Daniel that completes my picture of the man, then so be it."

Samuel uttered his special chortle and sipped from his vodka. "Vigorous patience," he repeated.

Maggie recalls the conversation with Samuel as she drafts a response to Daniel's email suggesting times for another Zoom session. The afternoon slot tomorrow works for her. Her uncle's reference to the two brothers being Irish twins makes her speculate their lives share more consistency than he suspects. How ironic if she sharpens Daniel's conception of his brother more than he does for her.

The conversation with Samuel fresh in her mind, Maggie covers her shoulders with a sweater and steps into her backyard, smiling as sunshine warms her face. Daffodils and crocuses daub their colors along the fence line and she fears a late frost will wilt the flowers. Staring at the blue sky, she imagines how a half-hour drive into the surrounding farm country provides scenes of tractors dredging furrows in the earth, the preparation for planting. Each spring she and Samuel drive in the country, meandering off the highway onto gravel county roads to witness the farmers' ritual. The ride has become their ritual, a reminder of where they live, that the enclave of the university is a comforting fiction within an overall less idyllic reality. History, she understands, means little to the bulk of the population that surrounds the nub of Iowa City, and neither she nor Samuel clings to any illusions about the nobility of the rural folk who regard the university as the owner of a football team, and who annually complain to the legislature about the amount of tax dollars spent on frivolous, *aka liberal*, education. And lately, fascists leap beyond ambivalence about the study of history, they're dictating to local school boards what exactly a teacher can say in a classroom. American history is horrible, but these people assert a right not to be offended. The truth of history offends, Maggie thinks, and recognizes how the difference between truth and what people want to be true poses so much danger to her field. There was a book burning in Tennessee last month by a fundamentalist preacher striving to drive out demonic forces. Politicians banning books in schools and libraries. Controlling access to information. Conservative voices openly advocating a Christian theocracy for the country. She and Samuel joked when Trump was elected that they should leave the U.S., move to a liberal country like Denmark or Sweden, but weighing the toll of such an upheaval, opted for waiting him out. Certainly, they insisted, the country will come to its senses and remove him before he completed a full term. They now shake their heads at the breadth of such a miscalculation. Samuel returned home one night from work with detailed instructions for renouncing their citizenship and moving to Norway. Maggie studied the regulations and the costs involved, (the government charged a fee for anyone renouncing citizenship and Samuel balked at paying it while Trump remained in office), lamented the repercussions such a move would inflict on her sisters, but confirmed to Samuel that she found the possibility tempting for so many reasons, most prominently how it reinforced her intellectual principles. And then the COVID pandemic struck and they faced a plague mishandled by a corrupt administration, a pandemic that prohibited them from escaping to another country, even had they chosen to do so. A conundrum which allowed for derisive laughter but not much more. When Biden defeated Trump, they sighed with temporary relief, but realized after four years of watching the deplorables crawling out from under the rocks that kept them out of the public eye, nothing would ever again be the same. Maggie warned Samuel that the patterns of fascism in Europe prior to World War II now bubbled around them, and despite the hope sparked by Trump's defeat, they renewed their research into possible relocation, broadening their search beyond Norway and the other Scandinavian nations to include New Zealand, Canada, and Switzerland. She had said nothing to her sisters about these discussions and knew that if she and Samuel shifted talking into planning, the fallout from them would be emotional. Maggie expected Hailey especially would interpret their relocation as abandonment, would never accept that Maggie and Samuel were moving toward something rather than away from her. It might cause an irreparable rift.

Like between Daniel and his family, she muses, tugging the sweater more tightly around her shoulders as a chilling breeze raises goose flesh on her arms. A professor years ago in a graduate seminar asserted that personal interactions influenced history as much as wars and famines. Her father's prominence in the family history underpins her only resistance to leaving the country, a reluctance Samuel understands, even though it exasperates him. Should she mention this to Daniel as an instance of being like-minded?

When she crafts a profile of her uncle, a few overlaps in their circumstances stand out. She and Samuel live isolated in their Iowa City doughnut hole as Daniel does on the west coast of Michigan. Acknowledging that distance isn't solely physical, does he gain more serenity, even gratification, from his location than they do from theirs? She's more communicative, by necessity and choice, but sympathizes, (does she envy?), Daniel's choices. Or does she resent his ability to make those choices? He's unfettered. She's tethered. Those facts are irrefutable but they're not neutral. When she and Samuel debated leaving the country, they understood the strain such distance would place on their relationships with family and friends, never considering severing them. She wants and needs Samuel, her sisters, their friends. Unlike Daniel, the absolutist. She remembers all the photos in his living room: black and white prints. Too far-fetched an observation? To judge his character by his preference of photography? Decisions have been made on less evidence, often with disastrous results, she reminds herself. Vigorous patience. The advice makes her smile as she returns to the house.

She calls Hailey, who answers with, "Hey, Sis."

"I was thinking about you," Maggie says.

"That's a coincidence," Hailey says. "I was telling Paul last night about the spring break trip to the Ozarks we took when I was little."

"You remember that?" Hailey was three or four years old at the time. The last trip they took as a family before their father left.

"Jessica doubted I had any memories," Hailey says. "But I remember the cabin Dad rented. Its musty smell."

"Yeah," Maggie says, certain this memory is a story their mother told Hailey years after the trip.

"There were canoes," Hailey continues. "And we explored a cave."

There had been a cave tour, Maggie recalls, during which the guide cautioned everyone she was going to switch off the lights, and then Maggie heard gasps as a blackness more complete than she had ever encountered swallowed them. The guide instructed everyone to place a hand before their faces and strain to see their fingers. People laughed but Hailey began to cry, insisting her hand had disappeared, until the lights were turned back on. She wept in their mother's arms as they resumed the tour. How could her sister possibly remember that?

"Yes," she says. "There were canoes. You went out with Dad."

"You made me a dream catcher for my bedroom window, remember? In the crafts class. White feathers and turquoise beads."

"I do," Maggie says. "You don't still have that, do you?"

"God, no," Hailey says. "I tossed that years ago."

From the dismissive tone of her sister's voice, Maggie understands that Hailey never valued the dream catcher beyond denying Maggie its possession. She remembers decorating the willow hoop, how Hailey begged her for it when they returned home. She'd never intended for it to be a gift for her sister but their mother pressed Maggie to placate the girl, and it occurs to her that no one ever demanded sacrifices of Hailey in support of family peace. Might she harbor some resentment towards her sister for that?

"I thought maybe it was something you'd kept, as a memento," Maggie says.

"No," Hailey says. "It got lost in one of the moves."

"How's the family?" she asks.

"All's good," Hailey says. "But I have some news." She pauses. "Paul and I are moving to Texas. Austin. His company is transferring him at the end of summer."

"Texas," she says, not bothering to hide the derision in her tone.

"Austin's not like the rest of the state," Hailey says, the snippy tone in her voice warning Maggie that she's rehearsed this conversation.

"Austin's where they make the hateful laws, Hailey. All the racist, white supremacist laws." It's certainly not Norway, she thinks.

"It's a promotion," she says. "More money, more responsibility. Paul's excited."

Maggie says nothing for several moments, imagining her sister's unease at the silence.

"I didn't call to ask you to be happy for us, Maggie. I wanted to let you know."

"I'm sorry, Hailey," Maggie says. "How do you feel about the move?"

"Oh," Hailey says.

Maggie thinks she sounds surprised by the question.

"The boys are grown. I'll miss Jess. But this is a fantastic opportunity for Paul." She pauses. "And the company made it obvious it's a take it or clear off situation."

"They'd fire him if he didn't go?" Maggie says, her face folding into a grimace.

"His boss avoided being that blunt, but Paul understood the message."

Maggie wags her head. "So they sweetened the deal to take the sting out of it."

"It's a promotion, Maggie," Hailey insists in a tone of voice that warns Maggie her sister is on the verge of another tantrum. The kind of outburst their mother smothered by demanding compromises from her and Jessica.

"Have you told Jessica?" she asks, hoping to forestall a petulant eruption.

"A few days ago. I asked her not to say anything until I could talk to you."

Hailey keeps her tone even, no inflections, a sign, Maggie knows, that although forestalled, a tantrum remains possible. Suddenly she questions Hailey's recollection of the trip to the Ozarks, how the memory casts their father in a positive light, behavior unlike Hailey, who never had a good word to say about the man. Did the story figure in Hailey's news that she was moving?

"And the boys?" she asks.

"Ben has already interviewed with companies outside Missouri," she says. "He was never going to remain in St. Louis. Tommy's looking at master's programs in New York."

"That's wonderful," Maggie says.

"I think I'll go back to school," Hailey says. "It's not too late, is it?"

Hailey dropped out of college after marrying Paul to raise their family, never expressing regret about her decision, but Maggie wondered from time to time if Hailey envied her sisters' careers. Their mother had worked by necessity, even after marrying Scott, but relentlessly grumbled about it, and Hailey, as the youngest, absorbed the longest stretches of that grievance. Maggie wonders if Hailey accepted her domestic role without complaint as a reaction to that unfairness. To insure her children never experienced the neglect she felt as a child. After the debacle of her marriage to Aidan, their mother wanted to be kept and cared for, felt she deserved pampering, but she and Scott learned that entitlement carries a price tag; they needed her mother's salary to afford what she demanded. Maggie knows if their mother had curbed her excesses, she never would have had to work.

"It's never too late, Hailey," she says. Encourage her, Maggie thinks. "There's a sizeable adult student population here. I'm sure it's the same at the University of Texas."

"I was thinking of a community college to start out," Hailey says. "Tiptoe back into it."

"I think that's wonderful," Maggie says. "What do you think you'll study?"

"Languages. I've always loved languages. Spanish, maybe French."

"I'm sure Spanish would be helpful in Texas." She pauses. "Daniel was a linguist in the Air Force, did you know that?"

"I think I did, but I don't remember," Hailey says. "I was never clear on what he did in the war. Dad never said much about it."

"I think he was jealous that Daniel was in the service," Maggie says.

"I do remember that," Hailey says.

"Grandma Breedlow says Dad threatened to join the Marines when Daniel enlisted in the Air Force. To one-up him."

Hailey snorts. "I can't imagine Dad surviving Marine boot camp. More of his moronic blustering. The man was a chronic liar."

Maggie smiles at Hailey's comment, recalling her sister's own fanciful relationship with truth when she was a child. Her embellishments and exaggerations, as their mother called them. Bald-faced lies she and Jessica labeled them. "She'd tell a lie when the truth would serve her better," Jessica once said when Hailey was in high school and agonized over the backlash of having invented a boyfriend who wasn't aware he was in a relationship with her. Typical of Hailey, she lied her way through the ridicule, shifting all accountability to the hapless boy.

The boyfriend debacle paled in comparison to the lies she constructed to explain their father's absence. Logging giant redwoods in northern Canada. Mining rare metals in South America. Captain of a fishing boat in the Indian Ocean. Every tall tale Hailey employed to explain their father's disappearance involved distant, exotic work, but the mom network at their school had already confirmed the scandalous reasons for Aidan Breedlow's desertion, and Maggie felt sad imagining her sister bragging to her classmates when they all knew the truth from overhearing the gossip among their mothers. The meaner girls surely challenged Hailey's claims. How did those encounters affect her sister? Was she humiliated by the assault on her claims or did the attacks fortify the conviction of her lies?

"Will you be able to come home before we move?" Hailey asks. "It'd be nice for everyone to get together."

"Of course, we'll try," Maggie says, imagining her sister's expression at not receiving a commitment. "Except for my trip to Michigan, we have no other plans."

"We hope to get all the cousins together, so I'll let you know when we settle on a date," Hailey says. Her tone warns Maggie of the peril of disappointing her.

"That's great, Hailey," she says. "Good God, it just occurred to me. You'll be moving to Texas in August!"

Her sister chuckled. "Paul already talked about how he's not going to miss winter. Said he's going to leave the snow blower and shovels to whoever buys the house."

They wish each other hugs and kisses and then Maggie sits at her desk, experiencing an epiphany of how she relies upon her sisters to anchor St. Louis as home, how their presence where she grew up provides a counterpoint to her ramblings. The opposite of what happened to Daniel, when his family moved to Arizona while he was in the war. Did he accept that as serendipity or an omen? According to Grandma Breedlow, his dissociation from the family began before his enlistment, and Maggie wonders what could have motivated him to use the Air Force as a way of fracturing those family bonds. Why resort to such a drastic move in wartime?

She winces as the notion that Hailey and Paul moving to Austin signals the spark of a chain reaction within her family. An inevitable scattering of nieces and nephews. Jessica's daughters all live within an hour's drive of St. Louis, but Maggie knows this is an American anomaly. After college and graduate school, she relocated for jobs without feeling any qualms about her absence's effect on her mother and sisters, all to advance her career. The four-hour drive from Iowa City to St. Louis owes more to chance than planning. She would have tolerated any distance from her family for a tenure track position. Does her ambition parallel Daniel's path? Which was more of an imperative: securing a lucrative career or distancing himself from his family while he pursued it?

The contrast between the brothers continues to surprise, but not shock, Maggie. Her aunt filled in many of the blanks for much of what she knows of them when they were children. She was the youngest of the first three, admits she was treated by their father as a princess until Elizabeth and Luke were born, and that Aidan resented their father's regard for her more than Daniel had. Aidan often spit the word "Princess" at her whenever he sensed their father's favoritism.

"I never tried to provoke that reaction," Laura told her. "Danny didn't try to provoke Aidan either. Danny was whip-smart. He got *As* on his report card without really trying and that always pissed off Aidan. He struggled in school. But I still don't know which was the chicken and which was the egg. Did Aidan give up because of how he was compared to Danny or was he never capable?"

"Your mother thinks he suffered in Daniel's shadow," Maggie said. "That he tanked his grades on purpose."

Laura laughed. "She's invested in that image of him. Anything else casts her in a bad light, right? I've given up trying to make her see that his flaws were inherent, not reactions to Danny, but she'll never unlink them, I'm afraid."

When Maggie told Laura that Grandma Breedlow said she had hoped giving Daniel space after he returned from the Air Force would help improve their relationship, but only later understood why he craved that space, her aunt sighed. "She never says he returned from the *war*, always that he returned from the *Air Force*," Laura said. "Isn't it interesting how she avoids that word? Like she fears that when Danny came home, we were just another battle in his war."

"A war of attrition," Maggie said.

"Absolutely," Laura said. "There are the dead and then there are those who are dead to Danny."

"Thar's an unsympathetic assessment, Laura," Maggie said.

"Don't be fooled. Danny talks to Mom and to me, but it's all superficial," she said. "I know nothing about his life since we were kids except broad outlines. A *Cliff's Notes* of *The Life of Daniel Breedlow* would have more detail than what he lets us know."

"Holy shit," Maggie said.

"That's the hill you plan to climb," Laura said.

Her aunt wasn't the only family member to misconstrue her intentions in reaching out to Daniel, and she wondered if the confusion was intentional. She sought Daniel's memories for intuition into her father's personality, into what drove him to make the decisions he made and how they affected her and her sisters, but Jessica and Grandma Breedlow persisted in believing that to be a secondary goal. Her uncle's mystique drives their conviction that he's far more interesting than her father, who to them seemed a simple story. An unprincipled man guided more by lust than by loyalty. Even Laura admitted that Aidan "let his dick lead him, until he found Jesus." She had paused. "And I always suspected that was a scam, too."

8.

Sandrine Vincent. An event planner in Chicago, booked by cultural nonprofits whose boards boasted executives' wives from the North Shore. If you worked in the city's charitable world, you knew them. Black-tie fundraising extravaganzas. Glitz and glamour for a worthy cause. These North Shore mavens acquired status through their husbands' careers and flexed their cachet in competitive oversight of social events benefitting the symphony, the opera, art and history museums, dance companies, choral groups, all within a structured hierarchy, ranging from long-established, blue-chip organizations to fledgling groups operating on shoe-string budgets. Their "one-up-woman-ship" taxed the patience of development staff at those organizations but defying them could be costly.

Sandrine earned favoritism in those circles for her inventiveness in staging elegant, creatively-themed events and for her willowy manipulation of the mavens. She'd cajole, seduce, charm, flatter, and if necessary browbeat any maven in service of the impeccable event. Grayson and I interacted with her through our pro bono work, leveraged by our association with the mavens' husbands. Scratch my back. The circles we entered heightened our visibility.

Maggie reminds me of Sandrine, tangentially. They resemble one another in attitude and mannerisms. Sandrine telegraphed a tender reproach with a sighed “Oh,” an appreciative nod, and then she’d bite her lower lip, pause, say “Except…” and the maven never understood the caress she felt was a hammer blow to her suggestion. She never could have sustained her reputation without results and Sandrine produced them until her prestige approached legend. Our affair began when the firm coordinated the public relations for a photography museum fundraiser, featuring an exhibition of work by local street photographers. A small organization by Sandrine’s standards, so her involvement surprised me. Grayson didn’t think we’d mine new clients from the event and although we’d ordinarily assign a senior associate to the work, with my enthusiasm for photography, he understood when I assumed the responsibility. During a visit to the exhibit space, a refurbished warehouse on a derelict stretch of South Michigan Avenue, Sandrine impressed me: a firm handshake, slim smile, and unflinching eye contact, held for an instant longer than demanded by cordiality. When moments of mutual attraction occur, it’s refreshing when both parties acknowledge them. Each of us later admitted we’d sensed our future trajectory at that meeting. One time I called her Sandy and she lifted herself from the mattress onto an elbow and told me never to call her that again if I wanted to continue enjoying her. Those were her words: “enjoying me.” Being with Sandrine broke a pattern of sleeping with women who expected more from me than I wanted to give. Of relationships I ended when the woman began presuming, clinging, or despairing at the dreadful apprehension that she’d invested time in an “us” that never existed. Two to tango and she’d been dancing alone. I’d caused mawkish breakups, dismissed my remorse, and refined my search for a new lover, a like-minded woman, who wanted a no-strings-attached fuck buddy.

Maggie’s forthrightness reminds me of Sandrine, who could pivot from indulgent kneading of the mavens to aggressive directness with me in an instant. I chuckle at asking Samuel if he’s ever gotten on her bad side and what that’s like.

In client debriefings, Grayson, shedding his suitcoat, sat with one leg crossed over the other at the knee, tapping his iPad, projecting a sense of informality. He wanted to differentiate for the associates the contradictory natures of each meeting: with the client and with one another. Our laidback, unconstrained behavior in one didn't cross over into the other. It was the same with Sandrine. When we coordinated on events, prim and proper regulated our interactions, even if later that night we fucked like rutting beasts. Sandrine once described our relationship as having a gym buddy, with the only workout routine being sex. We didn't shy from discussing our fondness for one another, our general compatibilities and admitted loving one another without being *in* love. The relationship confounded Grayson, who told me he was happy I'd outgrown the pattern of stringing women along until they loved me and then leaving them, an assertion I denied.

"Come on, Dan," Grayson said. "It's what you do. Make them love you. Like that's the only reason you're with them."

I brooded that night, contemplating words I'd dismiss from anyone but Grayson. Was he right? Was the goal of my relationships making the women love me? Once a lover crossed that line, was it a signal? A trigger? Love me, *love me*, so I can leave you. What disturbed me most about his observation was the inference that if I didn't gain a woman's love, I'd failed. I couldn't deny the pattern after he so plainly stated it.

Sandrine and I remained "together" for years, enjoying a non-exclusive attachment. Something I've never replicated. Break-ups where the lover groveled made me question what had first attracted me to them. Called a bastard, a prick, a dick. Sandrine smiled when we traded stories of ending past relationships, how jilted lovers labeled her bitch, cunt, and slut, and we debated whether men's terms for women in these situations were coarser, more insulting. She argued the intention of all the terms was identical, that judging one gender's insults more offensive than the other only served the patriarchy. "You'll always be a member of that club," she said.

She moved to Los Angeles and whenever work took me to California, I'd spend a day with her. We catch up on social media, comment on one another's posts. She admires my photography and for her seventieth birthday, I sent a framed print of La Salle Avenue during a nighttime snowstorm, at the corner of West Washington Street, looking south to the Board of Trade. An otherworldly, black and white image of the street lamps casting unfocused cones of light through the falling snow, the indistinct buildings in that canyon looming like mumbled words. Like me, she lives alone, and in her last email suggested we write a book espousing the advantages and rewards of the genres of solitude. She liked my novel and was one of only two people I recall from my professional life who never sought to identify themselves as characters. Grayson was the other.

Maggie's accomplishing what she wants: I'm revisiting my life if not recalling what she wants of it.

When my parents divorced, coinciding with one of Aidan's, I felt superior to both men, but that's like claiming I've never been sacked in the NFL when I never played the game. My relationships started as adventures, as I'm sure my father's and brother's did, although I want to believe our techniques differed. They were hunters, stalking women like prey; I was a trapper, enticing women to come to me. My mother, Aidan's wives, and all of the women I've wounded, would shred such a distinction. The last bastard-prick-dick alive. I'm curious to know how my brother's infidelities affected Maggie's relationships. Trust issues, naturally. Not married since she introduced Samuel as her partner, not husband. That's a line of questioning for future sessions. Maybe it's at the core of why she wants to know more about Aidan. Does she suspect he's responsible for a flaw in her character? A Breedlow genetic inadequacy? What about her sisters? Are they married? With happy families? She can't think only the firstborn inherits the flaw.

I assume Maggie's mother, Lisa, worked and I wonder if responsibility for watching her sisters fell to her, as caring for my siblings had to me.

Did the resentment of that task flow both ways for her, too? Aidan chafing at my assignment, Maggie's sisters at hers. There's so much to ask her that will provide insight into how much alike we are. My mother, I'm certain, advised her to scratch my curiosity as a way to open me up. It's exactly what I'd do. I still could have refused but I felt empathy for Maggie when she sat in my living room, trying to convince me that I could offer insight into her father, an absence she's identified in the story of her family. Like I feel for my father, a man I never bothered to know in the ways that could be helpful in my life, except as an example of behavior I shouldn't duplicate, and yet did. Does Maggie share the fear I had when I was young? That I was destined to become a copy of my father? Another recognizable pattern: rebelling against a parent, never once considering that the parent was once a rebellious child defying his own father or mother. Every other generation develops an affinity: a grandparent for a grandchild's struggles against the common denominator, and it's sad for the grandparent to watch the echoing cycle and know that any consolation offered will be rejected as a reflex. Children can't, or *won't*, countenance their parents' capacity for regret, the longing for a second chance at childrearing, the melancholy wish that they'd done things differently when they see their mistakes repeated in a son's behavior toward *his* son. But can being a good parent save the marriage of an errant spouse? My mother never tried.

The change in expression on Maggie's face when Samuel interrupted our Zoom session conveyed a partial answer, and ironically, it's an expression I never wanted. Well. That's not entirely true if I believe what Grayson believed. I wanted love right up to the point where I received it and then I rejected it.

My family regards me as a mystery, one I've reinforced since I returned from the war. When I was their caretaker, the younger two, unlike Aidan, admired me. Obeyed me. Their unformed personalities helped that dynamic work. I was the oldest brother, an authority figure with a more lenient touch than either Mom or Dad. Elizabeth and Luke saw me as a protector, as a heroic figure, especially after I enlisted. Mom's letters always included notes from them, urging me to be safe, hoping that I didn't have to kill any enemies. Mom never clarified their fanciful ideas of what I did in the Air Force. They were young and glorified serving in the military; nightly newscasts of battles and body counts reinforced their concerns, unlike Laura, who criticized my enlistment, condemning it one night before I left for basic training. She begged to know why I was doing it and I balked at telling her I knew of no other way to escape the family.

Has Maggie ever faced a similar decision or was mine a false choice? Did I need to abandon everyone in my family? Why such a complete rejection? My father pointed to the war as the cause of my distress with the family. This was years later, before his illness, at Luke's first wedding reception when we sat across from one another at a round table in the rear of the ballroom. In the dimmed house lights a mirrored ball rotated above the dance floor, firing bolts of jeweled light around the room, passing shadows across my father's face, reminding me that I'd never known the man. Each time a beam of light illuminated his face, I imagined highlighting insight into his thoughts, but I knew it was too late. My father crossed his legs and bobbed the hanging foot against the ruffled tablecloth. He'd switched from champagne to beer. I sipped ginger ale, adamant not to get drunk in front of any relatives. We each wore tuxedos, appearing to onlookers as the father of the groom and one of the groomsmen engaged in a casual conversation. No one would have imagined my father apologizing for what the war had done to me.

"You were different when you came back," he said. "If I'd known then what I know now, I'd have driven you to Canada to avoid the draft. It's not like when I was in the Navy."

I reminded him our times were different and weathered the tug of sympathy I felt for him in that moment. The opening for a heart-to-heart had passed, or as Grayson would say, I was too cold-blooded for any reconciliation. Laura had begged me to come to the wedding, to accept Luke's invitation to serve as one his groomsmen and I did so reluctantly, flying in the day before the ceremony and leaving the morning after, staying in a hotel instead of in my parent's guest room, which aggravated my mother. Listening to my father's alcohol-fueled lamentations convinced me I should avoid all family occasions, wanting never again to endure my father's self-serving candor. The next and last time I saw him confirmed what my mother suspected about my alienation: I was ashamed of my family, of where I came from. My father needed to believe, to soothe his conscience, that the war caused the changes he perceived in me and not the reunion with a family that embarrassed me.

But that was a long time ago.

Origin stories. Humble beginnings as code for surviving a broken family, where oral and physical abuse engendered fearful self-doubt, then morphed into resentful adult determination to escape the cycle of damage. Focusing too intently on one piece of a puzzle blinds you to the overall picture and the goal becomes a self-fulfilling prophecy. My father wasn't a beater, not physically, he berated his children by regularly mocking their ambitions. When Aidan, like every Catholic schoolboy, expressed interest in a religious vocation, of becoming a priest, my father declared he wasn't good enough to be a "pimple on a priest's ass." Some children would seize upon that derision as motivation, but Aidan crumpled, and I wonder if his vulnerability to my father's ridicule helped me grow inured to it. Ironic to consider I might owe my brother that debt.

Maggie's knowledge of my origin story: a jigsaw puzzle comprised of ill-fitting pieces from different boxes and she wants my help to swap counterfeit pieces for genuine ones. She's counting on my curiosity about the contradictions in the stories, those she heard as a child from her mother and father, and those she's heard from Laura and my mother, to draw me into revelations about Aidan. Or simply about myself. Does she believe I'm that different from her father? Two brothers of like nature living comparable lives even though they hated one another. Maggie might see her father's patterns of infidelity repeated in my relationships, except I never made the mistake of marrying any of the women I fucked. Aidan wouldn't be the first Catholic boy who rearranged the love-marriage-sex progression and fell in love with every woman he fucked. The love he felt was nothing more than gratitude. Thankfulness for access to sex. For all its teaching about the role of women as subservient servants, the Catholic Church couldn't avoid giving them supremacy over one critical aspect of a relationship: control over sex. A high school girlfriend once told me the reason she let me touch her breasts but wouldn't let me fuck her was because Jesus's legs were crossed on the crucifix.

The absurdity of religion, especially the ways its adherents interpret and practice its tenets, is ludicrous but for the danger it poses. When I read and post stories about global strife online, I feel we've entered an Age of Un-Enlightenment. People like Luke and Elizabeth glorifying prideful ignorance. Aidan jumped from the Catholic Church to an evangelical sandbox, waving the Bible in one hand and the flag in the other.

I imagine the expression on Maggie's face, telling her I keep survival rations in my garage. Probably similar to my face when Grayson told me that Costco sold coffins. Amazon sells the rations, with twenty-five year shelf life. Powdered. Dehydrated. Freeze-dried. Stored in packets, buckets. Formed into one-a-day pellets that meet a daily requirement of 1200 calories. Water purification tablets. Hand-cranked radios. Bring on the apocalypse. Laura said Aidan lived in a small town, on a cul-de-sac with other church members, and I imagined a cultish compound of end-of-days preppers, although when I read articles about fundamentalists preparing for Christ's return, I question the stockpiling of weapons and rations. Won't those true believers number among those ascending to the kingdom of heaven on Judgement Day? What need do they have for worldly goods? Taunting Aidan for the hypocrisy of his practices would almost have been worth the effort of talking to him. *Almost.*

How do I make Maggie understand how I don't make, haven't made, decisions about Aidan for years, because he wasn't a factor in my life? I need to work on the precise terminology to explain it. He wasn't an absence in my life since absence requires a consciousness of thought. Was Aidan a void? An unacknowledged emptiness? I *un-regarded* my brother. A deleted file. I imagine her hurried claim that no file is ever lost, that a trace remains, that it can be recovered, but those kinds of assertions serve her purpose. Can I ease her into understanding by explaining how I learned that rather than battling with my parents, and with their ally Aidan, accosting them with silence proved a far more poisonous tactic? Blocking my father from my emotions antagonized him more than any argument ever had and I relished his frustration. It saddened and depressed my mother, whom I never considered a protective hen prizing family above all else. I thought her complaints about our shortcomings exhibited selfishness, how every misbehavior reflected on *her*. Poor grades failed *her*. Misconduct embarrassed *her*. Naughtiness denigrated *her*. Mothers dominate a child's early life and the stories about the disappointment a mother feels as children grow apart from her are mythic, but my mother sanctified her martyred anguish into a fifteenth station of the cross. When I speak with her now, I imagine a disapproving grimace: none of us ever said enough penance to justify her absolution.

This relationship with Maggie strikes me as one unlike any other I've had with a woman. I shield my mother and sisters from the intimacy my niece seeks and with my lovers, except for Sandrine, when intimacy became a contention, it signaled the waning of my interest in the relationship. Was I too impulsive in agreeing to speak with Maggie? My enlistment in the Air Force was an impulse. My entanglements with women during my years at Northwestern were impulses. When I met Grayson at the firm where we both learned the basics of what became a lucrative craft, our mentor throttled the impulsive streak from me. He always insisted the "P" in PR should stand for patience.

Each day now epitomizes patience. There is nothing toward which I need to rush, to hurry. In my office, I lift my Martin D-45 and adjust the strings to open D tuning, first by ear, and then double-checking my approximation against a tuner. With a medium flat pick I strum the instrument, feeling the richness of the intonations rebounding against the exacting surfaces of the concrete walls. I glide my fingers up and down the fretboard, forming chord progressions, avoiding minor chords to partner the music with the sunniness of the day, tapping the strings at the fifth, seventh, and twelfth frets to produce resounding harmonics. I love this guitar's sound and close my eyes, blindly reiterating a chord progression, humming a melody to weave through its foundation. Prior to the pandemic, I occasionally played at a bar in Grand Haven that hosted open mic night on Wednesdays. I sang three songs, acoustic covers of singer-songwriters from the sixties and seventies, introducing myself as Daniel, beginning my selections without prologue, pausing after each song for the polite and sometimes enthusiastic applause, and then after the third song, rising, carrying my guitar to its case, and leaving the bar. The manager once told me I'd developed a following, intrigued both by my song selection and my post-performance mysterious departures.

Now I play for personal enjoyment. For gratification and to consolidate my thoughts. I bought my first guitar in Okinawa at a music store in Koza, a few blocks outside the air base. A bottom-of-the-line Yamaha six-string, which I still have, although I rarely play it anymore. It's not a well-crafted instrument. The action is high, the resonance tinny. But there's an emotional attachment to it as my first and when the mood strikes, I'll take it to the summer house and strum through several songs that I learned on the instrument. A woman renting the house to the south once heard me and stood listening, leaning against a tree trunk, startling me by clapping when I'd finished. "Lovely," she said. I thanked her, glanced at my watch, feigned surprise, and returned to the house. Audiences are superfluous. I played at the bar to experience the fullness of the music through its sound system. That's my story, and I'm sticking to it.

My childhood never exposed me to culture or the arts, except for church hymns, which I enjoyed for the opportunity they offered for harmonizing with melodies, for finding the complementary notes to a lead vocal. The nuns praised my voice and I remember feeling flushed with pride preparing for Christmas concerts. I marvel at the transition of that cherub-voiced boy into the man strumming the guitar today. A misanthrope with a castaway's beard bobbing his head in rhythm to a song no one else hears. Literally and figuratively.

The pro bono work at the firm nurtured a cultural education. Public relations professionals are broad generalists, deeply knowledgeable about their practice but embarrassingly shallow about other areas. Our essential preparation for a client meeting involved crash courses in that man's expertise. Farm equipment manufacturing. Accountancy. Hospital management. Grayson and I joked we should write a series of the "Dummy" books each time we crammed for a new client. What we lacked in our hasty research about a client's specialization we asked them to provide, playing to their egos as the "experts at what you do." So much smoke and mirrors. But when I donated my services to museums, to the symphony or opera, I tossed the pretense of even a rudimentary familiarity with the subject and listened to the curators, the managers, and the docents with obsessive attentiveness. My dates with Sandrine often consisted of visits to gallery openings, attendance at concerts, recitals, and performances, and she scoffed at any suggestion they were busman's holidays. She thrived in a cultural setting and that cerebral exhilaration always translated into sexual passion, prompting me once to joke that I was sleeping with my teacher. Rather than bristle at the comment, she smirked, sat upright in bed, and assigned me licentious homework.

Sandrine encouraged my photography, sometimes accompanying me when I walked along the lake shore or around the Loop, ventured into neighborhoods, or the many forest preserves around the city. She took pictures of me with her cell phone's camera as I explored subjects and compositions.

"Documenting the artist's process," she said, delighting me with the notion she considered my hobby as artistry. I remember the day I told Grayson Sandrine was relocating to Los Angeles. His face paled, fearing I'd leave the firm to accompany her; he later admitted he was surprised when I remained in Chicago, although he considered the decision a mistake. "I think you'll look back on Sandrine as the one you let get away," he said. For as much as he knows me, blind spots remain in his understanding of what motivates me.

Maggie may believe the same thing: there's a woman out there, the one who got away and I'm secluded here, lamenting that I ever let her go. I don't know why people can't accept that I'm not hiding from anything or anyone, I'm not in seclusion waiting for something momentous to happen. I'm not lonely. I don't feel non-existent by not mattering in the world anymore. I'm enjoying the absence of people wanting or demanding things of me and when suggestions to the contrary aggravate me, disappointment with my reaction aggravates me further. I live here to avoid that snowballing. It's why when Maggie tapped on my door, I felt my face morphing into a giant frown. My mother and Laura understand the rules of our interactions, what I'll tolerate and what will cause an outbreak of dead air between us. Maggie existed outside the rules until that morning, a circumstance my mother orchestrated.

I replace the Martin in its velvet-lined case and descend the stairs to the living room. Outside the patio doors, George scrapes a rake across the leaf-covered flower beds. He trims tree branches broken over the winter, a recurring groundwork on the cusp of spring, of renewal. I wave and he nods. He'll haul the leaves in his pick-up back to his acreage, compost them beside his shed, and return it to the beds next spring as fertilizer. I recall when my and the other fathers in our St. Louis neighborhood raked autumn leaves into rows along the street curbs, then set them alight, the scent of the smoke, unlike any other in my childhood, a harbinger of seasonal change.

9.

Maggie adjusts the headphones and scooches her lower back against the chair's lumbar support. She's adept at transcribing audio interviews, but never before transcribed a Zoom session. With her monitor divided into a split screen, the Word document on the left, the video recording on the right, she skips past their greetings and small talk, to her questioning.

M: How much do you think your brother's personality was determined by how he perceived you?

D: Gotta preface this with the stereotypical disclaimer: I'm not an expert in childhood psychology, but.... Of course we were both going to develop, individually, and as brothers, similarly. I've thought about why I don't remember much of the happy brothers phase of our childhood. A couple of possibilities for that: either it never existed, or the contentious phase overshadowed it to the point of obliteration.

M: You believe the latter, right?

D: I do, yes.

M: And you're willing to accept that there were happy times?

D: Accept or acknowledge?

M: Laura said you loved to parse language.

D: It was a habit long before it was an occupational hazard. Happy times. I know when you talk about them, it's in the context of my brother, but he's never figured in my happiness. Not then and not now.

M: Let me parse it then. I'm not implying that your happiness was caused by or linked to my father. I'm asking if you remember a time when the two of you got along. Weren't always fighting with one another.

D: That's the problem. My first memories are of us avoiding one another, which means the animosity already existed. How early in their childhoods do people have accurate recollections? I know it's frustrating for you, for Laura, and my mother, to accept that what you want me to recall is gone. You'd rather believe the memory is there to be recovered and you don't care whether I want to remember it. That even if I could retrieve lost recollections of Aidan and me as great friends, maybe I don't want to. And that I don't care if that's an inconvenience to you. I feel bad if this disappoints you, but can't you understand that my life's secrets stem from when I left my family, not from while I was with them. The people most interested in knowing what happened when I was a child. my mother and siblings, were there at that time. What can I add that they haven't already told you?

M: Fair point, Daniel. You're not the only person who thinks this is a fool's errand. But what you may not have considered is that while you remained incommunicado with my father, he remained in contact with Grandma, with your brother and sisters, even though he cut off all contact with my family. I want to compare impressions they have of him with what you can remember. Especially if you think you influenced what he became.

D: Let's back up, or slow down. I'm uncomfortable with the idea that I determined Aidan's personality.

M: Influenced, then. Your mother insists his reaction to you was severe. Laura, too.

D: Follow the money. I mean, what do they have to gain from insisting there's a link?

M: You must have an idea.

D: I suppose I could produce one, but why? No one wants to believe how uninterested I am in why Aidan was Aidan. And uninterested doesn't even approximate my indifference, my apathy. Those emotions require effort. I have to think about Aidan to be indifferent about him. I gave up wasting time on him long ago. It wasn't easy but I managed.

M: You understand how that reinforces the belief that you've suppressed memories, not truly forgotten them.

D: I'm not going to win on this point, am I? You want to play psychologist and lead me through memory recovery, but you haven't given me any motivation to do it. Imagine I'm a selfish prick and you need to give me something, anything, to convince me it's worth my while.

M: You're not curious how reacting to Aidan influenced your life? If you weren't so adamant not to be like him, what about you and your life would be different? Important decisions that affected you more than others?

D: Now you're homing in on what might work. Appeal to the old man who's naturally reviewing his life. That's a good tactic. Flip the narrative. Forget about how I determined Aidan's path and focus on how he narrowed mine. Shrewd.

M: Thank you, I think.

D: Oh, it's a compliment. Aidan influenced my behavior by forcing me to distinguish myself from him, and his behavior was a reaction to how I behaved. That puts the two of us in a maddening

whirlpool, doesn't it?
M: It's a workable theory.
D: More than a theory. Maggie. I think there's truth in it. But only to the point where I left home. Your theory requires presence to be valid. When I left for college, I stopped reacting to my brother's actions.
M: But he didn't. By leaving home, you only cast a longer shadow over him. Laura remembers your mother and father still pushing you at him not so much as a role model, but in contrast to his fuck-ups.
D: The impact of my leaving hadn't sunk in on them yet. They didn't understand its permanence.
M: That didn't matter for Aidan. You were still the stick they beat him with.
D: I never asked for that.
M: I know. But Aidan still heard it all the time.
D: So doesn't it follow that what he did with his life owes less to me than to how my parents, especially my mother, since Dad usually didn't give enough of a shit to get involved, treated him?
M: Of course, but how can you separate his treatment from how they treated you? From how they set standards for his behavior based on your achievements? Even if I accept you didn't give a shit about your brother, he wasn't allowed the same luxury. Every one of his fuck-ups triggered the same question: Why can't you be like your brother? That anger had to erupt. I find it hard to believe you don't remember that.
D: I remember anger. Arguments. Sullenness. Spitefulness. And I also remember escaping it all. My parents weren't content with using me as a passive example, they wanted me to help them solve Aidan's problems. Did my mother not mention that? How she lectured me about the importance of not only setting an example for Aidan, but pulling him along, convincing him of the errors of his ways. If she wonders why Aidan turned out as he did, she need look no further

than her nose.

M: I spoke with my sister yesterday and she recalled a trip we took as kids. Trouble is, she was four at the time and can't have the kind of precise memories she described. They had to be regurgitations of what my mother told her. Do you remember any trips your family took when you and Aidan were boys?

D: That's a losing setup for any memory I have.

M: I mention my sister because I'm cautious about over-relying on your mother and sister when they describe my father as a boy. I want perspective from someone who isn't tainted by what people have reinforced over the years until the fiction is now accepted as truth.

D: You think I'll be objective enough about Aidan to counter the family propaganda?

M: I think you haven't spent years spinning yarns into whole cloth.

D: That's a terrible pun.

M: Samuel says I'm famous for them.

D: I'm not sure my perspective is more accurate than theirs.

M: But perhaps less corrupted? Since you never dwelled on the rift, you never needed evolving excuses and reasons to explain why it began, why it persisted.

D: I see your logic but all I can offer is absence of memory.

M: You're a photographer. Do I have to remind you that absence is as important as presence?

D: So instead of drilling me for memories, you want me to guess why I have none?

M: That's a bit over-simplified. Can we start with my last question? Do you remember any trips when you and Aidan were young?

D: Like vacations?

M: Vacations. Weekend outings.

D: Dad loved going to the zoo. He'd sit and stare at the big cats until we pulled him to another exhibit. Aidan was always frustrated that the animals never reacted to him. Like they owed him some kind of acknowledgement for showing up outside their cage. There were places he wouldn't go. I remember that. The reptile house. Didn't believe that the snakes were locked away and couldn't get to him. When he got nervous, he bit his nails. Chewed them down to ragged nubs. Mom dipped his fingers in vinegar to get him to stop. Threatened to paint them with polish to shame him into breaking the habit. There's a question for Mom: did Aidan ever stop biting his nails?

M: I'll add it to the list. What was your favorite exhibit?

D: Of course, I pretended to love the snakes just to watch Aidan's face when I described how big the boas and pythons grew. How the eyes of the vipers behind such thin glass followed me when I walked pass their cages.

M: How old were you two then?

D: Maybe eight and nine?

M: In full feud mode yet?

D: Not fully. Aidan was a scared boy when he was young, bolder as a teen, but never brave. When the Gateway Arch opened, I was a sophomore in high school. The whole city turned out to see it. Crowds upset Aidan. He'd always feared getting lost or separated from our parents. Even though he was fourteen, he stayed home when Dad took us all to the opening of the Arch. Ask Mom if Aidan ever rode to the top. I'll bet he never did. Fear of heights. When we'd drive across the bridge over the Mississippi, he'd slide off the car's seat and huddle on the floor. He couldn't believe the bridge wouldn't collapse.

M: Nothing your sister or mother has told me paints this picture of my father.

D: I'm not the only one with blind spots. Memory reinforces preconceived notions.

M: Constantly.
D: Which means you're skilled at sifting through the contradictions.
M: I feel I am.
D: Aidan was susceptible to dares. The source of his fuck-ups could be other kids goading him. The threat of public shaming if he shied away from challenges, even knowing he'd get in trouble. You see. I'm not the only one who exerted peer pressure. Back to trips and his scaredy-cat nature. A summer vacation road trip to the Grand Canyon. Mom berating Dad about broadening our horizons until he relented. Three kids in a station wagon, Elizabeth and Luke hadn't been born yet, heading west to Arizona. Have you been?
M: Yes.
D: Then you know how when you stand on the rim and stare across that abyss, it truly is a breathtaking moment. We saw it on a day with a cloudless sky and what I remember most vividly were the colors. The rock striations. Gleaming in the sunlight.
M: Did you have a camera then?
D: We never could have afforded a decent camera and in my Dad's opinion, certainly not for a kid. But I know in that moment I was watching it all with a photographer's eye. Cropping different views. Noticing how the light fell on contours and surfaces.
M: What about Aidan?
D: Scared he'd fall in. Wouldn't get near the edge despite Mom coaxing and Dad threatening him. Laura promised to hold his hand the whole time they were at the railing but he never got closer than twenty feet to the rim.
M: Do you remember him ever getting past being so fearful?
D: By the time I graduated from high school, he put on a good front. But I'd be surprised if he ever stopped being that scared little boy.
M: You know what I'm going to say.

D: Yeah. It serves my interest to continue believing that. But only if I had any interest. And I should warn you that as I turn more sentimental in my old age, none of it gets directed toward your father.
M: Did you have any habits as a child that you grew out of?
D: Shyness. Believe it or not. It's convenient to think that Aidan and I constantly engaged in battles with each other, but it really was my nature to try to avoid them. I was withdrawn as a kid, a loner. I got good grades because I rarely socialized. When classmates were out partying, stealing booze from their parents' liquor cabinets, I was at home studying. Or in the library. I loved the atmosphere of a library. Silence and order. Libraries were the Internet of my generation.
M: How did you break out of that mold?
D: The war.
M: Do you want to elaborate?
D: No.
M: Can you remember what you did that never failed to inflame your brother?
D: Ignoring him. A mirror needs a reflection, right? He needed my reactions. Was really frustrated when he couldn't provoke me. It worked on my parents, too. Nothing pissed my Dad off more than pretending he simply didn't matter to me. The nearer I got to graduating from high school, the more I turned away from them.
M: Signaling a devaluation. But was it an effort more to convince them or to convince yourself?
D: Of course there was an aspect of self-reinforcement to it. Anyone at that age who's totally self-confident is arrogant. And stupid. College was my springboard and I had to work my ass off to get there. There was never any possibility my family could pay for college, so I worked summers, and saved what I could.
M: Dad told Mom you got a scholarship to Missouri.

D: Really? Well, that's a lie. I never received a scholarship. I worked in the campus bookstore part-time to make up the shortfall in savings and the loan I took out, which by the way I paid off while I was in the service. GI benefits paid for my degrees at Northwestern.
M: It seems important that you were independent.
D: I don't understand people who don't find that important.
M: Weren't my father's fuck-ups expressions of independence, too? Different in practice, but not in purpose?
D: Possible. But are you implying he sought independence from me, or from my parents?
M: They used you as the stick, and no one remembers them offering any kind of carrot. So is the difference significant?
D: Let's follow that logic. Aidan continued fucking up his life to be different from me. What he did wasn't as important as the reaction it provoked. Problem is, he had to escalate his fuck-ups. Constantly exceed every prior mistake. Go one better. So what did he do? Knocked up his girlfriend. Two good Catholic kids having a child out of wedlock. I can't swear your grandfather held a shotgun to Aidan's head, but you know what happened after that better than I.
M: So you're the reason I was born?
D: Of course not. Just trying to show that pigeon-holing my brother's actions into a narrow band of "but Daniel never" is too limiting. You need to consider that as I never thought about him, he probably did the same. He couldn't have had me in mind every time he acted.
M: Every time he fucked up.
D: I see what you're doing. No. I'm not the reason he crashed so many times. I don't believe anyone has that kind of influence on another, do you? Not a parent. Not a brother.
M: No. I don't. Do you think your ignoring him made him escalate his acting out?

D: Yes. In high school it was easier to escape the house. If he wanted an argument, I'd walk out. Nothing stings like being shown you're unimportant, that you don't matter.
M: Some would judge that to be calculatingly cruel.
D: It was.
M: You intended to be cruel to your brother?
D: I did.
M: How long did that last?
D: Until I left home. First for college and then to the Air Force. After that it didn't matter. Out of sight, out of mind.
M: Seems like he was that way, too. A similarity of siblings?
D: I'm sure it hurt when he left your mom, left you and your sisters. I see a difference. I never turned my back on responsibilities.
M: Can't we dismiss that as semantics? You can't abandon a commitment that you haven't made.
D: If we're going to play semantics, then it can be judged either as a failing or as a lesson learned. I don't find anything intrinsically malicious about knowing one's nature and acting accordingly. My mother thinks I'm horrible for disengaging from the family, but I think it's admirable that I know myself and live according to my principles.
M: So the differences are matters of perspective.
D: You tell me. Can you distance yourself enough from this morass to render an objective opinion?
M: The jury's out. And it isn't what I want to explore. My father is the focus.
D: As he links to me, though, right?
M: That can't be avoided.
D: Okay. Let's get back on track here. Yes. I do think how I treated Aidan provoked him. That was the intent and it worked. Mainly, because he was too slow to understand how easily I could manipulate

him. He was the poster child for reverse psychology. If I told Aidan I was going eat a banana, he'd eat the peel. Knee-jerk should have been his nickname.

M: What about his life after you left? Did your influence have that much carryover?

D: Maybe his reactions had become habits by then and he just never broke them.

M: I don't think coincidences are neutral. It harkens back to what Grandma said. You stopped caring about the family, but my father received a steady stream of news about you. Maybe that kept the fire burning for him.

D: His problem. Not mine.

M: Is that the chorus to every song you know?

D: It does make me sound selfish, so let's get back to what I said earlier about motivation. A simple question: What's in it for me? Self-discovery? How I formed my personality in contrast to my brother's? That's fine, but it's not something that requires a sacrifice from you. What chips are you going to throw into the pot?

M: You want the truth to be transactional?

D: Shouldn't we both be willing to pay something for seeking it? You want something from me. What do you have that I want?

M: Are you serious?

D: No, Maggie. I was trying to shock you, that's all. Regardless of what my mother thinks, I'm not that heartless. I'm sympathetic to how you and your sisters must have suffered. I like telling people I'm the product of a broken home, that my parents divorced. When they ask how old I was at the time, I tell them late thirties, and the expression on their faces is comical.

M: Has humor always been an important part of your personality?

D: Yeah. Class clown. Sarcastic son of a bitch in the service. The war turned my humor darker than it was before. Boosted all my cynical inclinations. I remember a joke the infantry told, a parody of an old TV commercial: Man from Glad. Man from Glad. Bodies all over the field.

M: I'll have to Google that reference.

D: I hope you laugh when you get it. Being funny was important to me. It helped me fit in, get noticed, back when I was shy. I later used it as a clue for finding like-minded people. Humor defuses anger, rescues hopeless situations. We needed that during the war.

M: Does your humor still run dark now?

D: Yeah. You should have heard me during the Trump years. I should go back through my Twitter feed and compile all those jokes into a book.

M: I don't want to sound like I told you so, but you are remembering things. Like the Grand Canyon vacation. And the picture of my father as a scared boy doesn't fit with what we knew of him.

D: I wouldn't expect it to. I'm sure he somewhat grew out of it, as I outgrew my shyness. Maybe he even overcompensated for it like I did.

M: From shy to confident?

D: More like obnoxious.

M: Is that why you suspected I was trying to lay the blame for my father's behavior at your feet?

D: Partly. Mom's made it a catch phrase.

M: Have you ever had a real discussion with her about it?

D: Nothing's going to shake her belief about Aidan. I know what she would've gained from the two of us reconciling, but she never could tell me what was in it for me.

M: Doesn't that contradict what you said earlier, about my father never being a presence in your life?

D: No. That's not a contradiction. Mom thinks I'm a selfish prick for cutting off the family. She'd never say it that way, but it's what she believes. That I didn't care. She can't fathom how not caring takes commitment. I've tried to clarify it for her. Laura, I think, gets it. But Mom's hopeless. Making up with Aidan was out of the realm of consideration, much less possibility. Whenever she'd plead that we were brothers, I shook my head on the other end of the phone, thinking about my real brothers, the men I knew in the war. Or the partner in my firm. I think this infatuation with a blood bond is so much bullshit. There are more traumatic events to survive in life than childhood.

M: You are cynical.

D: Scratch a PR man and you'll find a cynic.

M: Is that another trait that morphed from habit to occupational hazard?

D: Fair enough. No surprise that our character leads us to what we'll do best. Did you always have an affinity for history?

M: I did. As a child I loved reading biographies. Found the history textbooks too simple. The stories too broad. I loved libraries, too. On Saturdays, I'd pack a lunch and spend the day in the stacks.

D: Which branch?

M: The Mid-county branch.

D: I know it. I'd go the Central Express Library in the Post Office Plaza or the branch near Lafayette Park.

M: That one has beautiful architecture.

D: And now you're with a librarian.

M: Yes. Solidly. And you're alone. That sounded blunt. Sorry.

D: No offense taken. My choice.

M: Is that an area where you and my father had some similarity? Woman hopping?

D: Don't forget my father. But that kind of behavior, it's a gender thing, not a family thing, don't you think?

M: Yeah. I agree. Men are sluts.

D: I'm gonna use that. Count on it. But I'll admit what my mother insisted when she and my father divorced. Right around the time your mom and dad did. The Breedlow men can't keep it in their pants.

M: I'm sure she used different language.

D: You'd think so, but not so much. The woman who wouldn't say shit even if she had a mouthful of it let loose like I'd never heard before. A woman scorned, you know. I think what really angered her was that she couldn't lump me in with the two of them. I really believe she would have enjoyed a Breedlow trifecta, all three of us getting divorced at the same time. That's a righteous pile of shit she would have loved to preach from.

M: I think she's mellowed a bit since then.

D: Did your mother?

M: Once she married my stepfather, she dialed it back. It became an undertow. We knew not to swim too far from shore with her.

D: Elizabeth and Luke can give you a clearer picture of what my mother was like then.

M: Luke remembers more about Aidan than any of you.

D: He was three years old when I left home so he never witnessed much of the rivalry between me and Aidan. Like your sister, whatever he remembers probably comes from stories my mother told.

M: Actually, he stayed in touch with my father. He's the only one who ever visited him in Texas.

D: I didn't know that, but then, I don't talk to Luke.

M: He's got a theory about that, too.

D: Jesus Christ! I don't think I want to hear it.

M: You've earned a dispensation.

D: Back to humor, it occurred to me yesterday that if you're not careful, I'll start treating you like family.

Maggie pauses the video playback. Their conversation reverted to small talk, Daniel telling her he had started journaling since they last spoke, something he hadn't done since he was in the Air Force. When she asked if he still had those old volumes, he said they were in a chest in the basement, along with the uniform he wore on the day of his discharge, and the documents from his enlistment. On the anniversary of his discharge, he rummages through the chest's contents as a nod to nostalgia. When she expressed interest in seeing the material during her visit at the end of the semester, he said, "We'll see. That was a long time ago."

10.

I rise from my knees, blotting sweat from my forehead with a sleeve, waiting for George to round the corner of the house with the last wheelbarrow of compost. I turn the leather work gloves palms up: they are stained black by the fragrant fertilizer and the fingers permanently curved to fit my hands after seasons of repetitive use. George and I spread compost in the flower beds along the tree lines bordering the yard, from the patio to the bluff. During construction of the house, I directed the landscapers to plant perennials: black-eyed Susan, dianthus, hibiscus, blanket flower, garden phlox, butterfly weed, sedum, and yarrow. I pinned the planting diagram on the cork board in my office, admiring the designer's plan of successive blooming throughout the summer, continuous color through to autumn. On the bluff sloping to the beach, her crew planted clumps of dune grass, although the contractor warned that at some point in the future, erosion would reclaim the bluff and the land beyond it. Seawalls and boulder layers like the ones that dot the shoreline north and south of my property do more harm than good, he said, but my house rests more than a hundred feet from the bluff, so generations will still enjoy it before the lake swallows it.

"You're okay, Mr. Breedlow," he said, recalling projects he'd completed nearby, moving older houses back from the lake bluff. Homes built before the state established setbacks. "We'll watch the summer house, but it's on a slab and shifting it closer to the house, if that becomes necessary, won't be difficult."

George appears at the corner of the house, pushes the wheelbarrow and tips it, spilling compost. I kneel and fan out my arms, scattering it over the last square feet of flower bed along the north edge of the yard. When I finish, I slump onto my butt, rest my forearms on raised knees, and gaze out over the lake. In the cloudless sky, sunlight glints off the waves, radiant as sparklers. I enjoy the mindlessness of compost spreading. The manual repetition allows my mind to wander, to thread together disparate notions into something cogent. The Zoom session with Maggie the other day left several impressions. Some of them revelatory. Some of them reiterations of forgotten memory.

My mother is not like other parents who constantly have a favorable view of her children.

She was meaner toward her children when married to my father than after her divorce.

As a child I tried to do one thing each day that would piss off my father.

When Laura found some statement confusing or unbelievable, she squinted and wrinkled the bridge of her nose.

Because my favorite superhero was The Flash, Aidan had to choose Superman, because he was more powerful. I glance at the house and imagine Aidan envying my Fortress of Solitude.

After George returns the wheelbarrow to his pickup, we sit on the patio, chairs facing the lake. We finished past noon so I offered a beer and George, wearing his trademark olive drab zippered hoodie, holds his by the bottle neck.

"I'll haul a load of mulch over in a few days," he says, then pauses. "I saw you had a visitor some time back," he says. "Was driving by and saw an unfamiliar car."

It takes me a moment to realize he means Maggie, and that you can't see any parked cars from the road. George must have pulled into the driveway. I nod. "My niece." A ringed-bill gull flaps across our field of vision, disappearing to the south.

"Family," George says, his up-and-down tone elaborating his surprise.

"Arrived out of the blue," I say, explaining the reasons for Maggie's appearance, how we've stayed in contact. That she'll visit at the end of the May.

"Out of character for you," George says. We've discussed how ungrounded I am in family, a contrast to George's herd of siblings, aunts and uncles, cousins, and nieces and nephews, scattered through the lower and upper peninsulas. "We rent stadiums for family reunions," he once joked.

"She made it clear I couldn't get rid of her," I say.

"Old men get soft," George says, crossing one leg over the other. He toys with his beer bottle, balancing it on his knee, his hand encircling it to keep it from falling.

"Speaking from experience?" I say.

"Hell yes," he says, gripping the beer and sipping from it.

We sit silently for several minutes, listening to the waves break on the beach, a sound that sometimes evokes sadness, but at other times provides consolation. Earlier this morning, I descended the steps with a plastic bag and scoured a hundred yards of sand, picking up trash. I have a sense of ownership for this beach. Plastic bottles, straws, and cups. Food wrappers. Cigarette butts. Jagged chunks of Styrofoam. People can be obnoxious shit stains. I sort the recyclables and roll my bin to the road once a week for collection. George hauls the Styrofoam to a specialized recycler in Holland, near the outlet mall.

"Summer house could use a bit of touch-up paint," George says.

"Paint cans are in the basement," I say.

"So your niece is coming for a visit," George says.

I'm surprised. Mundane matters comprise our customary conversations. "Yeah."

"How long will she stay?"

It occurs to me that Maggie and I haven't discussed the duration of her visit.

"Uh," I say. "Maybe a week."

"So you'd never met her before she just showed up? That's freaky."

George understands my family picture in broad strokes, so he can appreciate the peculiarity of my compliance with Maggie's request.

"You weren't close to your brother?" George asks.

I raise my empty beer bottle and ask if he wants another.

"That kind of conversation, huh?" George laughs and nods his head.

In the kitchen I twist open the beers, pausing before returning outside, recalling a night in Tucson while on leave, sitting at the picnic table in my parent's back yard with my father. He had insisted the two of us talk. I remember smirking at his attempt at a sentimental father-son moment, the veteran imparting wisdom to a son at war. Nothing specific comes to mind from that conversation except my attitude: I always believed I was better than my family and in that moment acknowledged it as a cause of my alienation from them. A life-changing epiphany I mulled over on the lengthy flight from Travis Air Force Base to Okinawa, that I refined during the next two-and-a-half years. In San Francisco after my discharge, I debated flying directly to Chicago, bypassing Tucson, my family, but relented. Wanted a confrontation. To see the expressions on my parents' faces when I rubbed their noses in the fact that I was leaving. I was a haughty mother-fucker.

George accepts the beer and scrapes away a bit of the label with his thumbnail. Guys in the service did the same thing when we sat around tables in bars. Every scrape an identifying insignia for when drinkers and bar girls sat down after dancing.

It's happening, I muse. Talking with Maggie is unearthing scraps of memory, but they're not the recovered ones she wants to hear.

"Mind if I ask why you didn't get along with him?" George says. "Your brother?"

I wonder if he feels we've reached a stage of friendship where asking such a question won't jeopardize working for me. Then I realize such a question defines how I view the relationship and it shames me. "It's complicated," I say. "Doesn't everyone have one of those relatives?" I explain with merciless candor how I never felt I fit in with my family. "It was stronger than any teenaged angst," I say.

"All kids feel that," he says. "But they grow out of it. Like the old joke, 'When I turned thirty, I was surprised by how much my father had learned.' What was different with you?" George draws a long swallow from his beer. I do the same.

"Leaving my family was a natural trajectory," I say. "I've only recently begun analyzing why the bonds were never strong enough to hold me."

"So it wasn't you drifting away?"

"Oh no," I say. "I ran away as soon as I could." I think about those words, *ran away*, and the connotations associated with them: escaping, fleeing, cowardly. Maggie has me examining the intricacies of my language. Okay, I think, I fled, but like people flee oppression. Not like a disenchanted teenager.

"I can't imagine doing that," George. "No judgement, Dan."

"No offense taken, George. I've got people for that." We both chuckle.

"Now your family's stalking you," he says.

"I hadn't thought of it that way," I say.

"Have you asked yourself why now?" George stares toward the lake and I study his face. His nose turns up slightly at the tip. Boys in school teased one kid whose nose did the same, only more prominently. "Ski jump" they called him.

"Timing's always important," I say. "I think it's a combination of my mother's age, and mine. She's ninety-six years old."

"There's no longevity like that in my family," George says. "We hit seventy and it's adios."

"Hey," I say, raising my beer. "Maybe we'll go at the same time."

"You're not piggybacking on my funeral to boast about attendance."

He touches on something I've considered: when I die, who'll mourn me? Who'll attend my funeral? Grayson's the executor of my will and my assets get divided among charities. I envision Grayson and Iris collecting the urn with my ashes from the funeral home in Grand Haven, walking across the yard from the house, descending to the beach, unscrewing the lid, and then upending me into the surf. Will Grayson say anything? I've left no last words. When I asked him to serve as executor, Grayson insisted I make backup arrangements in case he died before I did. That stumped me. There was no one. My attorney said I could designate the firm to oversee all details if I desired, so I did. When I die, if Grayson's already dead, a nameless associate in the law firm will follow my instructions, distribute my estate.

"Why not give everyone a twofer?" I say to George.

He laughs and insists he be given top billing.

"I don't mind being an also-ran," I say.

"Ordinarily I'd invite you and your niece to dinner when she's here, but…"

He references the pandemic, how the Delta variant in January shook everyone's faith that the world had turned a corner on the virus.

"What'll they do when they run out of Greek letters?" he asks.

"Start naming variants after politicians," I say.

"Get the Fauci Ouchy for the…. Shit, what rhymes with virus?"

We fall silent. I run through names of GOP deniers and anti-vaxxers: Trump, McConnell, Graham, Cawthorn, Gaetz, Boebert, Greene, racking my brain for rhyming possibilities.

"The Hannity Malady?" George says.

"That works," I say, chuckling.

He tips his bottle and drains the rest of his beer, then rises from the chair. "I'll come back in a day or two with the mulch and touch up the summer house if you dig out the paint for me."

"Thanks, George." We bump elbows in lieu of a handshake and I carry the empty bottles into the kitchen, rinse them under the tap, and nestle them among the grocery bags in the garage recycling bin. In the basement storeroom, I locate the paint cans for the summer house. Light gray for the clapboards, deep charcoal for the trim. Colors suggested by the designer to connect the structure with the house, despite their architectural differences. She'd argued for a new structure to complement the house, but I resisted, wanting to maintain the link to the past. At the time, my nod to continuity with the past puzzled me. Maggie reawakens that confusion and the Zoom sessions with my Air Force buddies do the same, challenging my attitude that the past is past, the future is irrelevant, and only the present matters. Even when I recite that maxim, I smirk at my dishonesty. It's an outlandish assertion intended to deflect, to disrupt any serious discussion. Grayson once described me as too wrapped up in privacy, that by guarding myself from people, I fostered a mystique that wasn't always pleasant or complimentary. "You think you're being enigmatic, but you're just seen as a snob."

I didn't tell him that I'd accept whatever worked if people left me alone, but I suspect he knew.

On a shelf beside the stairs, I stare at the plastic storage bin where I kept my old journals, the ones I filled with scribblings during my years in the Air Force. They're on my desk now. I'm going to scan them into my computer. After the first Zoom session with Maggie, I decided to begin a new journal, but my first entry ignored meeting her. I chronicled my reactions to a Zoom session with my language school buddies. An historian, reading the first set of journals and then my newest, may consider the fifty-year gap between them, and marvel at how I seemingly picked up where I left off: impressions of an oppressive organization, (the Air Force then, the Trump administration now), and opinions of that organization from the men around me. I'd forgotten how many guys in the Air Force came from the South. Rednecks then, rednecks now. In one session, a guy from Georgia referenced the Chinese virus and suddenly all hell broke loose. I fell back into PR mode, masking internal turbulence with external composure, and listened as the debate escalated. Eventually the session host muted everyone's microphones, enforcing a de-escalation, appealing for civility by reminding us of those fifty-year-old bonds.

"We went to war together," he said.

That's a bone I chewed on after my discharge: our Vietnam experience. Compared to those who actually fought, our connection with the war was placid. The complaints about which they now reminisce have nothing to do with buddies dying, with wounds received, with PTSD. We suffered inconveniences, not trauma. We bitched about expensive or lousy weed. About GED lifers intimidated by our education. About the lack of good albums for sale in the base exchange. Fifty years on, if you listened to some of our Zoom sessions, you'd think we'd endured hell on earth, like overpaid actors bemoaning the intolerable conditions of a war movie set. Bellyaching about make-believe. A few seem unable or unwilling to let go of those years. I've given up seeking moral victories with them. With harmony restored in the Zoom session, I realized the parallel between the disgust I feel for some of those men and how my family views me: get over yourself.

Is Maggie my mother's instrument? Her Stanley to my Doctor Livingston?

Our last session was a duel that strained her patience. I'm certain of that. I fought reacting to her suggestion that all the effort I've put into tamping down memories now has the opposite effect: that talking with her sharpens those recollections. I'm remembering shavings. Several times I thought our conversation had entered a cul-de-sac, but Maggie coaxed me away from those dead-ends and I remembered moments when I visibly unnerved clients. I'd trained myself to blink slowly, maintain eye contact with them, and show no expression. A tactic I rehearsed first with my father, later modified with lifers, and finally perfected with clients. Impassive aggression, Grayson called it. He loved wordplay, encouraged associates in client debriefings to concoct the worst alliterations to describe our task. The all-time winner: Erase disgrace to save face. They'd abbreviated it to EDSF, and invariably someone would provoke laughter during a meeting by muttering it. "Sounds like a Myers-Briggs personality type," Grayson joked. Others began inventing other explanations for the letters: Erectile Dysfunction Stymies Fucking became the favorite.

Grayson and I understood that levity in the office kept morale high. PR can be thankless. Clients arrived resentful of their circumstances, interpreted our efforts as an assignment of blame for their crisis, refused to acknowledge any perspective but their own. In times of crisis, the petulant child within a person rose to the surface. The regularity of client annoyance wore on associates, the new ones especially. They required what Grayson labeled "attentive care and feeding."

Does Maggie presume that need in me?

Going into our session, I had one goal: make her understand that contrary to what my family believes, it's not animosity that keeps me at a distance. It's ambivalence. Elizabeth and Luke, particularly, believe I need enemies. They can't accept that suspicion isn't evidence of certainty. Mom said Luke was convinced I wouldn't mourn Aidan's death because it meant I'd beaten him in our lifelong conflict. She expected me to be sad when she told me that, but it left me unmoved. I missed Luke's childhood. Have no idea what kind of boy he was, whether my mother's and father's parenting skills had evolved after the mistakes they made with the first three Breedlows.

Maggie ignored a tidbit I floated for her: that my spiciest life secrets occurred after my Air Force service. It was a test. To determine if she really means to uncover memories about Aidan, her declared purpose, or to serve my mother's objective and delve into what keeps me from bridging the gulf between us. I should Google the quote about how burning bridges light my way forward and send it to my mother.

I open another beer and sit in the living room facing the lake, reflecting on the decluttered space. The perfect complement to a cluttered mind. I remember a night when I dropped acid with Tony Bergen, a constantly-stoned guy from Wisconsin, in his apartment in Koza, Okinawa, a space cluttered with black lights and day-glow posters, plastic toys, floor pillows, brick and board shelving, smoldering joss sticks, a glass bong, and massive stereo speakers. We watched back-to-back episodes of Bonanza on a cheap back-and-white TV. The show had been dubbed in Japanese and we cackled at Hoss Cartwright's dialog voiced by a high-pitched actor. "Holy fuck that's racist," Tony said when Hop Sing waved a cleaver at the Cartwright boys, his voice as guttural and clipped as a Samurai. "He shoulda wasted that entire fucking family."

Should I tell Maggie about these watershed moments? Their influences in my life dwarf the impact of my childhood. Real life began after I left my family. After the war. After college. After the relationships. After retirement.

The pattern of my life. Waiting for the next thing. Others found careers, married and raised families, provided for their children, and then enjoyed retirement with their grandchildren. My first time in college, I envisioned no career plans, never considered the ladder of advancement, wallowed in hedonism. The second time around, after graduate school, I sprinted toward a decent job and then settled into a pursuit of solitude, substituting temporary relationships for family. Marriage was another trap set by authority, like the Catholic Church or the Air Force. I shunned it. Judging by my Air Force buddies, aging numbs all emotions except for anger and mawkishness. I had a head start on them. It's probably the most opportune moment for me to reflect on the time I lived with Aidan. I'll never be more rational about it.

Being alone changes a person but not in the way loneliness does. Maggie knows the natural thing to do when you reach the end is to turn around and look back. She's depending on it. Memory is like approaching a door that has always been locked, turning the handle and finding it unlocked for the first time, but there's a contradiction: the door is random. What lies behind it is unpredictable. A moment of such acute happiness that I can't imagine ever being happier. Cynicism rising in volume from a child's whisper to the fury of a speeding freight train. Doubt that my interpretations of reality were unreal. Fear of saying I love you. Paranoia that the entire country is trapped in an escape room challenge.

In the Zoom session with Maggie, I was aggressively honest about certain things, toying with the notion that by agreeing to talk with her, I owe her that. Does she think I'm at war with my secrets?

Aidan. The synchronicity of his divorce with that of my parents always intrigued me. I accept the chaos of human behavior enough to believe in coincidence, but still wonder if my father or brother calling quits on his marriage emboldened the other. Laura was the conduit for information about the aftershocks of my parents' divorce. To the day he died, my father remained in touch with my mother. Thirty-eight years and five children left a legacy neither could ignore. At his funeral, Mom sat at the rear of the chapel, with all her children except for me and Aidan in the row beside her. Aidan delivered the eulogy, quoting from scripture, lauding my father as a godly man now in the arms of Jesus. He comforted Dad's second wife and the three children she brought to their marriage, offered Mom his condolences, and at the VA cemetery, tossed the first handful of dirt onto the casket, saying the bit about dust to dust. Laura told me the details in an acerbic tone of voice. "He acted like the head of the family," she said, and those words stung for the accusation contained within them. She might as well have demanded "Where were you, Daniel?"

For my father and mother, divorce was a dismantling, but for Aidan it was demolition.

In the next session with Maggie, I should ask her what she knows of Aidan, what Laura and my mother have told her, what she recalls from her childhood. If she expects me to fill in gaps, I should know what the gaps are, and if the other sessions are any predictor of what'll happen, I'll recall more snippets about my brother.

I drain the remainder of my beer, feeling an early afternoon buzz for the first time in years. In Okinawa, when we finished the last of three night shifts at seven in the morning, some of us would gather in a friend's apartment to begin three days off by drinking plum wine for breakfast. Our shifts were staggered: three 7 a.m.- 3 p.m. day shifts, 24 hours off; three 3 p.m. - 11 p.m. swing shifts, 24 hours off; then three 11 p.m. - 7 a.m. night shifts, 72 hours off. The Air Force's attempt to enforce fairness, with no one constantly working all night or swing shifts, meant no one ever established a rhythm to their sleeping schedules, and that drinking seemed acceptable at eight in the morning until the bars opened, shifting the party, crashing at three in the afternoon, waking at midnight, and starting it all over again. At Northwestern, adjusting to a schedule of what's expected during daylight and nighttime posed a challenge. Studying or partying begun in an evening often leaked into a post-midnight binge, threatening my determination to wake early each morning, a discipline I'd resolved to follow after the annoying fluctuations of the Air Force structuring my life. Always bucking the system. That's what drew me to journalism; PR, with its demand for outcomes, captivated me later. It seemed less passive than reporting, where objectivity suppressed my craving to express my biases. Grayson told me I'd grown frustrated with depending on others to do something with the information a reporter provides, aggravated that too often news is reported and ignored. PR, he said, is more active. "We're calling for action rather than just offering information," he said. Grayson and I have yet to sit down and discuss whether he believed everything he preached to new associates, if he understood the shallowness of the rhetoric. Those neophytes often found it stimulating that our work depended on other people's crises. Saw themselves as problem solvers, a more palatable term than fixers. I counseled them in weaving stories to take care not to fall into their webs, something to which I'd occasionally succumbed. It boiled down to avoiding laziness, to shunning the easy fixes. Clients wanted us to bend the limits of their perceptions to meet their expectations but bristled at the impression of being handled. Decisions spawned from impulses are double-edged: they can be detrimental or rewarding and most people never consider which will be the more likely outcome. I excelled at my job because I unearthed the concerns people only voiced reluctantly and then assisted their redemption. But never worrying about my own. A knee jerk reaction to eschewing anything associated with my Catholic upbringing. Even a single word. Words are like rocks; I need to turn them over to see what slug-like creatures they conceal.

Catholic school. Uniforms. Corporal punishment for misbehavior or underachieving. In high school, my parents gave my advisor permission to punish me with a meter stick, one slap for every point in every subject below a score of 90 on my report card. Was Maggie's school life similar? We're both the oldest, responsible for younger siblings, a burden imposed by mothers overwhelmed by obligations, charged with ruling the roost as the Queen's regent. I accept that I may have misjudged Mom's motivation then, and that her goal now is also not spiteful. She's more desperately maudlin now than aggrieved. Our relationship is better than it's ever been, because, despite wanting a more intimate connection, she's accepted my terms. We're as tethered as I allow.

God, I am a haughty motherfucker.

Uniforms in school. Uniforms in the Air Force. Clothing to define rank and role. Grayson didn't like me calling suits and ties uniforms, he preferred to call them disguises. It was the firm's job, he insisted, to remain invisible as we directed, or deflected, all attention to what the client wanted promoted or ignored. Yoga pants and t-shirts are my current disguise. Jeans and sweatshirts when I work in the garden.

11.

Maggie double-checks her remarks on the final essay among those submitted by her graduate seminar students, recording the grades in the *MyUI* portal. Samuel chuckles his signifying laugh when he sees she's printed out the online submissions, penned her comments, and then transcribed them back online. "My unredeemable Luddite," he whispers over her shoulder, stroking her hair. Grading this batch required intensified concentration as her mind wandered away from the essays to questions for her uncle.

"Should we go out for dinner tonight?" Samuel asks. Vaccinated and boostered, faithfully wearing masks and gloves at work, he'd begun pretending at times that he was immune to COVID. An attitude Maggie abhorred. His asthma ranked high among COVID comorbidities, making him susceptible to the most severe ravages if he contracted the virus. She suspects he intends the offer as isolation consolation. He leaves the house each day for the library, where in addition to his usual responsibilities, he also supervises the IT department's digitization of rare works. His contact with other people is restricted to a small group who, like him, received all their vaccinations, who practice all recommended safeguards, and undergo regular COVID testing. Samuel hasn't touched a human being other than Maggie since the pandemic outbreak.

She softens her gaze and shakes her head at him. "Eating at home is just fine," she says.

"Just thought you might want to get out," Samuel says.

"We can walk along the River Trail later if you want," she says.

"Maybe," he says.

"I haven't felt any cabin fever, Samuel."

"Just checking, Mags."

"And I appreciate that."

Among the accommodations demanded of them by the pandemic, thoughtfulness for one another was the easiest. The adjustments they've made deepened what she feels for Samuel, the solidarity of their relationship. When she thinks about her sisters' marriages, she wonders why their paths differed from hers so distinctly. They married and had children in their twenties; she found Samuel in her late forties and accepted childlessness as a choice her sisters might never understand. She muses at the equivalence of her and Daniel as the outliers of their families.

"How's your uncle handling the seclusion?" Samuel asks.

"He's a misanthrope, I think he welcomes the pandemic. He doesn't have to interact with anyone." She pauses. "I bet he wishes he'd been an only child."

"I'm glad he wasn't," Samuel says, bowing down and encircling Maggie in her desk chair. "How about a frittata for dinner?"

"Lovely," Maggie says, lifting her face for a kiss.

She logs out of the university intranet and double clicks on the folder containing the draft of her current paper, the decimation of social services provided by Christian churches during the Depression. Is she merely rehashing her dissertation? Prior to the bank failures, churches provided services for the poor and advocated for social reforms, but during the Depression resources for those efforts collapsed. While many churchgoers attended revivals, praying for rain, others turned away from religion in despair. What most interested Maggie were the new alliances, and battlelines, formed as both church and state examined their roles in reforming welfare, exacerbated by the major relocations of huge swaths of the population.

Maggie worries the attention given to her project with Daniel usurps the time she should devote to her scholarly research and writing. The deadline for completion of the paper is self-imposed but avoiding it in favor of Daniel chafes at her academic sensibility. At her discipline. The interaction with her uncle mirrors the steps she would take toward any academic inquiry: collecting evidence from sources, evaluating that evidence, using the evidence to answer critical questions. Her father's death means she can only understand him from the shadows he cast on others. Last week Samuel urged her to reapproach her father's third wife, Tiffany, to cloak her inquiry as preparation for a tribute to Aidan, rather than to satisfy her curiosity. Maggie appreciated his effort but doubted the woman would believe her. Her inquisitiveness about what her father told each successive family about his first nags at her. What reasoning had he concocted to defend such a desertion? Maggie was sure her father villainized her, her mother, and her sisters to the Bible-thumpers of his final family. She recalls their faces from the videotaped funeral. Grandma Breedlow had arranged to attend, Luke was going to accompany her, but a bout of pneumonia canceled those plans, and Luke went alone. Aunt Laura said the widow treated him as an outsider, despite how he and Aidan often spoke, how Luke had visited their West Texas home. Laura suspected Aidan's wife presumed her mother-in-law faked an illness as an excuse for not attending. "Mom watched the video of the funeral," Laura told Maggie. "She wept and called Tiffany to say what a beautiful ceremony it'd been."

"How was Tiffany?" Maggie had asked.

"You know Mom," Laura said. "By the time they hung up, both of them were crying."

Maggie wonders if Grandma Breedlow could get Tiffany to talk to her, if she has that kind of influence with the woman. Judging by the performance of her half-siblings at the funeral, she doubts any of them would speak to her, nor would she want them to interpret her approach as an invitation to maintain contact.

She assumes it's natural for divorced wives to demonize their successors, and for the new wives their predecessors. Interesting, she thinks. How does her father's second wife regard the other two? Ellen wasn't the woman her father was sleeping with when he divorced Mom. That was, according to her mother, "just some bimbo he used to slip out of the marriage." Mom said once the divorce was finalized, he left that woman, moved on to another, and then to Ellen. "I'm sure there was another one when he divorced from Ellen." Her mother said. "Your father lived like he was skipping across a stream: always had his eye on the next steppingstone."

What were Daniel's relationships like, Maggie wonders? He never married but did he repeat his father's and brother's patterns? Even Luke had divorced and remarried. Something intrinsically fickle about the Breedlow men when it came to commitment, as Grandma Breedlow preached? A generalized male thing? Laura and Elizabeth enjoy long-term marriages. How did they find husbands who avoided typical male pitfalls? Or perhaps they hadn't and never said anything to anyone about it.

Her mother's assessment of her husband as a coward reoccurs to her. He was too cowardly to commit. Too cowardly to address and solve their problems. Too cowardly to leave her without first lining up a new girlfriend. Too cowardly to love. Were her father's relationships attempts to distinguish himself from Daniel? Daniel professes not to care that his brother's life represented a renunciation of his, but how much did he know? Grandma Breedlow must have understood that relaying news of Aidan's follies would only strengthen Daniel's resolve to have nothing to do with his brother. Would she have censored what she told Daniel? She notes it as a question for Laura, smiling as she imagines creating a spreadsheet of all the characters in this drama, with a column for questions she needs to direct to each of them, another for the answers. Such a creation would elicit one of Samuel's trademark chuckles.

Thinking of him turns up the corners of her mouth into a smile and deepens the etched lines at the corners of her eyes, the roadmaps, he describes them, of how her life brought her to him. The first time they made love, in his bungalow on East College Street, each of them was tentative, taking care not to bruise the other's emotions. Months after that night, they marveled at the coincidence of their motivations. "I knew I wanted to be with you," Samuel said to explain his reticence to rush or coerce her to sleep with him, the gentleness of his touches, his whispers, asking if she enjoyed what he was doing, what she wanted from him. Maggie said she first thought him insecure and had grown annoyed at his cautious pace, but eventually understood that his sluggishness stemmed from attentiveness. He didn't fumble using his fingers and tongue, didn't grope her like a panicky teen. Her annoyance swung to appreciation and she became uncharacteristically vocal in guiding his touch, adjusting his speed. When later they lay in bed, listening to a student party down the street, Maggie dismissed an urge to thank Samuel, but mulled over how much of what anyone felt for a partner in the foundational stages of a relationship arose from gratitude not just for sexual pleasure, but for the attention, the singling out from the crowd. *You chose me.*

Maggie views each morning she wakes beside Samuel as reaffirmation of that choice, a romantic notion to which her sisters never thought she'd succumb. Jess especially expressed surprised happiness when Maggie told her she and Samuel had bought a home together. "I'd say it's overdue, Maggie," Jessica said. "But I never expected it to happen. I thought you'd be a spinster."

"Well, thank you," Maggie said, infusing her words with an overdose of sarcasm.

"Not in that sense," Jessica said hurriedly. "Poor choice of words. I always thought you'd be a professional woman who'd never depend on a man for anything."

"I still am," Maggie said. "Neither of us is doing this out of any dependence. We're choosing to be together."

"You're not a feminist traitor if you admit you need Samuel, and he's no less manly to admit the same about you," Jessica said. "Dependence doesn't negate equality. Especially when it's mutual."

"You understand," Maggie said, relieved Jessica didn't view her as some aberrant freak.

"God, Maggot," her sister said. "David and I are the same. Even Hailey and Paul. Mom taught some unconscious lessons, by example. Have you forgotten how changed she was after marrying Scott?"

Maggie remained silent, wondering how her impressions of their mother differed from her sister's.

"Sure, she bitched now and then about Dad, but her attitude before and after meeting Scott was night and day. He really calmed her down but I don't think we fully appreciated that at the time."

"Are you saying I ignored the difference?" Maggie asked.

"Why are you so defensive today?" Jessica said. "That's not what I'm saying. I'm trying to be neutral. Telling you what I observed. Scott wasn't perfect but he was good for Mom. That's all I'm saying."

They'd ended the call on a conciliatory note but Maggie spent the next hours analyzing her impressions of that time in their childhood. "The Scott Years," they called it behind their mother's back, who never tolerated any badmouthing of her second husband. A trait Maggie attributed to anxiety that her girls might drive Scott away, despite his obsequious attachment to her. Fool me once, Maggie reasoned, later recognizing how her mother's paranoia leaked into her own mindset about relationships. Until Samuel. Her passionate walrus, who approached the chaos of life with composure and a willingness to snicker at pandemonium, to jeer at turmoil. Was there something about being surrounded by the accumulated wisdom of humankind that allowed one to neuter madness with positivity, to inspire Maggie with his nonchalance? She felt a better person in his company. Was that how her mother felt about Scott? Did he better her nature or merely her circumstances? Parsing language again, Maggie thought. When she met Scott, it was her nature to be a mother before all else, improving her daughters' circumstances would have been foremost in her nature. She couldn't dismiss the notion that her mother's marriage to Scott was a bargain struck between them and that her relationship with Samuel was of a higher order. If she told Jessica that, her sister would accuse her of snobbery, of ivory tower pretentiousness, and Maggie would have difficulty disagreeing with her. Both Jess and Hailey were intelligent women, but Maggie often found herself torn by an instinct to dumb down conversations with them. Unlike when she spoke with colleagues at the university. Or with Samuel.

Or, she realizes, with Daniel, whose intellect zigzagged throughout their last session. A formidable mind, she thought when they severed the connection. Had her father possessed the same mental prowess? When he left, Maggie was too young ever to have had any conversations that would have hinted at his intelligence, in the way she now gauges intellect. His performance in school, Grandma Breedlow says, never matched Daniel's, but she attributes that to the cause and effect of jealousy. Furthermore, Maggie believes any adherence to religion, such as her father embracing evangelicalism, belies rational thought. Another snobbish trait.

"Dinner's ready," Samuel calls from downstairs.

"Coming," Maggie answers.

"Have you caught up with all your grading?" he asks when they sit down.

Maggie nods. "Just a conversation with one more thesis advisee and then I'm done." She pictures the woman: a triangular face, with wide-set blue eyes, her hair dyed black with violet streaks at the temples, soft-spoken yet assertive. She admires the woman. Her command of the subject matter is impressive. Her writing is taut, her research firm. Her conclusions anchored with evidence. It's an accomplished thesis and Maggie looks forward to when the woman goes before the examining committee next week. Then she's free to travel back to Michigan.

"Are you prepared for your trip?"

"I reviewed both Zoom session transcripts and listed some questions," Maggie says. "I need to speak with my aunt and grandmother before then."

"Are you finding it difficult to separate the niece from the professor in these conversations?"

With academic projects, Maggie often solicits advice from Samuel, suggestions for research paths, edits for cumbersome passages, but when he entered her office during the transcription of her last session with Daniel, she asked for privacy. He granted her seclusion and never questioned the reason for her request. Another of his traits that she appreciates: acceptance that her motives are never hurtful or unkind. She knows he intuits the curiosity surrounding her father is important as nothing else in her life has ever been. He won't intrude or interfere, will be present to offer support.

"Those two definitely interweave at times," she says. "I'm always the academic, but when we speak, I'm always aware of who he is. My father's brother. There's an emotional aspect to it that the rational part of me wants to dismiss but can't."

"And you shouldn't," Samuel says. "Your emotional entanglement is as valid as your ratiocination."

"Are all librarians part-time psychologists?"

"The bartenders of academia," Samuel says. "We hear it all."

"I'm excited and nervous," Maggie says. "Eager and a little frightened."

"Well I'm jealous," Samuel says. "I've never had an opportunity like this."

"That's because your family is nothing like mine."

"True, Mags. But all family closets have skeletons." Samuel clears the table, arranging the plates in the dishwasher so that none touch each another. When they first moved in together, Maggie discovered him reorganizing the machine's racks. She stood beside the dishwasher watching him as he explained how his method reduced cracking and chipping on the bowls, plates, and glasses. When he turned his head and looked at her, she folded her arms across her chest and laughed at his doggedness. Being set in one's own ways can provoke one of two reactions when confronted with another's ways: rejection, which results in fights over inordinately tedious matters, or acceptance that there is no one right way to do anything. She and Samuel enjoy the compatibility of the latter.

"My family's closet is a boneyard," she says.

"Makes me think of picking my teeth," Samuel says.

"I love that you're weird," Maggie says.

Samuel laughs as he refills his glass with tap water. "Are you going to work some more tonight?"

Maggie shakes her head, then flashes on a memory. "Before he left, my father bought us a dog. I say bought but he brought one home from a shelter. For years Mom insisted he'd left and only years later did we learn she'd actually kicked him out, so I assumed at the time that he provided the puppy as a substitute for himself. A few months later the dog died of distemper."

"That's Greek tragedy level happenstance."

"Hailey hated him so much when that dog died. Mom believed he'd known it was sick and Hailey treated that suspicion like gospel." Maggie pauses. "Mom never let another pet into our house."

"My parents believed every boy should have a dog," Samuel says. "Maybe it's a Midwestern thing. A childhood rite of passage. Teaching responsibility."

"What was your dog's name?"

"Roscoe."

Roscoe?" Maggie exclaims. "What breed?"

"Heinz 57, my father called it. He said they were the most loyal kind and hated the notion of purebred anything. 'We're all mutts, Sammy,' he told me."

Maggie grins, contemplating the ridiculous notion of her parents resembling the human equivalent of show dogs. More like strays encountering one another in a vacant lot.

Her cell phone trills and she lifts it from the kitchen island. It's Daniel. "Hello?"

"Dr. Breedlow," he says. "I realized I've never used your title."

"I'm more comfortable with Maggie," she says, glancing at Samuel who curls his fingers in a wave and skulks from the room.

"Just trying to be funny," Daniel says. "And failing, right?"

"I never think of myself that way when we talk, that's all," Maggie says, then falling silent, waiting for Daniel to explain his call.

"I suppose that's good and I apologize for the bad humor. I'm calling to nail down a date for your visit."

Maggie glances at the dry-erase calendar fixed to the door of the refrigerator. Despite the programs and apps on which she relies for classes, office hours, meetings, and other scheduled appointments, she still makes notes in the little boxes of the refrigerator planner. "The semester ends on the twenty-first. I thought I'd arrive on the following Monday if that works for you?"

"That's perfect," Daniel says. "Plan to stay for a week?"

"Sure," Maggie says.

"Any food allergies or restrictions?" Daniel asks, and Maggie smiles at the question. Organizers ask the same question when she speaks at conferences.

"None," she says. "I'm not a picky eater."

"Good. Then I'll see you soon. I'm excited."

"Me, too," Maggie says. "Bye now."

She ends the call and finds Samuel on the sectional in the living room. "That was odd," she says. "He sounded like a hotel clerk confirming my reservation."

"Is that different from his usual demeanor?"

"There was an artificiality to his cordiality," she says.

"Like a PR guy?" Samuel smiles.

"Just like that," Maggie says. "I felt handled."

"I assume not in a good way." Samuel rises and walks toward her, tucking a lock of hair behind her ear. "You're more than a match for him, Mags."

"Your mouth to his ear," she says. "Let's watch something frivolous on TV."

"Wouldn't you prefer something thought-provoking, something with subtitles? A German murder mystery?"

"How did I ever find you?" Maggie asks, laying her palm against the side of his face, feeling his mustache flatten beneath her thumb.

"Like all the best things in life, it was a library search."

They watch TV, a gritty BBC mystery with a soft-spoken but haunted Scottish detective, no subtitles, but the speed and heavily accented dialogue tempt her to switch them on. Maggie finds her mind wandering from the plot, imagining that episodes in the detective's life correspond to events in her uncle's past that made him welcome his isolation. She reminds herself to consider differing perspectives. She's in a happy relationship and shouldn't impose that as a standard when judging her uncle. Living alone must be the right choice for him. That she cannot imagine coaxing happiness from solitude doesn't exclude it as an option for Daniel. Perhaps it's simply undisguised narcissism, as Samuel suggested: "You really have to be your own best company to love living alone." Thinking about degrees of solitude, she realizes the extremity of Daniel's. On a lonely bluff above a barren shoreline. He examined the geography of emotion and put a pin in an isolated corner of it.

Their earlier conversation puzzles her. Cordial and straightforward, none of the sparring from their Zoom sessions. Saying he was excited for her visit was unusual. One impression she takes away each time they speak: he loves to talk, despite telling her that listening was his most valuable skill as a PR professional. Perhaps she's the beneficiary of years of a torrent of repressed conversation spilling over the dam of listening.

Maggie glances at Samuel, sees the rising and falling of his shallow chest. He's asleep so she lowers the volume on the TV and poses the question her uncle has consistently asked: what does she want from this? What is her desired outcome? The answer belies the simplicity of the question. It's a Gordian knot of her desires, Grandma Breedlow's hopes, Jessica's curiosity, and a need she suspects her uncle has for connection. She imagines his life's slate covered with chalk scribblings and wonders if he believes talking will wipe it clean. What's written on that slate? Why would he share that with her? She wags her head, chastising herself: don't assume and then find evidence to fit the assumption. Daniel has offered nothing to support a theory that he is more complicated than a misanthrope, but Maggie feels his situation must be more convoluted than that, and that it can't all stem from animosity between him and her father. She needs to talk to Laura. And to her grandmother. She senses they're holding something back, even though there's no evidence they are, and can't dismiss the possibility that Daniel's hermitage is as simple as he claims.

Samuel grunts in his sleep. Maggie studies him for a few seconds, wondering if he'll wake and ask her what has happened with the detective show, to which she'll reply she's paid no attention, and then they will both laugh. But he slumbers on, his hands clasped over his belly.

Her inquisitiveness as an historian aligns with her uncle's as a former journalist. She thinks that but then questions: did he ever work as a reporter? He said he found public relations after earning his master's at Northwestern. With those credentials, surely he could have found a position in journalism.

What had changed for him to switch paths? Wouldn't a witness to the Vietnam War and Watergate want to remain a passionate reporter? A professor in one of her undergraduate classes told them that to be human is to be corrupt. "To understand history, you must understand that," he said.

It still angers and saddens her when events prove him right.

Then what about Daniel is or was corrupt? And has he decided to use her as his confessor? To absolve him and wipe clean whatever is written on his slate?

Is she off base with these suppositions? Is her uncle simple? An uncomplicated misanthrope as Samuel suggests? Or Western Michigan's Machiavelli? She giggles at the thought and Samuel jolts awake, sniffing, wiping his eyes, asking what he missed. She gazes at him as he raises his arms above his head in a yawning stretch.

"We could still go for a walk along the river, if you want," he says.

Maggie shakes her head. "You're tired," she says. "Go on up. I'll be there after I make some notes."

"About work or your uncle?" Samuel asks.

"My uncle," she says.

"I know you've probably considered this, but what will you do when he tells you something that contradicts your own memories?"

Maggie compresses her lips into a thin line and raises her eyebrows. "Memory," she says. "Dueling unreliability. I always consider the source. There have already been instances. Daniel has corrected lies my father told us. Deceptions he might actually have believed. It's hard to tell."

"It was a long time ago," Samuel said. "How can you be sure your uncle isn't doing the same thing? Rewriting history to undercut your father?"

"I've considered that," she says. "But from what everyone in the family says about him, Daniel doesn't care."

"Or he didn't care until you started asking him about it."

"I won't rule that out," Maggie says.

"He might have thought he'd go to his grave with no one caring about his version of the story. Now you've given him an opportunity to use the present to change the past." Samuel grips the bridge of his nose with the thumb and forefinger of his left hand, closes his eyes, and grimaces. It reminds Maggie of when he concentrates on a menial task: his mouth open, lips curling away from his gums, squinting his eyes, wrinkling his nose. Scott made the same expression of exaggerated pensiveness when he repaired loose cabinet knobs or creaky door hinges around the house. Another intrinsically male habit, she wonders?

"That's history," Maggie says. "Writing the past is so often rewriting the past."

"But this is personal."

"Sounds like a cliché, Samuel, but all history is personal to someone."

"Agreed," he says, pushing himself up from the sofa cushions. "But you're *my* someone. I don't want you to lose your grounding just because he has none."

Maggie beams a smile at him, suffusing it with warmth she hopes he can feel. "Never gonna happen," she says.

12.

I'm sitting at my desk, scanning posts in the Facebook group of my Air Force language school classmates. Bitching about mask wearing and vaccination requirements. Updates on health conditions. I sort through reminiscences, like epiphanies, of funny times, departures from the tedium, when I scroll to a post from three days earlier. Justin Cowart's post on the anniversary of the day the flight he, I and others crash landed at Cam Ranh Bay when the landing gear on our RC-130 failed to lower and lock properly. The pilot declared an emergency, jettisoned excess fuel over the bay, and we all put on our helmets, swiveled our seats to face the rear of the craft, and waited for impact. There were no windows in our section of the aircraft and Justin, sitting beside me, shook his head, cursing, "Mother-fucking-son-of-a-bitch," he yelled. I laughed as he repeated it like a song's chorus, and soon every man in the rear of the craft was chanting it in unison until the belly of the aircraft juddered and shrieked on the tarmac, a metallic beast in agony, a sound unlike any I'd ever heard. We'd stowed as many loose items as possible in preparation for the landing, but helmet bags, pencils, coffee cups, even a boot, flew around in the confusion. The aircraft twisted and skidded sideways, a wing tip dipped, caught on the turf beside the runway and ripped the wing from the fuselage. A propeller flung from an exploding engine scissored through the side of the aircraft. When we skidded to a halt, the silence shocked us. Justin and I unbuckled from our seats and rushed toward the rear of the plane. He reached the hatch before me and struggled to lift it as smoke began filling the bay. I screamed for someone to lower the cargo ramp but received no response. Justin and I leaned our combined weight onto the hatch's lever and it gave. We lifted it and jumped to the tarmac, scanning behind us for others. I couldn't remember exactly how many crew members flew on our missions. Linguists and flight crew, maybe thirteen or fifteen. Smoke spiraled from the right side of the aircraft where the engine lost its propeller, and Justin and I began a head count of men in flight suits scurrying from the plane. Less than a dozen. "Let's go," I said, turning toward the craft. "You're fucking crazy," he replied, in lockstep as we reboarded the RC-130, coughing in the smoke, making our way along the line of intercept stations, searching for friends in the smoky interior. On either side of the fuselage gash, we located men slumped at their stations. Three in all. Justin and I dragged them to the rear hatch, passing them to the rescue teams, who then pulled us from the wreckage, guiding us a safe distance from the smoldering aircraft. From the grassy median, we watched them extinguish the flames with foam. The scene at the end of the runway was surreal. Ambulances and fire trucks with flashing lights. Men shouting. Bursts of radio transmissions. No fatalities. The three men Justin and I hauled to the hatch sustained minor injuries and recovered, but one of the firefighters told us if we hadn't acted quickly, they might have been seriously burned, perhaps fatally.

Justin's post commemorates the fiftieth anniversary of that day. Certain dates stick in my mind. Birthdays. My parent's anniversary The date of my discharge from the Air Force, and I'm surprised I forgot the date of the crash. For years, on that date, wherever I found myself, I'd lift a glass to the men on that plane, to our having survived. The pilot witnessed Justin and me racing back into the aircraft and recommended us for medals. Our squadron commander read the man's affidavit to us and it made us sound like superheroes. "At risk of their own lives," "With no regard for their own safety," "Saved the lives of their fellow crewmembers." He recommended us for Silver Stars, but the Air Force reasoned that although our flight that day qualified as a combat mission, at the time of the crash landing, we were not engaged in combat with enemy forces, and thus Justin and I were awarded the Airman's Medal. I cut my hip on a jagged section of fuselage, which required stitches, and was awarded a Purple Heart. The three men we rescued that day, Harry Bischoff, Mark Clancy, and Stan Galvin, all commented on Justin's post. They frequently add photos of family to their annual words of gratitude, and Stan, who lives in South Carolina and describes himself as a Christian Republican, (but not a Trump fanatic), posted a photo of a his eighth grandchild, a girl so committed to her smile that her eyes nearly closed from the effort. Justin and I had not been close friends before that mission, but afterwards we acknowledged the bond secured that afternoon, and during the group Zooms, we always share a nod to one another, chatting in private messages about the oddity of our bond: we don't owe one another a debt for saving the other's life but share the act of saving other's lives. We wag our heads when buddies reference us as heroes but have confessed to one another that neither of us feels that way. Returning to the aircraft that day was reflex. There was no discussion, no debate, just reaction. We weren't under enemy fire. We didn't rush into the proverbial hail of fire. Instinct drove us and I suppose that makes us heroes of a sort. Justin lives in Washington state, where he worked in a Boeing factory building 747s, but is now retired.

I'm contemplating why I failed to remember the anniversary, especially the fiftieth, when the telephone rings.

I barely answer and Laura's telling me that Elizabeth is in the hospital with COVID and demanding to know what I said to Maggie?

"She isn't vaccinated, is she?" I ask.

"Of course not," Laura says. "She's in the ICU on a ventilator."

"How's Mom?"

"Upset," Laura says. "Confused. I'm worried about the strain on her heart. And what did you say to Maggie?"

My mind juggles several thoughts at once: concern for both my mother and Elizabeth (despite her arrogant stupidity about the virus) and searching for what I said to Maggie that she relayed to Laura that has so aggravated my sister. "What exactly is Elizabeth's prognosis?" I demand. I rise from my office chair and walk into my bedroom, standing in front of the window wall, hoping the vista of the lake will calm me. "What have the doctors said?"

"Critical," Laura says. "They won't let Hank in to see her."

I picture Hank, my sister's husband, an insurance company executive who religiously wears a Stetson and cowboy boots, consoling their children by assuring them of God's mercy.

"Has Mom shown any symptoms?" I ask.

"She's been tested. Negative so far," Laura says. "The home's strict about visitors. If you haven't been vaccinated, you can't enter."

"What about her heart? Is she showing signs of another attack?" I am unsure which development warrants more of my attention.

"Not yet. I'm worried that the strain of the situation will be too much for her."

I imagine my sister dying from COVID, the logical irony of her flippant attitude toward the virus and then succumbing to it, a viral video of Hank saying he never understood the danger of the pandemic and how he wished she had heeded the warnings. That he and his children, in the wake of their mother's death, were now vaccinated and boostered. My folly. More likely, Hank would remain steadfast in his belief that the claim of a pandemic was a hoax and that God had called his wife back to his fold.

"Shit, Laura," I say. I feel no words of consolation. The sky today is azure and cloudless. It was like that the day of the plane crash. But the bay at Cam Ranh was bluer than the gray lake beyond the bluff. My instinct is to tell Laura to keep me updated on what happens, but I know my sister is not going to end this call without extracting from me an explanation of what Maggie has said to her. "What happens now?" I ask, realizing how lame I sound.

"Really?' Laura says. She doesn't pause for long before adding: "We wait and hope. That Elizabeth recovers. That Mom doesn't have an attack." She pauses longer this time. "That you…" Laura falls silent.

"You're not optimistic about Elizabeth, are you?"

Laura's sniffling makes me grimace. "The doctors have told us to prepare for the worst. She'd been ignoring the symptoms and didn't go to the hospital until she'd been sick for more than a week."

"Stupid," I mutter. Except for Laura, who visited me once while attending a conference in Chicago twenty years ago, I've not seen any other family members since my father's funeral. I picture Elizabeth's face, which resembles my mother's. Wide-set, dull blue eyes, high cheek bones, thin lips that I cannot remember ever smiling. She and Hank have three children. Two girls and a boy. The boy is named after our father and is called Little Eddie. That seems an unnecessary burden to place on a child. I envision him leaving home and demanding of everyone that they call him Edward for the rest of his life. Never Ed. Never again Little Eddie. Has Maggie spoken with her cousins?

"And every time I get a call from the home, I fear it's awful news about Mom," Laura says.

I realize that whenever Laura's number appears in my caller ID, I fear the same. I spy a white sail on the lake, distant from the shore. Visualize myself on the craft. The raspy whisper of the wind in my ears. Unlikely because I don't sail and have no affinity for boats. In fact, I fear the water. It doesn't stem from childhood trauma of near drowning or an inability to swim. In Cam Ranh Bay, with its notorious undertow, I often swam parallel to the shore for exercise and in Chicago at my health club, swam laps in the pool. Grayson asked when I retired if I would buy a boat and then balked when I confessed my fear of being on water. "Most people who fear water retire to the mountains, Dan," he said. "There's bears in those woods," I replied in a folksy rural accent and we both laughed.

"How are *you*?" I ask, knowing Laura has assumed the responsibility of caring for everyone. It's her way. Her default status. The "matriarch in waiting," Mom calls her.

"It is what it is," she says, waiting for her to add that I'm no help, then realizing she and Mom learned long ago that I don't respond to their barbs, so tossing them is counterproductive.

"So, what did Maggie say that has you so anxious?" I ask. Perhaps pestering me about Maggie will take Laura's mind off Elizabeth's situation. I hear Laura inhale and then exhale noisily.

"I spoke with her this morning before she left Iowa City," Laura says. "She didn't sound very enthusiastic about the trip."

"What did she say?" I press.

"Nothing specific. It was her tone," Laura says. "She was subdued. None of the enthusiasm she's expressed when I've spoken with her before."

"That's it?" I ask, not bothering to hide my surprise at the paucity of what she said.

"You must have said something to dampen her enthusiasm," Laura says.

"If I did, I don't know what it was," I say. "I've been honest and accommodating with Maggie."

"Your standard of accommodating leaves a lot to be desired, Daniel," Laura says.

I know she's venting frustration about Elizabeth's hospitalization and her fears for our mother's health, banging me like a drum to alleviate her feelings of helplessness.

"I'm sorry you're upset," I say, falling silent, allowing Laura an opportunity to pile on more criticism or take time to reflect.

"I know you'll be no help in this," she says. "I've known it for a long time and yet it still angers me. You haven't even asked how Luke and the rest of the family are. You don't even care."

I refrain from confirming what she says, that my involvement will not involve anything beyond receiving information.

"You wouldn't have come to Elizabeth's funeral even without a pandemic, would you?" She pauses. "Just like Aidan."

I close my eyes and wonder how much longer Laura will flay me for what has been our relationship for decades, tamping down my irritation that the two of us once again repeat this same conversation from our history. Long ago I believed she'd moved on, had accepted our new world order, and that I'd never again have to endure a rehashing of weary arguments and pleadings.

"I've told Mom we should just cut you off, give you what you want," she says. "A black-out. No communication." Her voice slices her words, like knife thrusts. "But she said that wouldn't be the punishment I thought it would be."

I chuckle unconsciously.

"That you are the only person she knows who doesn't need to be needed."

"I'm not going to change, Laura," I say, leaning my forehead against the cool glass of the window.

"I know," she gasps, "but you were my big brother, Danny." I hear sobs and remember her as a young girl, quietly studying me and Aidan as we played together, as we sat beside one another at the dinner table.

Rather than soften my resolve, Laura's emotional outpouring angers me. Reminds me that I have anticipated such a confrontation, but always believed my mother's death would precipitate it. That when she died, the détente among us would collapse as either Aidan (had he lived), Laura, Elizabeth, or Luke would castigate me for not attending our mother's funeral. An assumption of which I've done nothing to dissuade them. Mom said she knew I'd sever all contact with the family after she died and joked that she stayed alive to postpone that moment.

"That was a long time ago." I strive to keep my tone dispassionate. To make my words a statement. Not an excuse. Or a justification. I need neither.

"I've never understood how you feel no guilt, Dan," Laura says.

"Why should I?" I ask, feeling my patience crack.

"What did we ever do to you?" she asks. "What was so traumatic that you turned your back on all of us?"

I doubt telling Laura she is collateral damage will make her feel better. That as my battle with my parents and Aidan spilled over, it sucked her and the younger two kids into the whirlpool. Relating to her separately from my parents would have been impossible. Only a complete disjointing from them was tenable. For me to survive. I've never expressed it to any of them in those terms: my survival. The smothering. The claustrophobia of being among them. The irrepressible urge to escape. I felt all of that but never bothered to explain it to them. Why? Because keeping them in the dark about my needs and desires was integral to the punishment I envisioned my absence represented. Spiteful seemed rightful. Being absent from their lives was insufficient: I needed to know my absence harmed them.

"It wasn't that dramatic, Laura," I say, contradicting our history.

"Maybe for you," she says. "But there was too much drama in the void you created."

I want to tell her that wasn't my intention, but she'd immediately sniff the stench of that lie.

"I'm not sure how you thought Mom and Dad would take it," she says. "You were home for three days before you left for Chicago. After being gone for four years."

I want to say that three days was too much. To inflame this conversation. To erupt with such vitriol that Laura might never again call. It's an old itch I've never scratched and I'm unsure why. I turn from the window and walk to the stairs, gripping the handrail, pausing. "Classes were about to begin," I say. "I wanted to get as far away from anything that reminded me of the Air Force. To immerse myself in a new place, with new habits and new routines."

"It was more than that, Dan," Laura says, her voice almost a whisper. "You ran away. As fast as you could. You've always been running from us. How much distance is enough?"

"I've asked myself that same question," I say. I carefully place a foot on each tread and watch the view of the patio and yard emerge as I descend. A lone sparrow perches on the feeders as a pair of squirrels scratches in the grass beneath them, and I can't help but perceive a parallel between my family situation and the image. That my family forages and scrounges for my scraps. Christ, what an ego. Had I been a client sitting across from myself in our conference room listening to such bullshit, I might have signaled Grayson that the firm should pass on the assignment.

"I'm not going to ask you come down here," Laura says. "I know you won't, but you need to call Mom today and speak with her. For some reason, and God knows why, she's better after she talks to you. Less depressed."

"Depressed?' I ask, remembering what Maggie said during one of our Zoom sessions.

"She'll never say anything to you, Dan. Even with all you've done, you're still the golden boy."

"I never asked for that, Laura. I don't want it."

"I know," she says, exasperation thick in her voice. "Fucking ironic, isn't it? For all your distancing, your isolation and downright hostility toward the family, she still has you up there on a goddamned pedestal. It's infuriating."

"I'm not responsible for that, Laura," I say, understanding that no denial will defuse this exchange.

"Oh, I know. You're completely *irresponsible*, Dan."

I don't tell her that is unfair. In her state of vulnerability, Laura wants reassurance and agreement, not argument. My role here is to play the bogeyman to her fears. She doesn't want my truth; she'll adhere to whatever truth she needs. As much as she loathes me keeping such a distance, I think she fears more that I'll become the prodigal Breedlow. Laura enjoys her status and is happy I'm a passive presence, but the doubled strain of Elizabeth's hospitalization and Mom's fragility might compromise her capacities. It occurs to me she believes I escaped to avoid such an occasion, one that demands sacrifice. Selflessness not selfishness.

"I know better than to rely on you for anything in this," she says.

"Yes, you do," I say. Fuck this reticence to respond. To accept her accusations limply. "You shouldn't be surprised, Laura. I've made it clear for more than fifty years that I'm out." I hear Laura gasp in the receiver and expect an expletive and then a hang-up.

"Dan," she says, her voice calm. "You can run as far and fast as you want, but you'll never be out. It just doesn't work that way."

We are silent for several moments.

"Call Mom. I'll let you know what happens with Elizabeth." Then Laura hangs up.

I lower my arm, wincing at a pain in my elbow from holding the phone fixed to my ear for so long.

With the phone returned to its cradle on my desk, I sit before my monitor with my hands folded in my lap, feeling exhausted by the toll of the call with Laura, angry that it exhausted me. Is it pretense that my family holds no power to affect me? Grayson preached that people don't change, they merely pretend. I find myself gritting my teeth. Clenching my jaw. Throwbacks to my teens when I'd seclude myself in the basement of our St. Louis home to avoid the rest of the family. Usually in the wake of an unsatisfying confrontation with either of my parents, who in my frustration seemed interchangeable as the reasons for my unhappiness. I rarely, I realize, ever categorized my state of mind at the time as unhappiness. Being happy seemed beneath the level of outrage I felt then. The personal tectonic plates grinding against one another during my teens relegated concerns of happiness to self-centeredness. The national upheaval, the assassinations of the Kennedys and Dr. Martin Luther King, the demonstrations against the Vietnam War, civil and women's rights marches, riotous cities burning. Happiness as a desire was vanity personified. I sought the nobility of principled rebellion but floundered in the middle class coziness of my suburban home. The proverb about all politics being local succinctly describes family dynamics. I seethed about the nonchalance in my family toward the national turbulence around us. Why wasn't every family dinner a forum for outrage? Whenever I tried to mention my nascent politics, Dad cut me off. Wouldn't discuss it. Liberals received no voice in his household.

Skimming Twitter posts about the expected resurgence of the virus as summer nears, I inhale a deep breath I hope will cleanse me of anger, of a rising sense of frustration that Laura is right. Family just doesn't work this way.

I expect Maggie after lunch. The poor woman has no inkling of the morass she's approaching. What did Laura mean by saying Maggie seemed subdued? Is my niece having second thoughts? Journeys of self-discovery can't guarantee happy endings.

Mom. Nothing to gain by delaying the call.

"Daniel?" she answers her phone.

I lean back in my chair and glance at the clerestory windows in my office, high enough to allow in natural light while affording privacy from my neighbor's eyes. Tree branches shift in the view, moved by an offshore wind skimming over the bluff.

"Laura called me," I say. "Are you alright?"

"I think your sister is going to die," she says. Her voice, though tinged with its usual raspy wheeze, is not urgent. It's calm.

"Laura says she's critical," I reply.

"Stupid girl. The old man who lives across the hall loves to say people 'fuck around and find out.' Can't help but think Elizabeth's going to find out and I'm sick about it."

I remember Mom saying when Aidan died that no parent should live longer than her children and grimace at the prospect that she may relive that pain once again.

"I spoke with Hank," she continues. "They're not letting him into the ICU and he's agonizing because he won't be able to see her before she dies."

"Is it that bad?' I ask, leaning over my desk, bracing the elbow of the arm holding my phone on the black leather desk blotter.

"The doctors have told him they don't have much hope," Mom says.

"I'm so sorry, Mom," I say, doubtful of the sincerity of my own words. I don't know how to tell my mother how for me Elizabeth's death will differ from Aidan's, though it will. The animosity, however dormant, I felt when Aidan died is absent in my relationship with Elizabeth. She and Luke, the two youngest, were the "also-rans" in the family for me. Still preschoolers when I left for college and then the Air Force. Mom often joked that I never spent enough time around them to dislike them. I did not grow up with them, nor them with me. When they entered their teens, I founded the firm with Grayson in Chicago. We never shared any meaningful overlaps.

"It'll be another funeral I won't be able to attend, Daniel," she says. The wheezing intensifies. I sense her impending grief.

I realize the pandemic affords me an excuse for not traveling to Tucson for my sister's expected funeral, had I need for an excuse beyond having no desire to attend. It occurs to me that I'm also not expected and that I'll willingly fulfill that expectation.

"Laura's worried about you," I say.

"She told you, huh? I'm fine. They monitor my blood pressure and pulse oxygen every day. I get an ECG every month. They watch me like a hawk." She pauses. "There's no need to panic and come visit me just yet."

"All right, Mom," I say. "Maggie will be here this afternoon."

"Do right by her, Daniel. Do you hear me?"

I nod and then grin at the useless gesture. “I will.”

“I’ll call if anything changes,” she says and then hangs up.

I refrain from stating the obvious, perhaps because I’m beginning to doubt it, that nothing ever changes.

13.

Maggie leaves pothole footprints in the wet sand as she tiptoes away from breaking waves that threaten her bare feet.

"It's cold," she says.

"Even in summer it never gets really warm," I say.

She pauses and holds a hand to her face, shielding her eyes as she gazes out at the lake. "This kind of flatness would be plowed with rows of corn in Iowa," she says. "We get dramatic skies but I imagine they're more gorgeous over the lake."

I snap a photo, then study the image on the camera's screen. It's a 35mm lens that renders Maggie as a minor feature of the landscape. The clouds are slow-moving, bulbous, piled atop one another in a cobalt sky. She stands alone at the edge of the water, peering westward with the bluffs diminishing into the horizon. Early evening sun throws lengthening shadows on the beach and the lake flashes like polished jade. I turn and frame a photo of the lake in the viewfinder, raising and lowering the field of vision, alternating between a predominance of sky or water, snapping photos, then abandon the rule of thirds for one shot and settle the horizon line in the middle of the view.

After my telephone call with Mom this morning, I considered calling Sandrine, imagining her answering the phone by stating my name as a question, chuckling at her surprise, assuring her I was fine and that I only needed the sound of her voice as a palliative for family drama. Talking for half an hour and thanking her for being the kind of friend who knows when to listen. But I refrained and instead ticked off items on my checklist for Maggie's arrival. I prepared with a thoroughness that sometimes irritates me for its rigidity. Grayson once asked me jokingly if my uber-competence ever annoyed me, then immediately told me not to answer the question. When I asked why, he said it wasn't that he already knew the answer, but that he wasn't prepared to hear one that contradicted his estimation of me. "I like the predictable you," he said, grinning with an ambiguous smile that left me confused about whether he was teasing or being truthful. I suppose he might have been both.

Maggie and I spent the early afternoon talking about Elizabeth and the factions within the country that deny the reality of the pandemic. I asked her impression of my sister and she winced.

"I've spoken with her," she said. "But she was standoffish."

"How so?"

"Polite but not forthcoming," Maggie said.

As we sat in the living room, I tried to gauge her demeanor as she repeatedly shifted her gaze from me to the lake vista.

"I get the impression that she and Luke feel speaking to me somehow makes them disloyal to my father's other families."

"Other families," I repeated, focusing on the phrase as a double entendre. Maggie's family is *apart from* mine, and yet she is *a part of* mine.

"Like they're an 'other' family to you."

"You've been talking with Laura too much," I said.

"Guilty. I spoke with both her and Grandma Breedlow after you did this morning. They felt I should know they'd spoken with you."

"You've earned a soft spot in my mother's heart," I said. Maggie rose and walked to one of my lake photos, a black and white shot of a gale last November, a rhythmic tempest of curling waves capped with silvery crests beneath a murky sky, dozens of gulls huddled on the shore. She turned and faced me.

"And she in mine," she said.

"I think connecting with you makes her happy," I said, studying Maggie's face for any indication that Laura's observation she sounded subdued was accurate and not merely projection.

"I hope so," she said. "I was worried at first that your family would see me as an intruder."

Your family, she said. Did she intend it as a criticism? An indictment?

"They're both so worried about Elizabeth right now," she added.

Wouldn't that be the reasonable explanation for Maggie's bearing when she spoke with Laura? A thoughtful, compassionate reflection of Laura's concern for Elizabeth and my mother? In character with the woman who wore a mask when she appeared at the patio door. I appreciated the gesture but told her we'd dispense with them during her visit.

"It's tough to be normal when everything's so abnormal," I said.

"I don't think when it comes to family that there is a normal."

"You know I won't disagree with you," I replied.

"Do you feel like what's happening in Tucson is somebody else's story, not yours?" she asked.

I paused, wondering if saying "not enough" was an acceptable response, and Maggie waved off the need for an answer.

"Why don't we put off talking about family until tomorrow?" she said.

Maggie praises the photo of her gazing at the horizon and asks if I will take a portrait of her while she's visiting. As a gift for Samuel.

"You could make a print for Grandma Breedlow," she adds.

As we climb the steps to the house, I grow irritated at the frequency of my recent contact with my family. The woman climbing ahead of me is the catalyst but I don't blame her. Maggie is my mother's pry bar. At the edge of the patio, I indicate the chairs and Maggie slumps into one, extending her legs, crossing them at the ankles.

"This place is amazing," she says. "I was so nervous when I was here before that I didn't fully appreciate what you have."

"Thank you."

She turns her head toward the house where the sunlight blazes on the glass, and like a child, raises an arm and waves at her reflection.

"What kind of house do you have in Iowa City?" I ask.

Maggie swivels her head back toward me and smiles. "An old Victorian painted lady, with all the ornamentation you'd expect. We've got a tower turret and a wrap-around porch."

"Sounds lovely. Appropriate for a professor," I say, chuckling.

"And a librarian," she adds. "I know we agreed not to talk about family, but my sister is moving to Texas," she says.

"Shit."

"I know. You couldn't pay me any amount of money to live there, but her husband works for a tech firm and they're pretty much forcing him to move or lose his job."

"Where in Texas?" I ask.

"Austin. It's better than some cities."

I don't know how to respond.

"That'll leave just Jessica in St. Louis. The last anchor to home."

I nod. "I was in the Air Force when my parents moved to Tucson," I say. "Visiting when I was on leave felt weird. I borrowed the car and drove around a strange city that felt nothing like home."

"Had you already made up your mind about what home meant to you by then?" Maggie asks. I wonder if she mentioned her sister's move as a lever, like Mom, prying open the subject we'd agreed to postpone. As though reading my grin, she adds, "Talking about each other isn't covered by our agreement, is it?" She laughs.

"By then I knew what home didn't mean to me," I say.

We settle into silence and a few cautious sparrows descend from the trees to the feeders. They poke their beaks into the metal mesh, scattering seeds to the lawn. As wasteful as humans. I glance at Maggie. She's closed her eyes and folded her hands across her belly.

"Not asleep," she says and I wonder again if she's borderline psychic.

"It's okay to nap," I say.

"If I do, I'll be up all night," she says. "Samuel can nap for hours and still fall asleep when his head hits the pillow. I don't know how he does it."

"You're happy with him."

Maggie opens her eyes and studies me. "Yes. I'm happy with him." She pauses and pitches her head to one side. "You know what I'm going to ask."

"Would I be happier with someone?"

"Close," she says. "My question was: are you happy with you?"

"Yeah, that is a different question." I stare at her. She returns my unblinking glare. I break the deadlock. "My first night here, sitting in this very chair, watching the sunset, I felt a spring uncoiling. I hadn't known it existed."

"How are you different now than before you retired?"

"I'm more numb, I suppose," I say. "People get that way as they grow older, but I had a head start. These days I direct my anger toward things. Politics. Not clients."

"Did you enjoy PR?"

"Is this going to devolve into an interview?" I ask, smiling.

"A niece's curiosity," Maggie says. "Nothing on the record." She grins, the expression narrowing her eyes.

"I enjoyed aspects of the work. The sensation of accomplishment, of problem solving. But I also quite early concluded that I'm a misanthrope, and that's a drawback in PR."

"Do you blame your family for that?" she asks.

Waves breaking on the beach frame my silence. "Not sure I think in terms of blame anymore."

"But you did?"

"When I was young, I always got frustrated and angry with people who didn't say exactly what they meant," I say. "They talked around the point. It took a while for me to learn to interpret what they weren't saying. I developed an instinct for questioning them until they said what they meant. By then it seemed like an admission."

Maggie sits upright. "People disappoint you, don't they?"

A Cooper's hawk glides overhead, circling the lawn and then swoops to a corner of the summer house roof and perches. I've spied the bird before. It's tawny with a white underbelly. A three-foot wingspan that scatters the squirrels and chipmunks across the lawn when it appears. The sparrows escape into the trees. In my solitude, I've grown susceptible to viewing such occurrences as harbingers. The hawk's arrival foretells a revelation.

"And one another," I say. "My displeasure is perhaps a little more finely tuned. When someone fails a test he doesn't know he's taking, I admit I think less of him. Is it a lack of awareness or dishonesty? I'd rather people be silent than lack candor." I pause. "I really hated those who forgot their lie halfway through telling it."

"Can you imagine a different path that would make you less cynical?"

"Is that your classroom voice?" I ask. "I imagine you standing at a lectern with a sheaf of notes." I pause. "Do professors still use seating charts?"

"It's all on my laptop," Maggie says, then points toward the lake. "Are we going to get some rain?"

Turning in my chair, I gaze to the west. where a darkening plane defines the horizon. "Could be a storm forming," I say. "It's disorientating when the sky and the lake are the same tone of gray, when you can't tell where one ends and the other begins. I've sat through storms so intense that I felt like a ghost."

"My house talks to me during thunderstorms," Maggie says. "It creaks and moans. Sometimes it sounds like it's complaining, other times like it's enjoying it."

"That's oddly specific," I say. "My concrete box makes no sounds at all."

Maggie rises and the Cooper's hawk lifts from the summer house, flaps its wings and swoops down the bluff. "I've gone back and forth about what it reminds me of more, a prison or a fort."

"Probably a little of both," I say. "Depends on which day it is as to whether I'm locking people out or locking myself in."

Maggie examines the horizon. She's right, a storm front is approaching. We rise and I mention that I never check the weather since moving here. "It's irrelevant," I say.

"Doesn't affect your routine?" Maggie asks.

I shake my head. "Not at all. Even before the pandemic, I cloistered myself here."

"Did you do any writing when you lived in Chicago?" she says. "I imagine the isolation here makes it easy to focus. The lack of distractions."

"The thing about distractions," I say, "is that they exist everywhere." I wave an arm to encompass the lake. "That's a magnificent distraction. I can walk on the shore for hours and never see the same scene. But I get your point. It's easier to be a hermit here among fewer people than it was when I huddled in my Gold Coast home."

"What would you be doing if I wasn't distracting you?"

Maggie locks her gaze on the bird feeders as a pair of sparrows descends from a nearby oak.

"If you weren't here," I say. "I'd be reading, trolling people on social media. Chatting with Air Force buddies. Watching mysteries on TV."

"Journaling? You mentioned you were keeping a journal again."

That's her point, I think. She's hungry to read them. The old and the new.

"Yes," I say, then rise from my chair. "Come with me." I gesture toward the house and begin walking at a pace that'll require effort to match. Passing through the living room and into the foyer, I open the basement door and switch on the stairway light. "The castle catacombs," I say, descending the steps.

I turn on the fluorescent fixtures and Maggie pauses at the bottom of the stairs and scans the space. The cement walls of the foundation lack the smooth finishing of the upper floors.

"It's smaller than upstairs," she says, noting the width of the room.

I point to a door. "The garage is on the other side."

Maggie walks toward the stacks of shelves, fingering several of the plastic bins and bankers boxes, each labeled with the contents. "This is so organized," she says. "Samuel would love you."

I smile and guide her toward a shelf on the north wall. "USAF Memorabilia 01" reads the printed label on the bin from which I retrieved my 1971-72 journals, which I've been rereading. Reminding myself of events from fifty years ago as I reflect on that time's mindset in contrast to my outlook now.

"The Daniel Breedlow archives," I say.

Maggie paces along the aisle. She pauses and lifts her finger, counting the boxes and bins.

"Eighteen," I say. "Financial records. Client files. Cards and letters. Backups of hard drives." I pause. "When it comes to paper, I find it difficult to throw anything away."

"Not like people," she says, as I expected she would.

I nod. "Paper is manageable."

"Has anyone ever asked if you're borderline OCD?"

"Many have hinted," I say. "I like order. I *need* it."

Maggie laughs. "That's one reason to avoid family," she says. "Wait," she says, spying the shelves against the west wall that contain my survival supplies. "Holy shit. You're a prepper!"

"I'm not a prepper," I insist. "I'm prepared. There's a difference. For one thing I don't have any firearms down here. It's food, water, and medicine in case there's a shortage."

"Stored in the basement of your bunker," Maggie says, chuckling.

"Tease me if you want to, but there are militias in this state that are out of their fucking minds."

"Then why live here?" Maggie asks, turning away from the shelves, fixing me with an impassive expression I imagine she uses to challenge students.

I'm not inclined to explain to Maggie how I decided to retire here. A familiarity from summer vacationing in nearby Saugatuck and Grand Haven. Geographic and social isolation. The people here respect my privacy if I respect theirs. A realization that my tenure here is not long-term, but temporary, coupled with the hope that I die before confronting the necessity of moving to a care facility like my mother's.

"Personal reasons," I respond, hoping the rigid tenor of my voice stymies any further inquiry.

"Message received," she says, and we fall into an awkward moment of silence until she points to another bin, this one labeled "Family Photos."

"Mom sent photos over the years," I say. "I kept the prints after scanning them all."

"Can we look at them while I'm here?" Maggie asks.

I nod and gesture that we should return upstairs.

In the kitchen, I place a stock pot on a burner for pasta as Maggie retreats to her room to call Samuel. We agreed Maggie will stay three days, not counting today. Our discussions will begin in the morning and I've let my imagination conjure our conversations. How Maggie will attempt to serve both her and my mother's purposes and how I will divert her focus from the latter, although with the drama unfolding in Tucson, it might prove difficult, even fruitless. I check my phone: no messages. Outside the wind increases as the storm front nears. A bruised sky approaches the bluff and I retrieve my camera, stand on the patio and take several photos of the menacing turbulence, noting how the feeders rattle in the wind gusts.

The water boils and I add angel hair pasta, set a timer for four minutes, then light a burner beneath the tomato basil sauce. The routine settles me. Garlic bread in the pre-heated oven. Salad removed from the refrigerator and placed on the table. A bottle of Cabernet breathing in a crystal decanter. A block of parmesan ready for grating. Cloth napkins. Hand-painted pasta bowls from Italy. All contrived to make an impression on Maggie, one I had not known I would need to distract from what she assessed, after our descent into the basement, of a paranoid Doomsday prepper.

"What are you going to do with all that stuff in the basement?" Maggie asks from the bottom of the stairs. She's changed from her wet-cuffed jeans into black sweatpants with the Iowa Hawkeyes logo on the pants leg. "Tell me you're not going to toss it all."

I gesture toward a stool by the island and pour wine into her glass. "Maybe I'll have Samuel curate it all," I say. "Actually, there are no more than four boxes of family material, much of it things Mom and Laura sent me. I kept newspaper clippings of some of the more interesting and successful client campaigns. And they're duplicates of files the firm also has."

Maggie settles on the stool, sniffs the wine, and then sips, nodding her head.

"Some of it is unique. Memorabilia from the Air Force. Journals." I strain the pasta and add the sauce, combining them in a large bowl. "How's Samuel?"

"Keeping busy. Did I mention that he's digitizing old books and manuscripts in the reserved collection?"

"So there's a parallel between the two of us," I say. I place the garlic bread in a bowl lined with a towel on the granite island.

"You're a worker bee. He's a supervisor," Maggie says, chuckling as she lifts salad onto a plate. "But really, your collection is a treasure trove for an historian."

"I'll keep scanning photos and documents, but I don't know what I'll do with it." I pause. "What'll happen to it after I die."

"Would Laura want it?" Maggie asks.

"She's only four years younger than me and I don't think her kids want the archive of an uncle they barely know."

"You're a successful alumnus, would Northwestern be interested in acquiring them?

"Maybe if I sweetened the gift with a healthy donation," I say. "But the university isn't in my plans right now."

"I'll take it all," Maggie says, gazing at me across the island. I don't doubt the sincerity of her offer and wonder if she believes I revealed the cache to her to elicit such an offer.

"That's not why I showed it to you," I say.

"I believe you," Maggie says, as I scissor two forks into the pasta bowl and lift a nest of it. She holds her bowl beneath the drooping pasta.

"There's nothing about your father in any of it," I say.

Maggie twirls a fork in the steaming angel hair and lifts it to her mouth, sniffing the pasta.

As she chews, I muse about the contradiction the basement archive represents: a misanthrope striving to be remembered. The arrogant assumption that anything important to me will be of interest to anyone else. The irony reminds me of Zoom sessions with my Air Force buddies, how one man's memory becomes another's epiphany. Setting aside the vagaries of lapsed recollections, the remembrances we express when chatting with one another illustrate the varying experiences we each had. The different circles of friends. The activities in which we indulged. The differences seem most acute between the men who at the time were married or single and I realize how little time I spent with friends who brought their wives and families to Okinawa when we lived there. The dope-smoking, acid-dropping, bar-hopping, and whoring existence is alien to those men when we reminisce. I sometimes sense an undercurrent of moral disapproval when we relate stories of those pursuits with fondness or wistfulness. I remember a faction in language school of devout Christians who never set foot in an off-base bar and conducted prayer sessions in the barracks day room. Several of them join the Zoom sessions and remain silently stone-faced when others recall our debauchery, laughing at our youthful exploits.

My journals from those years contain descriptions of those adventures. How would it feel to let Maggie read those entries? To afford her insight into the strain of hedonism I and so many others practiced, diverting our attention from the war. By the last year of our enlistments, many of us regretted the bargain we'd struck with the Air Force to avoid the draft, the infantry. The extra years we served began to feel burdensome, especially for a cadre who always opposed the war but lacked the courage to burn our draft cards, face prison for resisting. Our principles were malleable and bent toward convenience when challenged. In our final year, we directed all that self-loathing outward without restraint, airing our disgust with the military, the government, and every institution under which many of us had chafed, because of a simple epiphany: the Air Force needed us. The cost of recruiting and training a linguist bestowed on us an extraordinary status: the Air Force was reluctant to get rid of any of us for petty violations. We grew our hair longer than other airmen on the base. Decorated our barracks walls with *Playboy* and *Penthouse* centerfolds. Smoked dope at the far end of the squadron compound with impunity. Pushed the limits of tolerance with underground newsletters produced on the same machines where we transcribed reel-to-reel intercept tapes to fuel the war.

My journals detail it all.

It was a long time ago.

Rereading them makes the memories of those escapades so vivid that they've slithered into my recent dreamscapes, memory and fiction interweaving to form fantastically erotic scenarios. A redheaded summer college intern at the firm. We're both high on an unspecified substance. My hardon never softens, her desire never lapses, and the fucking seems endless. We're a pair of rutting creatures. A graphic spectacle of performative lust so forceful that upon waking I remain confused about what was real and what was invented with a sensation that I've done something criminal, and question what moral deficiencies fester within me to conjure such repulsive scenes.

Morals. I can't dismiss the notion that sticky Catholicism influences these decadent constructions.

Maggie rests her fork in her pasta bowl. "I'll take it all," she says again.

"Why should I give it to you?" I ask.

"Why have you kept it all these years if not to give to someone?"

"I like sparring with you," I say, sipping wine. "We'll talk more about it tomorrow. Tonight we'll watch a storm and drink wine by candlelight." I pause. "Tell you what, every time we see lightning on the lake, you get to ask me a question and I promise to answer."

"No subject off limits?" Maggie asks.

"Nothing," I reply.

"Complete honesty?"

I nod.

"Because my curiosity about you might take us into uncomfortable areas." Maggie spears greens with her fork, chews them while staring at me, but I present her with my "client face," as Grayson described it. Gentle impassivity, an indistinct smile, unblinking attention to the speaker.

"Things have been uncomfortable since you turned up at my door weeks ago," I say. "I can deal with uncomfortable."

Maggie's expression falters for a moment and I see Aidan in her face, a hint of a wounded grimace. Did I fracture her assumption that our relationship is no longer adversarial? It's not admirable to admit I want to keep her off balance. Even just slightly.

She recovers and bites into a slice of garlic bread, chewing slowly, and speaks around the food. "It's no picnic for me either, Uncle Dan."

14.

Maggie grips a mug of cinnamon-flavored tea and gazes up toward the trees bordering the yard, enjoying the calm infused by the steam shower in Daniel's bathroom. She wonders how much it would cost to retrofit her bathroom in Iowa with such a luxurious feature, rehearsing arguments with Samuel to justify the expense, knowing if the installation pleased her he wouldn't care. Leaves shiver in the breeze from the lake and she turns her gaze to the horizon. Does her uncle ever tire of this vista, she wonders? Ever fail to notice each day's changes in the scene? The waves today approach from the Southwest. Yesterday's raged from the Northwest, the storm that swept across the view from the patio doors. She and Daniel finished the bottle of wine he opened at dinner, sitting in candlelight, chatting about the similarities between corporate and academic politics, until a fissure of lightning illuminated the gloomy lake.

"One question," Daniel said.

Maggie eased into the research about her father. "Was my father more like your father or your mother?"

"Huh," Daniel said. "I think each of us was a combination of both of them, but Aidan was more like my mother than I was. He clashed with Dad all the time and Mom defended him. I always thought he was her favorite between the two of us, so yeah, he was more like Mom than Dad."

"People often clash more with those most like themselves," Maggie said.

"In my experience, that's true."

"But with siblings, a sister often allies with one of the parents because another sister doesn't. It strengthens that rivalry between the two of them."

"And sometimes," Daniel said. "A brother forms no parental alliance. How does that affect the sibling rivalry?"

Maggie watched the tree limbs flail in the gusts from the lake, hoping for another lightning strike. "I imagine it exacerbates the conflict. How frustrating do you think it is to have an enemy who won't engage? Not with you specifically, but with the game, with the competition for creating partnerships in the war."

"Wouldn't Aidan have liked it more if I was totally unallied?"

"But then he couldn't rely on the adage about the enemy of my enemy," Maggie said. "He'd face a one-on-one battle. That could be frightening."

Another lightning strike, far to the north that lit up the sky and highlighted the wave crests.

"Not my night," Daniel said, then chuckled.

"You're not averse to truth, are you?" Maggie sipped wine, gazing at Daniel above the rim.

"There's truth and then there's *my* truth," he said.

"Your rules," Maggie said, as Daniel raised and tipped his glass toward her. "Do you remember any of my father's girlfriends? From high school."

"That's not what I expected," Daniel said. "That calls for some deep dredging." He paused. "Short answer? I don't. I mean, he dated, but he was two years behind me and that gap imposed a social as well as age distance. Seniors didn't associate with lower classmen. My friends were not his friends. We certainly never double dated. Have you asked Laura and Mom?"

"No," Maggie said. "Just a spur of the moment curiosity. I've often wondered if Dad ever dated anyone before he got Mom pregnant. If they were each other's first, that might explain why he cheated on her so much."

Daniel scratched the side of his nose with his index finger as he stared at the candles scattered on the hearth. "He would have cheated eventually, regardless. It was his nature."

"Your nature, too?" Maggie asked. "Grandma Breedlow's been candid about your father's issues with fidelity."

"That's a wonderfully benign way of putting it," Daniel said. "Your words, not hers, right?"

"I cleaned it up a bit."

"Watching her and Dad made me think that you could get used to almost anything," Daniel said. "That her tolerance was endless. Then one day, it wasn't. I was long gone by then and I don't know exactly which straw was Mom's last. She and Dad divorced about the same time your parents did. She swallowed a lot of bitterness then."

"That's what Aunt Laura said. Lots of cursing about the Breedlow men."

"Bred-low, did Laura mention that?" Daniel chortled.

"Bred low?"

"Mom's variation of low-bred to describe my father. And your father. Luke got thrown in, too, when he screwed up his first marriage."

"How did you escape?" Maggie twisted in her chair to view Daniel's profile. Candlelight highlighted his beard in amber tones.

"Lack of commitment," Daniel said. "Or, to rotate the perspective, an explicit commitment never to marry, coupled, of course, with a commitment never to tell my family about the details of my life. Especially my love life."

"They wonder why you never married," Maggie said.

"I'm counting that as a question, regardless of how deceptively you phrased it," Daniel said.

"The contrast between how you and Dad related to the women in your life fascinates me," Maggie said. "Mom said he fell in love with every woman he fucked and wanted to marry every woman he fell in love with. It was a compulsion."

"Our father was one hell of a role model," Daniel said.

"Yet you went to the other extreme," Maggie said.

Daniel nodded but remained silent.

"I keep wondering to what degree my father's character was determined by an effort to differentiate himself from you."

"Maggie," Daniel said. "That's a rabbit hole."

"Alice had fun in her rabbit hole," Maggie said.

"Lewis Carroll was rumored to be a pedophile," Daniel said.

"That's been debunked," Maggie said. "It's based on a lack of understanding of Victorian morals. Where child nudity was regarded as an expression of innocence."

Daniel held up his hands in a gesture of surrender. "I'm not going to argue history with a professional."

"Good instinct."

Maggie sniffs the tea, remembering an article she read years ago about the poignance of scent, its power to evoke memory and emotion. Cinnamon, she realizes, recalls weekend breakfasts, when cinnamon toast was served as a treat, by her father, offered as an apology for the tension of a Friday or Saturday night argument with their mother. The three sisters sitting at the Formica topped table with the chrome legs, still wearing their pajamas, watching Dad feed slices of Wonder bread into the four-slice toaster, his manner hyped cheerfulness, while Mom remained in their bedroom. "Let Mom sleep late today," he said, and Maggie remembered how her parents bickered, her mother crying audible through the house's walls. The pattern played out: eating the toast while watching cartoons if it was Saturday, or Mom interrupting and hustling them to prepare for church if it was Sunday. Her father never attended Mass. He'd sit in front of the TV with his feet on an Ottoman, smoking a cigarette and drinking coffee as they strode in single file to the car. Maggie snuck glances at her mother when she knelt and lowered her face to her crossed hands, wondering if she prayed for their father to change his behavior or to die. Death, Maggie thought, would solve their problems. Would eliminate the chance that her father, who she'd heard guarantee a change in his behavior too many times to take the words seriously, would renege on his promise and relapse. Death would put an end to the predictable skirmishes heard from their parents' bedroom. That battle zone would then become their *mother's* bedroom. Maggie wonders if those moments when she imagined her mother praying for her father's death coincided with or prompted her abandonment of faith. She'd love to know the age at which most people begin to doubt the dogma that regulates their behavior. The age at which rationality casts doubt on doctrine. When faith ceases to be a divine mystery and is revealed to be a far too human ploy to keep the believers in line. Her mother died a believer; so did her father. Jessica and Hailey remain religious, but they're passive in their faith. They never proselytize or judge. Maggie grins, realizing she resembles Daniel: her family either takes her as she is or can fuck off.

"Morning," Daniel says, opening the patio door. He holds a glass of ice water with a slice of lemon. "You looked lost in thought."

"I was. Thinking about faith."

He smiles. She wonders if gray yoga pants and T-shirts are his uniform. "Not much on faith, but I like the idea of hope."

"Isn't hope the practice of faith?" Maggie asks.

"I don't associate hope with religion." Daniel settles in a chair beside Maggie, cradling the water glass in both hands.

"I made tea," she says, raising her mug.

"Later," Daniel says. "Cold water every morning first."

"Did you follow a strict routine when you wrote your book?" Maggie asks. "Or were you loose with it, writing when the muse struck you?"

"The true muse is discipline," Daniel says. "I got up each morning at seven, brushed my teeth, ate a banana and a slice of rye bread toast, took my ice water to the office and wrote until I completed a minimum of a thousand words."

"That's admirable," Maggie says. "I asked before, but are you considering another novel?"

"Undecided." Daniel glances at the bird feeders. "I thought I'd said all I had to say in the first."

"Calling it the 'first' is a give-away," Maggie says.

"Maybe the next novel will pick up where the last left off. I'll have my main character seeking redemption for his mistakes. Making amends."

"Can there be redemption without faith?" Maggie asks.

"Let's not call it redemption. Too religious. How about I have him seek recovery or emancipation?"

"Still sounds like atonement."

"Noted," Daniel says. "Needs work." He pauses. "I always clean the beach after a storm. Are you up for some trash collection?"

"Sure."

"We can chat while we work, or do you want something more formal. You can record our conversations while you're here."

Maggie had not asked but assumed since Daniel allowed her to record their Zoom sessions that he would not object to her recording her interviews. "Thank you," she said. "We can do both. My memory's good so I can make notes after beach duty."

"I thought about what you said last night," Daniel says. "About legacy, which is what all those boxes represent."

"If you don't leave it to someone, then what's the point?"

Daniel stares at the lemon slice floating in his water glass. "It seemed important to save those photos and documents, even if I wasn't certain what would happen to them when I die."

"I don't believe it," Maggie says. "You're smarter than that."

Daniel chuckles, lifting the water glass to his lips.

"You must have some kind of a plan." Maggie imagines she and Samuel spreading the contents of the boxes and bins on tables in the basement of the university library, dismembered skeletons of Daniel's past. Reconstructing from his parts a semblance of his whole.

"Not really," he says. "And that's totally out of character for me."

Maggie gestures toward the house. "Have you considered that you built a box for your boxes?"

"That's occurred to me," Daniel says. "It wasn't entirely unintentional."

"You're organized. Efficient to the point of compulsion. Everything ordered and labeled, but you have no plan for what happens to your archive when you die." Maggie paused and stared at Daniel, studying his face, waiting for the contradiction to affect his expression. His face revealed nothing. "You must have been formidable with clients," she says. "Never giving anything away."

"At poker, too." He pauses. "Teens always think they're different from everyone else, but I went beyond that. I believed I was uncommon. Do you understand the difference?"

Maggie did understand, having experienced similar feelings when younger, but she shakes her head, anxious for Daniel to continue.

"Feeling different from everyone else," he says, "not just feeling freakish or unaccepted for being uncool. I always felt exceptional. Superior as well. And shy. Until I enlisted."

"That strains credulity," Maggie says, smiling.

"Grayson said the same thing to me once, but it's true," Daniel says. "It's not like I never spoke out or stood up for myself when I was kid, but I was never assertive. Grayson said I must have over-compensated for it at some point."

"In the Air Force?" Maggie sips from her mug. The tea has cooled.

"I found my voice, so to speak," Daniel says. "There's a buddy from our Zoom sessions, Mickey Phillips, who roomed with me in language school and in Okinawa. He credits hallucinogens."

"LSD?" Maggie asks.

"A true disciple of Timothy Leary," Daniel says. "I dropped acid half a dozen times in Okinawa. The first time with some friends in San Angelo, Texas." He pauses and Maggie watches his pensive expression dissolve into a smile. "And that was a journey into unexpected elation. We dropped tabs of Orange Sunshine at nine o'clock. All night I kept saying how amazing it was that the music was dancing around me like fairy lights."

"I've never," Maggie says.

"Now they're experimenting with hallucinogens for PTSD treatment," Daniel says. "And the music we played that night is used in TV commercials."

"You're the demographic for what's being sold. And your generation has all the disposable income," Maggie says, grinning.

"Yeah, yeah," Daniel says, waving an arm toward her. "The children of the Greatest Generation fucked it up for everyone else."

"Trump's a member of your generation," Maggie says, smirking.

"That's a low blow," Daniel says. "You'll carry the bag while we pick up trash." He rises from the chair. "I'll get some gloves from the garage."

Maggie returns her mug to the kitchen. Wondering if Daniel will allow her to skim some of his older journals. Wondering if he recorded his impressions from those acid trips. Had her father ever used drugs? She doubts it. His religion forbade sex outside marriage, but that hadn't prevented him from getting her mother pregnant with Maggie or repetitively cheating on the woman, and she imagines him relying on his faith in shunning drug use, imagines him preaching against it in his West Texas home, conjoining religion and hypocrisy forever in her consciousness. She rinses the tea mug and wonders if all first-borns are natural cynics.

She scans the beach to the south, her hands loose in leather gloves. Daniel walks beside her pausing to lift debris washed ashore by the storm. So much plastic, she thinks. Racoons get an unearned reputation: humans are the planet's true trash pandas.

"I usually patrol down to that root stock," Daniel says, pointing to a large tipped-over tree lying on its side at the base of the bluff. "It fell over the bluff two years ago. Most of it's been cut up into firewood. The owners use it as a windbreak for beach fires now."

A hundred yards distant, three people stroll near the water's edge. Two women and a man. The younger woman tosses a stick into the surf and a brown Labrador chases it, bounding into the waves.

"Some of the first renters," Daniel says. "The season's begun."

"You said you vacationed near here," Maggie says.

"Down in Saugatuck and up in Grand Haven." He approaches with a collapsed plastic water bottle and Maggie holds open the trash bag for him.

A pair of gulls glides in place above them. "Tell me something about my father," Maggie says.

"He was stupid," Daniel says without hesitation.

"That was unexpected," she says.

"A generalization, but mostly true," Daniel kicks at a piece of driftwood with the toe of his shoe.

"He wasn't perceptive or clever. A dullard, my father said. Too quick to react."

She lifts a crushed beer can and drops it in the black plastic bag. "Did your father praise you?"

"You mean to piss Aidan off?" Daniel points to a bottle cap beside Maggie's feet. "I'm sure he did, but I didn't care."

"You often seem angry when you talk about your mother, but maybe that anger should have been aimed at your father."

"He got his share of it. It might seem Mom got more but that's just because she was around more."

"A convenient target?" Maggie deposits the bottle cap in the bag and steers toward the water, where a chunk of Styrofoam bobs in the surf.

"She earned what she got."

"Was she as hard on my father as she was on you?" Maggie rejoins Daniel. She tilts her head to study his eyes as he considers his answer. This morning there's a gray hue to his irises mixed with deep blue striations.

"Ask her what she thinks," Daniel says. "I'm sure in her memory the discipline was distributed equally. But Aidan and I, maybe even Laura when she was older, probably felt we each bore the brunt."

"You said Dad was too quick to react. I never thought of him as impulsive," Maggie says.

"Maybe your mother tamed that part of him."

Maggie laughs. "I don't think my mother tamed any part of him."

"She must have had some influence."

"In between the criticism and the belittling?" Maggie asks. "Dad was a serial offender as far as she was concerned. But there must have been more to him."

"There was, I'm sure. No one, even my brother, could be so one dimensional." Daniel pauses, and then indicates they should turn northward. "It circles back to my not caring, doesn't it?"

"Fair enough, but while you were not caring, what did you notice?" Maggie shakes the trash bag, gauging the bulk of what they've collected.

"Giving Mom and Dad the silent treatment centered their enmity on me, so I guess it spared Aidan some unwanted attention," Daniel says. He chuckles. "He never thanked me for that."

"Now you're just being glib."

"I'm sorry. It's a defense mechanism." He hesitates, bending over to retrieve a bleached length of wood, and draws a circle in the sand. "Aidan acted out a lot, but he also retreated into himself little by little." Daniel pokes the middle of the sand circle with the stick. "Closed himself off from the family."

"Like you did," Maggie says.

"My reflex, of course, is to say: 'not like I did.' But there's some truth in that. Let's say we retreated in opposite directions."

"They seem parallel at times."

Daniel gazes at the clouds. "I see so much sky here," he says. "Reminds me of Okinawa at times." He pauses. "Remember: don't take what Laura and my mother say as gospel. What they know of my life is what I let them know."

"It's amazing how you can be wistful one moment and kind of a dick the next," Maggie says.

Daniel laughs, throwing his head back. "That's an acquired talent. Highly effective with certain clients. Invariably white men reluctant to assume responsibility in a crisis. Eager to blame anyone else rather than admit they fucked up and resorted to using Grayson and me to minimize the blowback. Compounding their moral failings."

"Moral failings?" Maggie says.

"We should never have allowed religion to hijack morality," Daniel says. "Never should have linked it to anyone's idea of sin. There can be good without God."

"My father," Maggie says. "Godliness without goodness."

"Prime example."

The chocolate Labrador races past them in the wet sand, startling Maggie, who clutches the trash bag to her chest. She giggles as the three people she'd seen earlier pass them. The youngest apologizes for the dog surprising her.

"No problem," Maggie says.

Daniel nods to the older couple and then tells Maggie they should return to the house. "No masks," he whispers as they approach the stairway to his yard. "There'll be another surge in infections this summer. People are stupid."

"I'm still stunned that people make political decisions about a health issue," Maggie says.

"Fuck 'em all," Daniel says, pausing beside the summer house to scan the beach. "July's the most popular month for families," he says. "Parents with small kids, teens with fires partying all night. None of them will take precautions."

"Does everything make you angry?" Maggie asks. She studies Daniel's face, his head backlighted by a shaft of sunlight through the trees.

"Most everything," he says, smiling. "But it wanes and then I just feel sad. Wisdom makes sadness plausible."

"But not bearable?"

"Oh, Maggie, anything's bearable. You just need the courage to be a coward."

Maggie wags her head. "That's a curious concept."

"When people cite 'the courage of your convictions,' well, what if your conviction is to mind your own goddamned business?"

"Always an observer, never a participant?" Maggie asks, striving to keep her tone of voice neutral. "Like you are with your family?"

"Haven't you just defined an historian? Watching but never getting involved?"

Maggie grinds her teeth at the barb, aggravated but cognizant that she should avoid reacting to Daniel's skill at nudging the conversation away from himself. "Professional detachment," she says, "doesn't prevent emotional engagement."

"I believe you," Daniel says. "I bet you and Samuel donate to the correct causes, sign the correct petitions, and carry the correct signs in the correct demonstrations. And while it may sound like I'm attacking or criticizing you, understand that I'd do the same if I had any desire to leave here." He lifts an arm and points toward the house. "But I don't so I confine my rantings to online forums, where I never shy from telling people how wrong they are, and how much I enjoy that no one has ever told them that before. I enjoyed sitting in client meetings, just staring at ego without flinching. No need for that restraint anymore." He pauses and runs a finger over one of the summer house clapboards. "Total freedom, which comes from loving nothing. Just ask my family."

"Wow," Maggie exhales.

Daniel laughs as he pivots toward the patio. "This is the time of day when I'd normally be screaming on Twitter. But today you're my audience."

"I'm so fucking honored," Maggie says, walking past him, dragging the black trash bag to the patio, where she releases it. It collapses and some of the trash spills on the bluestones.

Daniel replaces the spilled trash in the bag and then faces Maggie. "Are we going to have a fight?" He stares at her with an impassive expression.

She feels as though it's a test. She returns his glare and then says, "We might."

"When I punished my parents as a teenager by withdrawing from them, it set a pattern of never revealing more than I needed to. Maybe like my shyness, I'm over-compensating for all those years of reticence."

"No more filters?" Maggie asks. "I don't think so. Every word you use seems well chosen. You're not flippant or unfiltered, you're calculating."

Daniel carries the trash bag to the side of the house, down the stairway to the garage. Maggie trails him. "My clients never wanted theoreticians, they wanted practitioners. They didn't want academics, they wanted applications. Grayson and I had to remain unemotional even during their hysterics. Only a few of them ever expressed interest in the journey. They always focused on the destination. I sense you're a process person. How I got to be who I am fascinates you, even though you cloak it in curiosity about your father. Right?" He pauses at the bottom of the stairwell and punches a code into a keypad. The door opens and Maggie sees a silver Range Rover parked on a polished concrete floor.

"History is process," Maggie says. "So, yes."

"My father viewed my ambition as a criticism of his life," Daniel says. "Isn't that sad? To send a child that message?" He deposits the trash bag in a blue, wheeled bin. "That's process. It still makes me mad when I think of how little ambition that man had for me. If you asked him, he'd brag about being self-made and he could have applied that lesson to his children in one of two ways: pave the road for them so they didn't have to experience the same setbacks he suffered, or step aside and let them fend for themselves as he had because having no one else to rely on but yourself builds character. You can guess which he chose."

"Is that why you never wanted children, to avoid repeating your father's mistakes with you?" Maggie crosses the space to the door to the storeroom and leans against the wall.

"Some people shouldn't have children. I'm one of them."

15.

Maggie's in her room, typing notes of our conversation while I retreat to the summer house, giving her "space" to analyze my mood shift. It wasn't an arbitrary shift, of course, it was purposeful, which does make me the dick she accused me of being. I wanted to make her angry, which would also make her vulnerable, and I'm not certain why. She didn't say anything to provoke me. Didn't goad me into it. Didn't quarrel about something I said. The term "free-fire zone" surfaces from my days in the Air Force and that's the best description of Maggie this morning. Wanting to make her angry was a way of draining my own anger that I'm drawn into Elizabeth's condition, my mother's fragility, Laura's guilt trip, pretending I'm unaffected by the concurrence of everything happening, but it weighs on me and Maggie is innocent…but here.

The mesh in one of the screens is new. George must have replaced it when he repainted the clapboards. The space reminds me of the porch at the back of our family home in St. Louis. A concrete floor painted gray on which Aidan and I played board games and raced toy cars. During Chutes and Ladders, when Aidan lifted his piece and tapped the count of his spin on the board, he often double tapped on a space so he'd land on a ladder square or avoid a chute. Cheating. Even at something as insignificant as a board game, but I guess to him, beating me was never insignificant. Neither was cheating. One year for his birthday. Aidan received a slot car racing set. He laid out the figure-eight track in the porch and the two of us raced competing cars, although our contests soon devolved into anarchy. I strove for faster and faster times while Aidan accelerated on the straightaways, propelling his car off the track when it sped into a sharp curve, staging spectacular crashes. As Maggie would say: he wasn't even playing the game anymore. Because he could never win. We spent many afternoons on that porch and they weren't all moments of conflict; it's simply that conflict is more memorable than contentment.

Several people walk along the beach. None wearing masks. Not the older folks who walk on dry sand or the small children who tease the waves. George jokes that the pandemic affects me least of all the people he knows. Until now the two years of the pandemic have cost me nothing. He wonders if I'm in a love/hate relationship with my solitude. Pre-pandemic, we discussed it sharing beers and he alternated between envying and deriding me being alone. A cautious man, he never confronted me with his theory that I'm hiding from something; he danced around the suggestion, asking questions about my life in Chicago, the women I'd known then, because in his experience only a woman could provoke extreme isolation like mine. Only a disastrous relationship could force me to cross Lake Michigan in search of solitude and he wondered about the kind of woman I fled. His circumspect questions betrayed vicarious, almost prurient curiosity. Restrained by his natural reticence to pry, the conversations proceeded like a comedy, with George inquiring about the kinds of women I'd met in Chicago. Did I have a type? Favorite hair color, eye color, height, or personality? He reminded me of a patient hunter stalking a clearing where his prey grazed. Circling downwind of the quarry, waiting for the optimal kill shot.

I told him about several women I'd dated, although for an adult, the term seems juvenile. They were women I fucked. I detailed several red flags for ending relationships: her asking me to meet her family; my repeatedly saying "That's not what I meant;" her stopping along a lake walk to hover over an infant. George snorted when I admitted I often grew bored with a lover and I remembered wondering at the time whether I was bored with the woman or myself, and whether a new relationship would distract me from that realization. Following a pair of acrimonious break-ups, I tested honesty, where I'd tell prospective lovers that any relationship would be transitory, that all I sought was an interlude of mutual fun. If she sought a long-term partner or a husband, she should move on. Many did and some didn't, most memorably, Sandrine. She exemplified the difference between moving and moving on.

Maggie asking about the girls Aidan dated reminds me of my senior prom, picking up Jenny Bishop at her house, driving home for Mom to take pictures in our living room, and Dad standing beside Jenny for the photos. In one of the prints with my parents, she's blurred as she stepped away from my father; she moved, she later told me, because he'd placed a hand on her ass. That night at the dance, I kneaded my anger at my father, reminding myself that in a few months, I'd leave for college, that my father was a temporary fixture, that when I left home, my real life would begin. Jenny remained angry all night, both with my father and with me, for doing nothing to "avenge her honor." I scoffed at the notion of confronting my father to satisfy her aggrievement, and we broke up soon after the prom. Other boys staring at me in the school corridor convinced me she'd electrified the gossip mill, but like my family, high school was a temporary inconvenience.

George is the only person to whom I gave a copy of my novel. I told everyone else who expressed interest that I'd autograph any copy they bought. After the novel was published, my conversations with George often revolved around how I would fill my time. I noted how at this stage in my life, time tugs in two directions. Longevity ticks like a raucous clock and yet each day seems comprised of endless hours to be occupied. He wondered how I endured unstructured days with no obligations. George is the kind of working man who associates being idle with laziness, so the notion of me sequestered in my concrete box with nothing to do seemed foreign, decadent, and (with some prompting from me), his confidential aspiration. Our difference, of course, is means. On a handyman's earnings, George will never afford to retire in the luxury I enjoy, yet like a spoiled child, I fret about legacy. About whether a life without a legacy is a wasted life.

Maggie hurries across the yard, waggling her phone, and a shiver crawls up my spine. Reminiscent of late night telephone calls when I was a child, it signals terrible news. My maternal grandmother woke the house when she called to tell my mother that her father had died. My father grumbled that she could have waited until morning to relay the news, that the man wasn't going to get any deader if she waited a few hours until a decent hour to call. It was one of the atypical moments when my mother left his complaint unchallenged. A lesson for me of the effects of grief: it alters instinct and behavior.

"Your sister," Maggie says, opening the door of the summer house, extending the phone. It's an older Android model, unlike my up-to-date iPhone.

I can't read her expression. Her face is impassive: neither grim nor encouraging. I place the phone against my ear. "Laura?"

"Mom's been taken to the hospital," she says. "Her ECG was all over the place. It's time for a pacemaker."

"That's a simple procedure, right?"

Maggie hovers at the doorway, swiveling her gaze between me and the beach below.

"There's no such thing as a simple procedure for a woman of her age, Dan," Laura says. "It's worrisome."

"I'm sure she'll be fine," I say, uneager to rehash our wearisome argument, resolute that I'll not travel to Tucson.

"From your mouth," she says, her voice trailing off.

"How's Elizabeth?" I ask, as Maggie sits beside me on the wicker love seat, the compression of the cushions makes me lean against her shoulder for a moment before I right myself.

"Getting worse," Laura says. "The doctor's not hopeful."

"I'm sorry, Laura," I say, as one would to a friend, not a sibling.

"Mom wanted you to know," she says.

I imagine their conversation: my mother telling Laura to call me, both of them knowing the call will be informational. It won't stir me to any action. I glance at Maggie's face. She's more affected by this news than I. Her lips compact into a hard-pressed line and her brow hoods her eyes.

"What's Luke doing through all this?" I fear asking because Laura will assume I'm trying to pass responsibility back and forth between the two of them while I perch up north, distant and detached.

"He's trying to console Hank and the kids," she says. "But everyone feels so helpless. And now with Mom, so hopeless."

I fight the urge to end the call by telling my sister to keep me informed, both for how it will affect her and Maggie's opinion of me. That realization, that I care about what Maggie thinks, catches me off-guard and I hear Laura repeating my name in the receiver.

"I'm here," I say.

"Right," Laura says. "I'll call after Mom has the procedure."

"Okay."

No exchange of sentiment as she severs our connection. I lower the phone and stare at the screen, which reverted to the call keypad. I return the phone to Maggie, who pockets it.

"Are you worried?' she asks.

Shouldn't she know my concern is unemotional?

"I mean," she says, "within your capacity to be involved."

I grin, considering the taunt justified after this morning's conversation. "I'll be sad when I need to be. Despite what my family believes, I'm not heartless."

"Then why cultivate that image?"

I say nothing.

Maggie sighs and rises. "There's a dead squirrel beside the patio."

"Is it intact?" I ask.

Maggie pauses and regards me with a quizzical expression. "What?"

"Does it look like something's been eating it?' I ask. "There are foxes and even coyotes have been reported."

"It looks undisturbed."

"I'll take care of it," I say, gripping a love seat arm, pushing myself up.

"Reconciling with your family might actually benefit you more than them," Maggie says, then pivots on her heel and walks toward the house.

I admire the tactic of forcing me to address any retort to her retreating form.

Seclusion suits me because I can't change anything meaningful in anyone's life, but Maggie implies I'm robbing myself by remaining isolated. That I'm myopic, inured to any joy my family could bring me. Having someone need me never appealed to me. Not my family. Not my clients or coworkers. Not my lovers. Solitude balances me. Harmonizes me like disparate voices fabricating improbable beauty from ordinary melodies. I know my place at this stage in my life and have no my patience with people who cannot recognize or acknowledge that, whether stranger, friend, or family.

It's a black squirrel, still limp, and its tail droops over the edge of the shovel blade as I carry it to the garage. No indication that a predator killed it. Hawks, foxes, and coyotes kill for food. This body bears no wounds or evidence of feeding. Illness or old age, I think as I lift the lid to the garbage bin and flip the shovel.

Maggie stands at the patio door with her back to me. "Do you want to talk some more?" I ask, and she turns toward me.

"I'm thinking of flying to Tucson," she says.

I nod, crossing to the sink and washing my hands.

"I'd have to drive back to Iowa and then fly from there." She studies my face as I lather and rinse my hands.

"That's your choice," I say. We stare at one another across the open space, listening to screeching gulls and the high-pitched voice of a child on the beach through the open patio door. "But you could stay until something happens." I'm careful about what words to use with Maggie following our earlier confrontation on the beach. It would be more honest to ask her to stay so I can both make amends for my attitude and allow her to browse some of my journals.

Her expression remains stoic, reinforcing my feeling that she tunnels more deeply than mere observation when she looks at me. She studies me. Assesses me. With eyes so dark brown they seem black. I examine her features again, searching for similarities between her and my brother. I can't recall her mother's face. Have no way of knowing how much she resembles the woman. Her hair, parted in the middle and tucked behind her ears, reveals gray at the roots.

"I feel being here inconveniences you," she says. "That anyone's presence would be an inconvenience. You're invested in and fond of isolation, but I'm questioning whether it's to protect you from the outside world or protect all of us from you. It depends on how much credit I want to give you for being self-aware. You pretend to be so calm but there's anger running underneath that façade."

I remain silent, braced against the kitchen counter. Maggie said it all with a poker-faced expression. Said it all matter-of-factly.

"I didn't intend for my visit as a platform for your historical grudges," she says.

"That's fair," I say. "I apologize and won't make any excuses."

"Thank you."

Our silence feels like an impasse so I add: "Living alone is an indulgence, I admit it."

"This anger belies your insistence that you don't need anyone." Maggie walks to the kitchen island and places her hands palms down on the surface.

"Laura called me once my freshman year at the University of Missouri. In those days, the dorms had a pay phone in a booth on each floor. The poor guys that lived in the rooms at the end of hall ended up answering it all the time. She called to tell me that Aidan had been arrested for stealing from the register in the sporting goods store where he worked." I chuckle. "We're talking about less than ten dollars. My parents reimbursed the owner and talked him out of pressing charges, but Laura worried that Aidan might run away from home rather than suffer my father's punishment. He was sixteen, broke. The idea of this spoiled, middle-class teen running away was ludicrous, but Laura was distraught and made me promise I'd call if Aidan showed up at my dorm room. Aidan running away, much less running to me, was laughable."

"I never heard that story," Maggie says.

"Mom would never tell you. Laura either. I bet your mother never knew." I pause. "The point is, Laura has always been a worrier. And a peacemaker."

"Are you that cynical?" Maggie asks. "You think she's manipulating you with what's happening?"

"Not manipulating," I say. "Being opportunistic."

"One of the pitfalls of constantly being alone is believing everything revolves round you."

I laugh at the accuracy of Maggie's statement. "All right. That's true."

"When I talk with Grandma Breedlow and Aunt Laura, you're not the center of our discussions."

"I'm shocked," I say, trying to foster an atmosphere Maggie will find amiable. That might convince her to stay.

She continues staring at me. "Sarcasm. The recourse of a remorseful mind. Do you have a plan for your life beyond resentment?" Maggie asks. She inhales and holds that breath for a moment before exhaling.

We've moved beyond any impasse to a junction. What I say next will determine whether she stay or goes. "I'm sorry, Maggie," I say. "I've treated you unfairly." I fall silent. The best apologies don't have a "but" or an explanation she might construe as an excuse. Apologies should be abrupt.

"Thank you," she says. "For admitting it. Now tell me why?" Maggie thumps her thumbs on the island surface.

"Let's sit down," I say, gesturing toward the sitting area. I wish she had bluntly accepted my apology, but she's earned the right to an explanation. We sit in the chairs that flank the fireplace and I note wax from last night's candles on the hearth stones.

"Whether or not it's justified, I've tethered you to my mother," I say. "To my family."

"I *am* your family," Maggie says. "That's the point, right?"

I nod. "Fair or unfair. Because I don't know you."

"Transferring your anger toward your family onto me makes me wonder if the anger you feel toward them is a transference of anger toward someone or something else."

"That's another rabbit hole," I say, deflecting. "I could insist there's endless transference."

"Except it all seemed to start with your family."

"Ground zero," I say, resting my hands, resisting the urge to drum my fingers, to remain calm, although my stomach flutters.

"What did they do to you that was so terrible? That doesn't happen in all families?" Maggie asks.

"Oh, there was no abuse, if that's what you mean," I say.

"It's not. I never thought that." Maggie crosses her legs, resting one hand on top of the other in her lap. It's a self-possessed pose that conveys calm, self-confidence, and patience.

I lower my eyes as I consider my words. "Did you feel the *other* in your family? The one who never fit?"

"I know where you're going with this, but doesn't every child feel that at some time?" Maggie shakes her head. "It's a little predictable."

"There are degrees," I say. "I felt it more deeply than anyone else I knew."

"So you talked a lot about that with your friends?"

I pause to let the reflex for sarcasm dissipate. "No," I say. "Maybe I was no different than any other boy my age. But it still was the way *I* felt. And it seemed more intense than just a generational difference."

Maggie nods. "Okay. That's valid. But you never outgrew it."

I grimace and she notices.

"That was a poor way to express what I meant," she says. "Not like it's a childish phase. But you clung to it. You're still clinging to it and I wonder if it's too much of a convenient bogeyman."

"Maybe it seems like I'm clinging to it because they won't leave me alone. It's like a scab they constantly pick."

"I love parsing language," Maggie says. "And it's fascinating you'd use an analogy that concerns healing."

"So my family is an open wound."

"Nothing that simple," Maggie says.

She glances at the driftwood on the mantle and I flash on its resemblance to bleached bone. I recall a lover who, when we broke up, leveled accusations much like those Maggie now poses: self-loathing is the motivation of all my anger. I flinched at the notion of self-loathing. I conceded self-*dis*satisfaction but balked at self-hatred.

"My parents never tried to understand," I say. "They, *my father,* mocked my opinions, never sat down and talked with me. It was dismissal."

Maggie dips her head. "My father did that, too," she says. "But he had moments when he went overboard being kind to us, usually because he'd been arguing with Mom and didn't want her turning us against him."

"My Dad never cared if I turned against him," I say. "I think he enjoyed knowing I hated him."

"What was his family like when he grew up?" Maggie asks.

"I have no idea," I say, realizing the void in my understanding of my father. "He never talked about it. We saw his parents on birthdays and holidays while they were alive and I never thought anything weird about the way he interacted with them." One person's memory is another's epiphany, but I never considered how the absence of a memory can also be a revelation. It's disturbing to believe I'm angry because of the way my father treated me. That he treated his children the same way his father treated him. What explains his poor parenting? His obvious resentment of his children?

"Did Laura ask you to come to Tucson?" I ask.

Maggie shakes her head. "No," she says. "It's my idea."

"I understand why you'd want to go rather than stay here and unpick my life." I grin to assure Maggie I'm kidding.

"It's a matter of who needs me more," she says.

Her words bite. I know she's skeptical about my insistence that I don't need anyone. I'm intensely staring at her face when my senses of perspective and balance falter, as though I'm slumping to one side but I remain upright. A hovering, buoyant sensation slides away and I re-center, still staring at Maggie, although my awareness of myself within the room feels like an echo. The manifestation frightens me, but also recalls an acid trip in Okinawa when I escaped my body and floated to the corner of the room, turned, and marveled at the sight of myself and three other buddies reclining on mats, talking about our fathers, all World War II vets, trying to find common ground by comparing their experiences to ours. We laid the groundwork for empathy that I never exercised.

"But I'm undecided," Maggie adds.

"Have you traveled?" I ask.

Her face reveals confusion at the question, like I've posed a non-sequitur.

"Aidan never traveled any farther than West Texas, I imagine. Even as a kid, he wasn't receptive to new ideas if they contradicted his beliefs. He was proudly insular, like a lot of religious people."

"Even as a child?" Maggie asks.

I roll my shoulders to rotate my head on my neck, reluctant to re-experience the troubling, disjointed singularity. "He played at being devout," I say. "Was an altar boy. One year he told everyone he wanted to be a priest, but that was a phase. The nuns tried to convince every Catholic boy he had a vocation for the priesthood." I pause, recalling Aidan telling us all one night during a commercial on TV that he wanted to be a priest. My father laughed and said he wasn't good enough to be a pimple on a priest's ass. My Mom spat my father's name as a rebuke and I watched Aidan's expression stiffen into a hateful glare so obvious that I feared he'd say or do something that would spark one of my father's frenzies, where he yelled over everyone to drown out any voice other than his own.

"Maybe that explains why he became born-again," Maggie says.

"Religion fills a void," I say. "An intellectual deficit."

"You don't respect any authority, do you?"

"I've learned not to. Family. The church. The Air Force. Corporate society. I don't see much to respect."

"And Grandma Breedlow is the last vestige of all that authority, isn't she? Even though the real antagonist in your family seems to have been your father." Maggie sits motionless and I imagine her agency in a classroom, how her manner would command attentiveness, how she would project authority. Much as my comportment in client meetings exuded authority.

"Do we all become what we once disliked?' I ask.

"Did you like the person you were before you retired?"

The question follows logically from mine. I wave my arm to encompass the space. "I like the comfort I earned."

"Not many people can claim to be comfortable and alone."

"I've always been different, remember?" I smile. "What are you going to do?"

Maggie purses her lips and blinks slowly. "Wait," she says.

"I'm sure my mother will be fine," I say. "Would you go for Elizabeth's funeral?"

Maggie rubs a finger along the chair arm. "We have such differing views of family, don't we?"

I nod.

"Her death won't mean anything to you, will it?"

Her question bares all the harshness of my regard for my sister. "She was five years old when I left home," I say. "I don't know her."

"You don't like her," Maggie says. "You don't like the person she is."

"No, I don't," I say. "I don't like what she believes, how she votes, her prideful ignorance, or her condescending superiority."

"That's a lot to dislike in a person you don't know."

"Point taken," I say. "I know enough, even if it's second-hand."

"I wouldn't be going because of Elizabeth," Maggie says.

"Of course not. You'd go for Mom. And Laura."

I remember Elizabeth as a toddler, mesmerized by her older siblings. Laura coddling the child when Aidan and I spurned her annoying presence, accepting the functions of a substitute mother when Mom worked. When Mom was expecting Luke, Aidan told me he wished that if our parents were going to continue fucking, they could at least use birth control. He was embarrassed to tell his friends that his mother was pregnant again. Never followed his own advice, I think. Sowing children in three different marriages.

"I doubt your mother's doctor will let her attend," Maggie says. "The risk of infection."

"I hope not," I say. "I left a journal from my Air Force days on my desk. You're welcome to read it," I say. "But remember, that was a long time ago."

16.

The text Maggie received from Jessica alluded to a rift with Hailey, but she put off calling until she read a few of the pages in one of Daniel's Air Force journals. The date on the first page, May 12, 1971, detailed a mission he'd flown where the co-pilot appeared beside Daniel's workstation, plugged his headset into her uncle's communications panel, looked out the hatch portal, and told the pilot that the aircraft was losing fuel. The man glanced at Daniel, shook his head and then raised an index finger to his lips, signaling Daniel to remain quiet.

She read in Daniel's tidy handwriting:

I nodded to him, a First Lieutenant. We never associated with the flight crew. Officers. He wasn't much older than me. Moments after he returned to the cockpit, the pilot announced we'd be diverting to the Philippines for an emergency landing. Clark Air Base was closer than flying back to Okinawa and I wondered why we didn't just land at Cam Ranh or DaNang, but I bet the Air Force doesn't want a spy plane sitting on the tarmac in a war zone. A juicy target for a rocket attack. We landed without incident and maintenance crews worked on the plane for hours while we sat in the shade of the revetment walls. I unzipped my flight suit, slipped it off my shoulders and tied the arms around my waist. Every time the air mission supervisor walked by someone would ask how much longer it'd be, and he'd bark "as long as it goddamned takes." He was a heavyset man and in the heat his flight suit had darkened from sweat patches under his arms and across his belly. No one liked him so no one cared that he was miserable. In fact, several of us enjoyed it.

We eventually returned to Okinawa rather than continue our mission over Laos. We sat on that tarmac for three-and-a-half hours. I napped for a while. It's a skill I've developed. The ability to sleep anywhere under any conditions. The first time I tried to sleep on the aircraft, the reverberating engines grated in my ears, but later, the droning sounded like a lullaby.

Back in the barracks, my roommate Stuart, asked if I'd been afraid when the co-pilot shushed me. Our flights are pretty safe. In pre-mission briefings, AAA and SAM sites are identified for the flight crew to steer around. MiGs don't enter our airspace and we have combat air patrols to suppress them if they do. If we ever go down, it'll be mechanical failure, so when he asked if I was scared, I said yeah. The whole time I squatted on the tarmac I hoped they'd put us on a different plane back to Kadena. Why tempt fate by getting back on the aircraft that tried to kill you?

Daniel's journal is a black notebook, long and narrow with lined pages. He began a new entry on each page. She rereads the entry about the aircraft mechanical problem, until the matter-of-factness of his language resonates: no emotion. When his roommate asked if he'd been scared, Daniel's answer was monosyllabic. "Yeah." No elucidation. No exposition.

There are gaps in the journal, pages where tape has been removed. She assumes he had mounted photos and removed them for scanning. Seeing him as a young man may remind her of her father. When she was a child, visiting her mother's parents meant she and her sisters could browse the old family albums, pointing at square photos on stiff black pages, the corners secured by adhesive triangles. It occurs to her that Daniel displays no photos of people. His photos depict sunsets and sunrises, shot in Michigan and Chicago, but there are no portraits. Not of family, of friends, or of old lovers. Samuel and she have converted their stairwell into a gallery of family photos, the framed prints prompting each of them at times to pause and smile at a portrait. Above their antique iron frame bed hangs a large black and white portrait of the two of them sitting on the front porch swing, taken by a friend from the university who works in the external relations department. Side-by-side, leaning their heads against one another, each of them smiles and looks down at the other's hands. Maggie loves the photo for the quietude and affection it portrays. After she and Samuel met, moved beyond the tentativeness of learning another person's tendencies and predilections, the fierceness of her attraction to him startled her. Such passion at her age seemed unseemly, more appropriate for a woman decades younger, and when she confessed her desire to Jessica, her sister scoffed at Maggie's reaction, expressing shock she'd fall into such an agist trope. "Good lord, Maggie, you're overdue. There's going to be a flood of craving behind your dam." She felt like a fifty-something teenager with Samuel.

Thinking of her sister, she calls Jessica, gets voicemail, chuckling at her sister's recorded instructions: "Leave a short message. No one wants to listen to your podcast."

"It's Maggie. Call me."

She assumes Jessica wants to vent about Hailey and Paul moving to Texas. She would not send a text message in an emergency, for which Maggie is thankful. One more emergency, no. When she and her uncle spoke by the fireplace, he studied her, gauging her reactions to what he said, examining how she responded to him. A professor in graduate school once described academics as "gladiators of rhetoric." He assured her their contests were also "battles to the death."

When she spoke with Laura about Grandma Breedlow's procedure, her aunt said Daniel had no capacity for guilt. The statement seemed harsh given the circumstances. Laura needed to vent her frustration, Maggie assumed, no doubt feeling overwhelmed by her obligations. Did Laura expect Daniel, as the oldest, to shoulder these responsibilities? Or as the oldest son? Her minimal and chilly interactions with Luke offered no clue as to how he was helping his sister cope with the crisis. Laura never spoke about her desire for reestablishing a relationship with Daniel, but of how it would delight and fulfill her mother. The inference being she needed to accomplish it before Grandma Breedlow died. The concurrence of Elizabeth's failing health and Grandma Breedlow's heart problems increases the urgency of engineering any reconciliation.

She returns to the journal. Date: September 23, 1971.

Badger's girlfriend introduced me to Kimiko, who spent the night with me in our off-base apartment. He said she was looking for a new boyfriend but was vague about why. We fucked but she was unenthusiastic about it, like it was payment for being allowed to stay in the apartment. Honestly...I didn't care. She wrapped her short legs around my ass and tugged me close, my chin resting on her shoulder. She didn't want to have to look at me, that was obvious, which was a shame, because she was pretty, with shoulder-length glossy black hair, and nice boobs. As soon as I came, she darted to the bathroom, returned shortly, lay on her side, and pulled me to spoon her, my arm curved around her, my hand gripping her boob. My nose burrowed in her hair and I sniffed, a whiff of something floral. I covered us with a sheet and woke several times during the night, unaccustomed to having another body in bed with me. In the morning, I woke first, propped my head on a hand, elbow on the mattress, and watched her sleeping. I guessed she was in her early twenties. She was beautiful lying on her back, her chest rising and falling in gentle rhythm. I brushed a stand of hair from her face and she hummed, turning toward me, snuggling. Minutes later she opened her eyes, flitting them around the room, and then pushed herself off the bed. I stared at her pubic hair, black, silky. She turned from me and pulled back the curtain to stare out the window. I asked if she was okay and she nodded.

She made it clear in her limited English that she didn't want to go out, so we spent the day in the apartment. Took a bath together and she beat me off with sudsy hands, dried me, and then we watched TV on Badger's small black and white set. Kimiko laughed at a slapstick sitcom, about a man and his three daughters, constantly conspiring against their clueless father. She sent me with a written note to a neighboring restaurant and when I returned with the food, I expected her to be gone, but she was there, and we ate the meal sitting cross-legged on the tatami mats in the tiny living room. Whenever someone walked by outside on the landing to another apartment, she tensed up. I wondered what frightened her. Who was she hiding from? That night, she told me she wanted to go to a club and we strolled to BC Street, where she walked swiftly ahead of me to a bar where several women hung around out front. She spoke with them, glancing up and down the street. They gestured with their hands and I understood nothing of what they said, but their tones were shrill, angry. Suddenly four men appeared, their haircuts pinned them as Marines. One of them grabbed Kimiko by her arm, spun her around, and demanded to know where she'd been. I stepped back as she pointed to me, muttering something I didn't want to hear. The man looked at me and then told me to get lost. I nearly ran down the sidewalk, ducking into one of the alleys that connect BC Street with Gate Two Street, and then hurried back to the apartment. Even if Kimiko told that guy where I lived, Okinawans constructed their buildings to withstand typhoon force winds, and the concrete walls, barred windows, and steel door would keep even four Marines from kicking their way in. I hoped getting his girlfriend back was all he wanted.

Hours later, she knocked on the door and I snuck a peek through the window in the kitchen. She was alone on the landing, but I ran to the bedroom window to look for the Marines, balking at unlocking the door. She knocked again and I let her in. "Where you go?" she demanded. "Why you go?" She was furious. Elbowing past me, she entered the bathroom, sat on the toilet pissing without closing the door, and berated me non-stop about why had I left her.

I told her I wasn't going to fight them alone and she shook her head, rising. I noticed she hadn't wiped but said nothing. "He not tough," she said, striding to the bedroom, where she stripped out of her clothes and waved me inside. She fucked me while I lay on my back, reaching down to massage her clit. She leaned forward and gripped my head in her hands and stared at me when I came and the intensity in her eyes fucking scared me. The whores I usually fucked rarely pretended it was anything but a job, and when they did pretend to be engaged, their acting was piss poor, but Kimiko fucked me that night like a girlfriend, and I panicked. Stories always circulated about girls in Okinawa who wanted to go to the States, hunting for husbands. I wasn't too worried about that, but it crossed my mind. More frightening was Kimiko assuming I'd protect her from her Marine boyfriend. No fucking way.

When Badger came home with his girlfriend later that night, I took him into his bedroom, closed the door, and explained the situation. I flew a mission the next day, slept in the barracks when we returned to Kadena, and on my next day off found the apartment empty.

Badger's girlfriend told him Kimiko had left Koza but offered no other explanation, and I didn't push for one because I didn't care. For the next few weeks, every time I prowled BC Street, I glanced over my shoulder for that Marine and his buddies.

Maggie's cell phone rings and she sees Jessica's photo appear on the screen.

"Is he feeding you well?' her sister asks.

"Like a chef," she says. "What's up?"

"Hailey's driving me crazy with this Texas thing," Jessica says.

"How so?" Maggie flips through pages of Daniel's journal, finding a photo of himself taped to the page. In uniform, fatigues, his name above the right pocket, walking along a sidewalk, his right arm raised in a fist, grinning at the camera. The similarity to her father stuns her.

"She's going along with it all, but she's not happy about it," Jessica says. "And instead of telling Paul, she's unloading on me."

Maggie traces the photo with a fingertip, wondering why Daniel hadn't removed it for scanning. "How eager would you be to move to Texas," Maggie says. "Missouri is bad enough."

"Like Iowa's a hotbed of socialist activism."

"Point taken," Maggie says. "You're the middle child, Jess. It's your job to be the peacemaker." The background of the photo includes ugly, two-story brick buildings. Barracks?

"Yeah, well who's responsible for my peace?"

"That's the point," Maggie says. "Let Hailey vent, but don't let it get to you."

"That's what David said."

"I know the move'll be tough on you," she says. "You'll be the last of us still there."

"There's that," Jessica says. "And I worry that I'll lose touch with her like I have with you."

"What are talking about?" Maggie says. "We talk all the time. We chat online. We email."

"It's not the same, Mags, you know that. That's all too easy, too superficial."

Maggie visualizes Jessica on the window seat in her bedroom, knees pulled up, phone braced against her ear, head turned to view the backyard. The swing set David promises to dismantle remains in the corner, where Jessica wants to plant a raised garden for herbs. She's the cook and the sisters' favorite house for family meals. "I'm sorry you're feeling abandoned, Jess."

"I had this fantasy about Hailey and me growing old together where we grew up."

"It's remarkable you've both stayed there so long."

"David and I have each had opportunities to move," she says.

"Why haven't you ever said anything?"

Jessica snorts. "I didn't want to leave Hailey here alone."

Maggie laughs, closing Daniel's journal. "Life bites everybody eventually."

"It's my pity party. I'm entitled to bitch." Jessica pauses. "How's it going there?"

"He's been trying to rattle me," Maggie says. "To keep me off balance."

"Means he fears you," Jessica says.

"He's letting me read his old journals, from when he was in the Air Force."

"Anything interesting?"

"Lots of sex," Maggie says, laughing.

"So he's like Dad." Jessica laughs.

"It's weird to realize that when he was writing this journal, I was an infant and you weren't born yet." Maggie hears the patio door opening downstairs. "Dad was nineteen. Mom was eighteen. What were we doing at that age?"

"College," Jessica says. "I'll give Mom credit for drilling into us that we'd all go to college."

"Grampa Breedlow never pushed Daniel that way," Maggie says. "He denigrated education."

"Is that the reason why he has nothing to do with his family?"

"His father's a big reason, but he spreads the blame around."

"To Dad, I imagine."

"I'm resurrecting a few stories from him. Oh, and Aunt Elizabeth is in the hospital with COVID. It doesn't look good. And Grandma Breedlow's having a pacemaker installed." Maggie pauses, considering that word. *Installed.* Like a furnace or a dishwasher. Not a life-saving device. *Implanted.* That's the word, she thinks.

"Shit. How's he taking it?"

"It's complicated, like everything to do with him and family. He tries to keep a distance but me being here doesn't help that." Maggie considers the entries in the journal, recognizes within his dispassionate descriptions of events early evidence of detachment. "He acts like it's all an inconvenience to him."

"Pretty egotistical," Jessica says. "Like Dad. Peas in a pod."

"And this place is so impersonal," Maggie says. "Minimalism run amok. You'd hate it."

"It's on the lake, right?"

"Yeah."

"Have you been to the beach?"

"He cleans the stretch in front of his house. There was a storm last night and we picked up trash."

"Good God, Maggie," Jessica says, laughing.

Maggie imagines her sister shielding her mouth with a hand. "Actually, it was fun," she says.

"What big revelations have you uncovered?"

Maggie considers her answer. "Daniel was more like his father, but he denies the comparison. Dad was closer to his mother and that drove the wedge deeper between the brothers. There were instances when they got along, but Daniel doesn't remember them lasting very long. His memory's locked on them always being in conflict because that suits him. I think they took their frustrations out on one another because they couldn't directly address what angered them." She pauses. "For Daniel it was his father. I haven't figured out what it was for Dad, even though Daniel thinks it was him. Always having to live up to what his older brother was doing."

"Older siblings are a real pain," Jessica says.

"Good thing I'm the exception, huh?" Maggie chuckles. "Sorry about Hailey. Call anytime."

"Love you, Maggot."

Maggie opens another journal. The inside page had the year "1972" drawn in colored ink, balloon numerals. She reads the first entry, a short paragraph dated January 6, 1972.

I'm in Nakhon Phanom, Thailand for the last year of my service. Not flying anymore. The Air Force set up a listening station here and the traffic we used to intercept is now being relayed here from a U-2 orbiting over Laos. There are still missions flown out of Okinawa, but fewer. Why pay us flight and combat and pay when you can stick us out here in the northeast corner of Thailand and save all that money. Cheap bastards. One year and I'm out. It's surreal. I'm not going to tell anyone my plans.

Maggie looks up from the page, smirking at the endurance and consistency of that last statement. She flips ahead to another entry. June 23, 1972.

Scowler Fowler, the lifer in charge of my flight, a tech sergeant, struts around the work area, his pot belly hanging over his belt. It's not as pronounced as some of the other lifers, more like the a training belly, like the additional wheels on a child's two-wheeler when they learn to ride. He's proud of his five stripes, earned after only seventeen years, and it must gall him that most of us have three stripes in less than four years. Never went to college. From Northern Alabama. Cocky. Loud. Stupid. And mean. Last week during a midnight shift, he crashed into the men's room looking for anyone sleeping in the stalls and surprised a captain. Got his ass chewed out, which he later took out on everyone else. But it earned him a new nickname: Cruiser. We all try to work the word "cruise" into our conversations whenever he's around, watching for a reaction, although it's unclear if he knows about the nickname.

Cruiser has it in for Jamie Grogan. Thinks he's gay. That Cruiser's Air Force shouldn't be polluted with people like Jamie. He singles Jamie out for extra duty, denigrates him in front of everyone, and yesterday, when he thought no one could overhear him, told Jamie he was gonna have his faggot ass dishonorably discharged. But Morris Tederman and I heard him and that night in the barracks, we talked about what we could do to protect Jamie, who we feared would do something rash and get himself in trouble. Morris said Cruiser would never let up. "As long as he's alive," he said. We sat in my barracks bay, talking by candlelight, listening to a Savoy Brown cassette tape. Morris sipped Jim Beam, easing himself into drunkenness, accepting in his state that killing Cruiser was our only option, expounding on the place, methods, and timing when we should "execute" him. "It'll be a mercy killing," he said. Morris decided it couldn't be done on base, that we'd have to surprise Cruiser when he was barhopping in the village, at night, on a stretch of dark road, where there would be no witnesses. We'd use a knife. Thrust it up into his chest, under his rib cage, straight into his heart. Drag the body into the roadside ditch and let it be found in the morning, long after we returned to base. In case anything happens to me, or for fuck's sake, Cruiser, and someone reads this journal, I think Morris was out-of-his-mind drunk and just letting off steam, not seriously considering murder. The specificity of his planning frightened me, as though he wasn't inventing the steps he'd take for killing Cruiser but describing some past murder. I told Morris I'm not a killer and he laughed. It didn't sound to me like a dismissive laugh, not a "shit, I was just kidding" laugh. More of a "never know what you'll do until the time comes" sort of laugh.

Nothing happened to Cruiser and he seems to have lost interest in Jamie, although I don't understand why. Someone says he received an anonymous note warning him to leave Jamie alone, but no one can confirm that, and the squadron is a cauldron for rumors. Every now and then, a typewritten note appears on the bulletin board in the work area, detailing a fresh rumor. Some are outlandish, such as when a note claimed the base commander had been discovered stoned and naked by security police riding a water buffalo down the runway. Others are political. Criticism of the war effort. Threatening war crimes trials for everyone involved after Nixon ends our role. The buddies I hang out with have always been left-leaning, but we maintained our opinions as undercurrents during the first years of our enlistments. Here, with one year to go, we grow bolder, expressing them as waves. Our squadron area sits on the edge of the base, bordering the perimeter, with two rows of barracks. The buildings at the end of row, where we live, are a no-man's land for the lifers. They don't venture down here. We smoke dope openly on the decks outside the barracks. Play our music as loud as we want. Party whenever we please. Cover our barracks walls with outlandish dayglo hippy posters. And cultivate political radicalism, huddling in circles, trying to one-up each other with our disgust for the Nixon administration, the war, the Air Force, American exceptionalism, and lifers. How we hate lifers. And eventually the talk turns to what each of us will do when we return to the "world."

The "world." A ghostly concept. More fantasy than reality for some. Married guys anticipate restoring stability in their lives, as though four years in the Air Force can be sloughed off like an old coat. Others vow to pick up interrupted lives where they left off, as though the rest of their world was treading water for four years in their absence. I listen to the ones who wish nothing more than to buy a van and drive around the country, their response to four years of being told what to do, where to go, and I feel sorry for them, fearing they'll find freedom illusory and depressing. When questioned about my plans, I shake my head and mutter that I'll go back to school. Nothing more specific than that.

And at every such gathering, fueled by dope and wine, people promise to stay in touch. A few plan to settle in Denver. I shrug when asked where I'll go. Everyone moves on.

Maggie closes the journal, considering how ungrounded, even in 1972, her uncle was with family. Or with his Air Force friends. She wants to ask him why he indulges in Zoom sessions with them now, when he seemed so intent on abandoning them when he left the Air Force. Then again, it parallels what he's doing with her. If she hadn't contacted him, he never would have reached out to her. Or would he? Is his resolve to remain secluded waning? Have her visits and the associated reminiscences awakened some impulse within him?

17.

I'm failing Maggie. I provide little information about Aidan and instead bicker with her like a schoolchild. It's petty and I spent the afternoon trying to fathom why. I stood on the bluff watching the waves, tame in comparison to those that pounded the sea walls in Okinawa. We'd sit atop the rocks, passing a joint, sipping from bottles of plum wine, damp from ocean spray, overawed with a perception of our tiny place in a massive world, belittled by the roaring power of an ear-shattering wave. Moments of introspective discovery shared with men with who I felt more kinship than my brother that I've tried, and failed, to replicate here on the beach during storms.

I showed her the Air Force journals. My matter-of-fact records of those years. There's little in them of family, of her father. Is the offering a bait-and-switch or a stalling tactic? I sense she feels pulled to Tucson, to Laura and my mother, but I want her to stay here. I'm reticent to tell her stories of Aidan that would embarrass me. How we compared masturbation techniques. Showed one another our first pubic hairs. Laughed when we woke with erections that made pissing almost impossible. Hyper-hormonal preteens floundering in shared ignorance. Or the moments when as young boys we united against parental rule, lying in our bunk beds belaboring the unfairness of some edict.

I hope Maggie gains insight about her father from what I reveal of myself, because I'm only singing half of the chorus.

Maggie's presence strengthens those memories and I should share them with her. But they're not the only ones. I've recalled and even dreamed about so many women, past lovers, nameless one-night stands, spurred by discussion of our fathers' failures as husbands. I'd like to explore her reasons for remaining childless, to see how they align with mine. As the eldest, are we more fearful of the kind of parents we'd be? Fated to repeat the mistakes made with us despite whatever best efforts we might have made to avoid them? "When I have kids, I won't treat them like this!" Yet the cycle repeats and it always seemed to me the only way to avoid the trap was not to play the game. I know I'd be a lousy father and besides, I had too much fun being unattached. The newness of a woman lured me, attracted me. New sexual preferences. New desires and practices. New vulnerabilities to identify and exploit. I catered to what a woman demanded of me sexually, asking what she enjoyed, shocking them at times when I asked what they did to make themselves come, and in spite of embarrassment, they revealed what they wanted, what they needed, and I gave it to them. I recall lying beside one woman who wet my fingers in her pussy and then directed them to her clit, which I massaged in a forceful circle while she held my head to the crook of her neck, murmuring "Oh God, yes," over and over. After she came, she straddled me and bucked up and down, begging me to come inside her. She wore her hair in a bob and strands slapped against her cheeks when she bounced. A nurse who swore she'd never marry a doctor. Our breakup was amicable. Attraction often expires as quickly as the wind dies.

Did Maggie cycle through affairs before meeting Samuel?

That's our divide. I have no Samuel in my life. Does she question why?

By getting Maggie's mother pregnant, Aidan adhered to the Breedlow pattern. Marry and then stray. Some don't possess the self-awareness to prevent them from marrying or fathering children. Our species would benefit from some men practicing childlessness.

I spent so much of my younger life pursuing sex, an irresistible urge from which I no longer suffer, but which I vividly recall. Getting fucked was my engine. Finding women to fuck consumed my non-working hours and I have Aidan to thank for debunking the idea that marriage was a necessary domino to sex. He confirmed the lesson taught by our father: you're only cheating if you're married, so I never felt any urge to marry every woman I fucked. No strings.

So much of the conflict between Aidan and me arose from striving not to be like one another and I've portrayed it to Maggie as mostly her father's effort. But I'm also culpable. Especially in relationships. I judged my little brother for marching lockstep in my father's path, but with a twist. Carnal self-indulgence wasn't wrong, the offense was disloyalty, unfaithfulness. Ergo. I heard stories about Aidan falling into relationships too quickly and I made myself unattainable as a result, but never considered those storytellers might be unreliable narrators, might have relayed those stories for a purpose. Certainly, Maggie understands this. The stories told to her have been filtered through the perspectives of two generations with different axes to grind. Her mother clung to victimhood and my mother clings to reconciliation.

Anger with my mother for using Maggie seems cruel considering her health, but as a child, when I seethed at her reluctance to confront my father, she threw Aidan in my path as a diversion, as a distraction. I saw through her tactics but played along, fighting with Aidan, my anger at her festering, when I should have passed the bitterness up the line to my father. I never centered my early fury on him. My mother, Aidan, and I carried the burden. He evaded that responsibility.

My journals may keep Maggie here a bit longer, but she will go to Tucson. I've nothing substantive to offer her about Aidan beyond opinions and conjecture. But maybe that'll satisfy some aspect of her curiosity. We rise from similar circumstances but we diverge when considering how we judge them. My family tethers snapped long ago; Maggie's bind her.

I took my guitar to the summer house while she read the journals. Strumming simple chord progressions, humming melodies, watching the beach like a sentinel, waiting for a call from Laura. In client meetings, silence fostered speculation, which could be useful. Men who approached us as though we could keep whatever they wanted hidden in a box had to be told that the scope of their problem would always exceed the volume of any box in which they tried to contain it. The summer house is my box today. A sense of inevitability hangs over me, as though Maggie's intrusion led to this moment and nothing I could have done would have altered events. This is a fulcrum moment when a nudge or a shift will upset my balance. My mentor told me the core of a client's problem often proved to be ego. Am I my own client?

I climb the stairs in the house to my office, pausing outside the door of the guest bedroom. Maggie's inside engrossed in a telephone call. Surely if something happened in Tucson, Laura would call me directly. Must be Samuel or one of her sisters. A lover once told me that in struggling not to be defined by my family, I also prevented being defined by a partner. Another explained that my selfishness grew out of being the first-born. I had been forced to share with my younger siblings and now wanted everything for myself, that I enjoyed *having* responsibilities but never *being* anyone's. When I replied that I never wanted to be responsible for anyone's happiness, she accused me of being as unfeeling as a sociopath, that I worked hard to prevent anyone knowing me. The *real* me. She likened me to Tarzan, swinging from one relationship to another, making sure I had a firm grip on the next vine before releasing the current one. "You treat relationships as though you're building a resume," she said. I smiled in response and she broke it off.

My family believes they know the real me, that they know me better than I know myself. I devoted years behaving like a chameleon in my professional and personal lives, understanding that no one's character is ever frozen, that no two narratives are identical. Guiding a client to accept differing perspectives often devolved into a tug-of-war, one Grayson and I often lost. My family engages in the same struggle and believes they will win. Then again, my parents had no expectations for me.

Maggie startles me by opening the bedroom door. "Were you eavesdropping?" she asks.

"Passing on the way to my office," I say. "How are you finding the journals?"

"Unemotional," she says. "Although in 1972 you begin to reveal more of your thoughts."

"The last year," I say. "All of us focused our energies on what we'd do after our discharge."

"But you kept your plans from your friends," she says.

I smile, remembering that year in Thailand, the swing in attitude of so many of us, from dwelling on an oppressive present to contemplating the scary possibilities of the future. "That was a long time ago."

"Always protecting your privacy." The etched lines at the corners of her eyes deepen when she smiles. I imagine my mother's lines only deepen when she frowns, but that might be unfair. "Any word form Laura?"

"Not yet," I say. "No news, right?"

"I was talking with my sister, Jess," Maggie says.

"Everything okay with your family?" I ask. "Mine's been such a burden."

"Hailey moving to Austin, Jess feeling like she'll be the last one living where we grew up." Maggie hesitates. "Like she's been abandoned by all of us." She glances at me. "Don't say it."

"Yeah, that'd be superfluous," I say. "Hungry?"

Maggie nods and we descend to the kitchen. She clutches her cell phone, placing it on the island top as she settles on a stool. "I expect it to ring every time I look at it," she says.

"Expectation warps time," I say. "Before your visit, every day seemed much like another. I'd often forget which day of the week it was. A concept so foreign to my life in Chicago, where I seemed aware of every minute of every hour. But here…time is transformed." I pause and glance toward the patio doors, remembering how even before the pandemic, it was a challenge to differentiate one day from another. "It might appear that nothing here changes, but that's a mistake I made when I first arrived, too. I had to match my sense of time to the pace of the changes around me. What's monumental is the level at which things here change. Tiny. Almost minuscule. The day I understood the passage of time here, when I harmonized my perception to the rhythm of it, was better than any rush I'd ever felt."

"That's quite a poetic way to describe the agony of waiting," Maggie says. "Are you sure you're not working on another novel?"

"If you stayed here long enough, you'd know what I mean."

"What's 'long enough'?"

I chuckle and ask what she wants for dinner.

"Something simple, I suppose. Sandwiches?"

"We can do that," I say.

As we gather the fixings on the island top, Maggie asks if I journaled while at Northwestern.

"I did, but they're lean compared to the Air Force ones," I say. "In Thailand, I had a lot more time on my hands than when I was in Evanston. But if you're interested, they're in the bin in the basement."

"What about the electronic ones?" she asks.

"I thought about making copies of those for you," I say, unraveling the twist tie on a bag of rye bread. "I have ham and smoked turkey."

Maggie pauses and I wonder if like me, she employs hesitation in her work as a default setting. "So how has this interruption in your routine affected your cadence, your awareness of time?"

"I know what day it is," I say, chuckling, but Maggie's face remains stoic. "I was a runner, did you know that?"

Maggie shakes her head.

"Sprinter. Wide receiver in high school. I loved faking out a cornerback, leaving him in my wake wondering how the fuck I was yards past him, praying he had safety help. In Chicago, I'd run along the lake for miles. Cleared my head. Liquified the stress into sweat. Here, I walk on the beach or sit in the summer house with my guitar. Sometimes I strum in open-D tuning until the instrument's reverberations synch with my body. Have you ever felt like that?"

Maggie shakes her head.

"Maybe it's nothing more than a mild flashback," I say, chuckling. This time she smiles.

"Did you ever meet a woman you thought you might want to stay with for life?"

"No." The speed of my answer surprises me. I thought of Sandrine as I replied, but we both knew our individual selfishness precluded any long-term partnership. "There's no one I ever wanted to spend that much time with. I'm sure most of the women I've known are happier forgetting me."

"That's pretty narcissistic." Maggie says.

"I think it's quite the opposite."

"Wanting them to forget what a dick you were?"

"What makes you think I was a dick?"

"I don't know," she says, laying tomato slices on ham. "Their absence? Did you always have a short attention span with them? Get bored easily? They never measured up to your standards?"

I recall my promise to be honest with Maggie. "Most didn't," I say. "And it wasn't quantity versus quality," I say. "Although I did enjoy the variety. The adventure of beginning a new relationship. Getting hot and heavy right from the start, whether it lasted a night, a week, or months."

"Wide not deep, right?" Maggie spreads garlic hummus on her bread, adds bib lettuce and slices the sandwich diagonally.

"Absolutely. I don't apologize for that," I say, and immediately know what Maggie will say.

"Telling that you thought it was an accusation," she says, grinning as she lifts her sandwich to her mouth. "And I don't believe you want people to forget you."

"Maybe just certain people."

She raises a finger as she chews. "I'll buy that."

"I find solitude quite bearable," I say.

"Were you a break-up artist?" Maggie asks.

"That's fair," I say. "There's artistry in making the woman initiate the break-up."

"If you're an asshole," Maggie says.

"I was an asshole." I bite into my own sandwich. "So I set boundaries," I say through my food. "Warned them that I wanted nothing long term. Just some mutual fun with no strings attached."

"And that worked?" Maggie's smile tells me she knows it didn't.

"More than you'd think. Hope sprung eternal for a few who believed they could change my mind. Change *me*."

"This is good ham," she says, holding up her sandwich. "As I read your journals, it occurred to me that you have an aversion to belonging. Your family. Your Air Force friends. Your lovers. Always keeping a distance. Even your home," she waves an arm, encompassing the open space. "Minimalism. But you can't minimize yourself, can you?"

"Just the opposite," I say. "What kind of person do you think surrounds himself with minimalism?"

Maggie laughs. "Okay. That fits." She pauses. "Talking with you is like entering maze."

"A former lover says when I open the door to a new room, I lock it behind me."

"Says?" Maggie asks. "Not said?"

I realize the slip of tongue and smile. "Sandrine. Lives in California. We stay in touch."

A screech from the yard distracts us and we hurry to the patio door. The Cooper's hawk stands on the lawn, its wings spread, a small black squirrel pinned in its claws. "The young ones haven't had time to learn the danger yet," I say.

My phone rings, startling both of us. It's Laura.

"How's Mom?" I ask, switching the receiver to speaker so Maggie, who grips my upper arm, can hear our conversation.

"The procedure was successful although she had a small stroke," Laura says.

"Shit," Maggie says.

"How bad?" I ask.

"Very minor," Laura says. "There are no lasting effects. She conscious, talking, asking about Elizabeth. The doctor says it's just something we have to be watchful about."

"And Elizabeth?" Maggie asks. She's close enough that I feel her body heat.

"Maybe today," Laura says.

I can think of nothing to say and Maggie moans, "Oh." I imagine Laura gripping her cell phone to her ear, head dipped, and wonder if she thinks about how differently Maggie and I receive this news.

"I'll call later," Laura says, disconnecting, leaving Maggie and me standing, shoulders touching, mulling over the brief call. I turn my head and the anguish registers on her face, the pain of connecting with a branch of the family her mother had shunned only to watch it disintegrate. I remain quiet, rather than utter some treacly reassurance. Nothing I say will offer consolation or comfort. The stages of life capture us all. My mother. Laura and me. Maggie. Elizabeth's children. Events overtake and envelope us, despite any attempt to insulate against them. When my father was dying, I capitulated to my mother's appeals and flew to Tucson. On the flight home, I wondered if it would have been kinder not to have come. I displayed the same indifference I'd employed as a petulant teen toward every member of my family, especially Aidan, and I knew that wounded my mother, who had hoped Dad's dying might affect a reconciliation. On that flight, I speculated about whether and how my mother had prepped Aidan for approaching me. Had she gotten him to agree to try and patch up our failed relationship? Mistake one: imagining even a failed relationship existed. Yet the thought caused wonder: did Aidan work as feverishly as I to ban all contact between us? Did he actively work to avoid me? Point of view, I muse, as Maggie releases my arm and walks to the sink, fills a glass with water, gulps until she drains it, then sets it on the counter, and heaves a breath.

Point of view, I think again. So crucial in my work. So difficult to convince clients to adopt. Had I really never wondered about my brother's point of view toward me? Toward our feud? Convinced it wasn't a feud because I refused to participate, had I fallen into the trap of self-delusion that so many of our clients had? That inability or refusal to contemplate someone else's view always frustrated Grayson and me. I never considered how Aidan viewed us in all the decades of our separation, insisting instead that I didn't care.

Maggie turns from the sink, bracing her hands on the counter behind her. Sadness exhausts her expression and stance. "I think I'm going to drive home and then fly to Tucson," she says.

"I understand." I brace for her to ask if I'll also fly to Tucson.

"I need to see Samuel." Her voice cracks and she raises a hand to wipe her eyes.

There's nothing for me to say. No kind way to tell her I will not go to Tucson. Not for my sister's funeral. Not to comfort my mother, who will surely not be permitted to attend her child's funeral. Not to unburden Laura. Or to console Hank, Luke, or my nephews and nieces, who don't know or care about me. Have I so completely succeeded in remaining a ghost that my appearance would cause more anxiety than my absence? Much as Mom threw Aidan at me to distract from my anger with my father, my arrival in Tucson would confuse everyone, sidetrack from their grief. It would be an unkindness, not solace.

Maggie pushes from the counter and walks toward the staircase. I watch her climb with nothing of the energy she's displayed since arriving. Does she feel defeated? Arriving with hopes for completing the imperfect puzzle of her father but leaving after suffering another loss. How can she judge me as anything other than a disappointment? The journals. I'll copy them to a thumb drive for her.

She pauses on the landing and turns back toward me. I expect her to ask me to join her, one last attempt to cajole me into acquiescing to my mother's wishes.

"I'm sorry," she says. "I know you put on a game face, but this must affect you."

Her unexpected comment confounds me. I'm so cynical. I falter. Is she sincere or manipulative?

I nod in response and watch her retreat toward the guest bedroom, remembering the pride I felt in readjusting a client's point of view, contrasting it with the earlier epiphany of never having considered Aidan's. When Mom relayed news of his life, she buried disappointment with his decisions, and never communicated any opinions he expressed about our dispute, which is how she regarded it. A disagreement to be solved, but for her benefit, not ours. Had I allowed this view to taint my own? That when Aidan was alive, Mom sought a burying of the hatchet for her own peace of mind, not ours?

What frame of mind do you have to adopt to believe that someone else's motives are always selfish? Or in constant conflict with your own?

Laura was the one to call when Aidan died and I wondered why it wasn't my mother, but only briefly. What did I think in that moment? That the responsibility for telling a son that another son had died should be my mother's responsibility? That amid the grief of losing a child, she should be the messenger? There's logic in Laura conveying all messages now.

I climb the stairs and pause in the guest bedroom doorway. "When Mom spoke about Aidan, I pretended not to care, but knowing we were still so disparate in our lives made me feel better than him."

She stands beside the bed, her suitcase open, rumpled clothes tangled within.

"I never missed him. Never missed the arguments, the confrontations, the constant tension and striving to be everything he wasn't."

"It feels like you're cramming for an exam," she says. "Now that I'm leaving, you're data dumping so I don't feel it's been a wasted trip." She balls a t-shirt and tucks it into a corner of the case."

"Wouldn't it be better to leave in the morning?" I ask.

"I'd like to have more time to talk about my father," she says. "Knew I'd have to be patient and let you set the pace for leaking information. Let you be in control. But there are some things you can't control." She scans the room and sighs. "One good thing about minimalism, you know right away if you've left anything behind." She zippers the case shut. "If you hear anything, please text me."

I nod as she lifts the case and wheels it past me toward the stairs.

In the kitchen she refills the glass with water and sips slowly. I glance to the yard but the hawk and the squirrel are gone. She upends the glass in the sink.

"I'm gonna have to make so many piss stops."

"I can't believe you're leaving so suddenly," I say.

"We had so much more to say, is that it?" She sets her mouth in a tight line.

Point of view again. She's no happier with the afternoon's developments than I. "Something like that," I say.

"Drips and drabs about Dad, right? Playing out the line. Using me for entertainment."

"That's not what I intended," I say.

She bobs her head, the sarcasm of the gesture unmistakable, walks toward the hallway, wheeling her suitcase, then pauses and turns to me. "Your mother and sister still love you," she says. "Do you want to matter to anyone? To them? We always fight the things we love and you've made it an art form. You could teach masterclasses in the duplicity of escapism. No one's completely untethered."

I remain silent; I'm not going to make this a debate.

Maggie stares at me. "You should write another book," she says. "Call it 'The Hermit's Handbook.' Make the main character an unadulterated misanthrope. It'll be more believable if he's an only child."

I follow her to the front door and step outside as she lifts her case into the trunk, slams it shut and then pauses at the driver's door. "Text me," she says. In moments, she's gone, and I'm inflamed by the abruptness of her absence, the assault on the constancy of our time together.

I return to the house, recalling that I have not filled the bird feeders. Hauling the seed bucket to the yard, I pause and examine where the Cooper's hawk snared the squirrel. Blood droplets and a tuft of black fur mark the spot. I scan the trees for any sign of the predator but see no birds of any species. Filling the feeders is a mindless task that allows my thoughts to ramble. Maggie's departure disturbs me. Did I keep our relationship as one-sided as with clients, with the men who overestimated the size of the bubbles containing their crises? Men who expected grandiose engagements rather than measured approaches. Grayson and I smiled when these men spent money at the firm to avoid spending more money somewhere else. It was always about the money. The greed. Some acknowledged their fear that whatever crisis drove them to us would harm the bottom line. The stock price. Their profits. Their bonuses. That they would not escape financial pain.

Like I feared I would never escape my origins. My family. For years I took neither pleasure nor any other emotion in distancing myself from them, but Maggie exposed that feigned neutrality.

I cover the bucket and replace it in the garage, then climb the steps to the hallway, retrieve a beer from the refrigerator and take it to the patio, recline on a chaise, and, while waiting for the birds to arrive, experience another episode of my peripheral vision wavering, my sense of balance fluttering, entertaining the possibility of an ancient acid trip unsettling my consciousness.

But that was a long time ago.

18.

Maggie left four days ago. Days during which I had more contact with my family than in the past four years. I took my camera to the beach each evening, flushed with the certainty that nature would reward me with an extravagant sunset, recompense for the day's conversations. Certainty or aspiration? The first night, I gathered driftwood, stacking the logs in a cone within a fire pit I hollowed out by hand, and lit a fire as the sun approached the horizon. I sat with the blaze to my back and shot photos every thirty seconds until a mere strip of amber on the horizon matched the color of the sparks rising in the dark sky, smirking as I correlated the dying light with my sister's life, cheap symbolism I could repeat the next night and the night after that. In Okinawa we often ended a night of debauchery viewing a sunrise over the ocean, went home, slept for eight hours, and then crossed the island to enjoy a sunset over the ocean. In Chicago sunrises captivated me and invigorated my mornings, but here I behold sunsets to mark my nights, accepting the difference as illumination of the two competing stages of my life.

Laura telephoned before midnight the night Maggie left with the news of Elizabeth's death and as I had in our earlier conversation sympathized as though she were a friend losing a sister, not a sibling commiserating a shared loss. People found it off-putting when I told them I didn't know my youngest sister and brother, but they were five and three when I left for the University of Missouri, to them a babysitter who happened to be an older brother. Luke, while I was in the Air Force, had a vague notion of where I was and what I was doing. Mom told me she shielded him from TV news of the war to keep him from worrying about me, but she was only partially successful. He understood I was at war but hadn't the capacity to comprehend what that meant and when I returned on leave, he quizzed me based on snippets he'd gleaned from movies, confusing World War II with Vietnam, mistaking North Vietnam for Japan. I was thankful he had not yet started school, fearful of the berating older kids would give him for being so off base with stories of his older brother.

I asked about Mom. Recovering. Stable. The doctor recommended waiting to tell her about Elizabeth until the morning.

"I already called Maggie," Laura said, and I glanced at the clock on the microwave. She'd be home by now, no doubt confirming a flight to Tucson.

Laura and I spoke for a few more minutes, avoiding the issue of me coming to Arizona. I carried the phone to the patio door and gazed at my yard, illuminated by the industrial light mounted above the summer house door, a fixture I found in a junk shop in Holland, tempered glass shrouded in a metal cage. George insisted I use an old incandescent bulb for its pale yellow light, rather than the austere white of an LED. "Atmosphere," he said, reinforcing the incongruities between the summer house and my concrete box. A glowing globe within the darkness of the lake beyond. My mind transformed mundane observations into commentary infused with implication. I resisted, hostile to living a life defined by metaphor, as the shimmering of my vision startled me, accompanied in this instance with tiny pricks of bright white light and a tingling sensation on the skin of my arms, like a tiptoeing spider; I wrenched away from the view and slumped on the sofa, leaning my head back, and clamped my eyes shut until the sensation passed.

I recalled two instances from my and Aidan's childhood. The first a moment when Mom took us to the neighborhood pool one summer, dressing us in identical swimsuits and white bucket hats to protect us from the sun. As she lounged on a folding chaise, watching us in the kiddie pool, a woman stopped and looked at us, turned to Mom and said, "Such adorable twins." Aidan and I had experienced this misapprehension before and usually raced one another to correct the speaker. But this time we exchanged glances and without speaking a word staged an on-the-spot performance as a two-headed entity. We waded to the side of the pool, rested our arms on the edge and spoke to our mother, alternating each monotonic word.

Aidan: "Mom."

Me: "Can."

Aidan: "We."

Me: "Go."

Aidan: "In."

Me: "The."

Aidan: "Grown-up."

Me: "Pool?"

The woman stared at us, her mouth gaped, and Aidan and I pulled our lips back in exaggerated, unnatural smiles.

"No boys," Mom said, dipping her head so the wide brim of her straw sunhat covered her attempt not to laugh. "Not today."

Me: "Aw."

Aidan: "Mom."

Me: Please."

Mom shook her head as the woman hurried away and Aidan and I kicked from the pool edge, splashing one another.

The other memory: a night we heard something crash in the kitchen. Aidan, five or six years old I think, grew fearful whenever Mom and Dad argued, but that night was the first we ever heard anything break. He whimpered and asked if he could climb into bed with me. I feared he'd pee on my mattress or fall from the top bunk, so I climbed down and burrowed beside him under his quilt. His body quivered and the annoyance I felt at having to calm him, this aggravating little baby, turned to sympathy at how acutely my parents' bickering frightened him. It wasn't always a battle between the two of us. Maggie should know this.

I wonder if he ever outgrew his fearful nature. Did he have moments of awareness during his heart attack of what he faced? That he would not be granted any reprieve? Did he think of his god? Of his family? Any of his families?

The day after Elizabeth's death, I emailed Maggie my digital journals and spoke with my mother, who sounded too subdued and restrained to attempt even her usual passive aggressiveness about my isolation. Despondent I'm certain by another child's death or her own approaching mortality. I felt empathy for her as I looked around my home, reflecting on Maggie's observation that surrounding myself with minimalism doesn't maximize me, and that if I inherited any of my mother's longevity, this box will not be my last residence. Sometimes I believe I could welcome death for the respite it would provide from thinking.

Mom confirmed her doctor banned her from attending Elizabeth's service, although Hank was trying to convince the pastor to allow her to watch it live on his cell phone. Holy shit, I thought, please don't make a video and post it online like Aidan's funeral. Elizabeth, she said, would be buried in the same cemetery as my father, though the graves would be distant from one another, and when I said, "How appropriate," Mom actually chuckled before chastising me. I wanted to know how she felt, a woman nearly a century old, who buried two husbands and now two children, also thinking the reflections on such a long, eventful life would be more insightful from someone other than my mother. I'm sure she would tell me I'm beyond redemption.

Elizabeth was much more Mom's baby girl than Laura, whom she resented as Dad's little princess. To me, she was the toddler underfoot when I came home from high school, the shy mop head who stood behind my mother when I left for college, the wide-faced girl who didn't hide her expressions of confusion when I visited on leave from the Air Force, and whose life after that remained a subject about which my mother provided intermittent updates when we spoke. I did not attend her wedding and struggle remembering the names of her children. We were siblings and strangers and I've mustered more grief for lost Air Force buddies than for her. I'll never experience the anguish of losing a spouse, which itself is mournful; it spares me the heartache so many people in Tucson feel now, but it also reinforces how I'm close to no one. That I choose to be alone, which evokes pity from my family. When I ended the call with my mother, I felt gratitude. If I flew to Tucson, my presence would be nothing more than a shallow public relations performance. An unconvincing charade. A provocation. For my family, absence makes the heart stay calmer.

I fear my solitude will not remain quiet anymore, that Maggie, even though I've been such a source of frustration, will remain a presence. We spoke after Elizabeth's funeral, while she and Samuel were staying at Laura's house, and I told her I was composing journal entries of memories of Aidan. She fell silent for a moment before thanking me. We avoided the barbed exchanges that marked our last conversation, but she shocked me, saying I should have had children and that Aidan should have remained childless. The inference that she would have preferred me as a father I left unsaid. She wondered if I'd slipped back into my daily routines since her departure and I assured her I was capable of being both alone and busy, and that I looked forward to talking with her when she returned to Iowa.

This morning while patrolling the beach, bagging trash, greeting strolling folk, I unearthed memories of Aidan, none with any more density than a shadow, but their emergence thawed me. In the afternoon, I telephoned Sandrine, who told me of the friend she lost to COVID, a watercolor artist who had developed cataracts, noting how her altered vision affected her painting, ascribing an ethereal impressionism to her landscapes, a progression Sandrine could trace as the cataracts worsened. When her ophthalmologist performed surgery to remove them, correcting her vision, her painting reverted to earlier form and gallery sales fell off. Buyers preferred the dreamy approximations of what she saw with imperfect vision to realistic portrayals. Sandrine lamented her friend's loss, sad that she died before regaining confidence in her artistic expression.

We reminisced about Chicago nights, gallery openings, concerts, author readings, waking in my bedroom to a Lake Michigan sunrise, and how we each marvel now only at sunsets, concluding with my promise that when the pandemic eases, I'll visit her.

I wrote the first entry in my Maggie journal detailing the two recalled stories of Aidan, hoping she will appreciate them, prefacing the recollections by saying that her visit had reawakened sections of my aging brain, mentioning the beach walk, and while typing, received an email alert for my annual physical. Mom refused to speculate on whether Elizabeth would have survived if she hadn't delayed seeking treatment, had received the vaccinations. George told me his father never went to the doctor for fear he'd find out he was dying and I believe that's a common defense against a pervasive fear, a corollary of "ignorance is bliss." Until it's too late and they recall the adage "an ounce of prevention." Even as I read the reminder of my appointment, I question mentioning the phenomenon to my doctor. Maybe it's low blood pressure or low blood sugar, something simple I can address on my own. When I moved here from Chicago, I asked my doctor, who had treated me for decades, for a recommendation of a local GP. He mentioned a colleague with whom he attended medical school, (I envisioned another elderly white man), who had a daughter who practiced in Grand Haven. She graduated from the University of Michigan Medical School and her office is festooned with maize and blue mementos. Each year when Northwestern and Michigan play, we wager a bottle of cabernet from a local winery.

I effortlessly snowballed Elizabeth's death, Mom's procedure, Sandrine's friend, the shimmering vision and balance issues into a stubborn knob of anxiety and paused at the computer reassessing time: how much longer I'll live in the concrete box; how many more times I'll clean up other people's trash on the beach; how many more sunsets I'll photograph; how many more memories of Aidan I'll recall.

Grayson swore the struggle with my family was a struggle for identity. "Every teen engages in it," he said. "But you've perpetuated the fight. You've never settled on who you are, either because you don't know or because you *do* know and don't like what you found."

I've thought about that during the past four days. Maggie's now a new conduit between me and the origins I loathed, from which I strove to distance myself in emotional, intellectual, and geographic terms. She's the only Breedlow with whom I feel any kinship, with whom I feel on equal footing. Sandrine once told me that feeling superior to others is only arrogant when it's expressed. She believed silence reaffirms true superiority and that the loudest voices pinpoint the dumbest people. "Listen and learn," she cautioned. I link that to Grayson's suggestion about my search for identity, Maggie's belief that my living alone is an indulgence, and characterize myself as a lifelong idealist battling unrelenting cynicism, a multi-millionaire in a luxury prison forged in compromise and fakery. I imagine Maggie smirking at such a chaotic judgement, accusing me of inflicting word-jumbling, sensory overload to confuse a client. So many people regarded my work as the business of obscuring truth with illusion, holding it in mild contempt, until the moment they needed our services. Like lawyers: detested until they're needed. Then the Shylocks become saviors.

I swallowed my loathing of hypocrisy to finance these years in my box above the beach, and among all the things I've done in my life that deserve an apology, this isn't one of them. Grayson touched on the truth. He recognized the struggle but missed a crucial detail: I kept moving as I rebelled, hopeful that in the next place I paused, I'd win the battle. So I moved and moved, settling in Chicago when I understood the struggle was internal, was within me. I need to explain to Maggie that I understand the battle never ends. Being static is surrender, which is death. I hope within the brevity of that statement is drama. Is truth.

On a visit during the construction of the house, I overheard a laborer say it looked like a tomb. A coworker laughed but I paused to consider how no two people ever hear words the same way. What they saw as a mausoleum, I envisioned as a refuge from the demise of a way of life. Of being a problem-solver in business who never accepted his role in the problems created in his personal life. Of being a coward who avoided risk-taking.

At times when I stand on the bluff, I imagine I'm an explorer arriving on the shore, my breath arrested not by a lake trapped by land on all sides, but an ocean I could sail through endlessly. When storms batter the lake, I imagine they're punishing the land, and I watch how the rain drives the downpour, understanding the phrase "sheets of rain," as though I can look along a plane of raindrops extending from the house to the bluff.

I receive an email notice, a reply to my message to Maggie.

She thanks me for the journals and attaches a photo of my mother, gripping the arms of a wheelchair, the tubing of a nasal cannula looped over her ears. White hair matted on one side of her head as though she'd slept on it. Her eyes bright and blue, as though untroubled by the apparatus surrounding her. Smiling. Her teeth yellowed from age. Sitting upright, her stature defies the grief of recent days, and I imagine Harriet Breedlow outliving me, presiding over a family gathering to memorialize my death, a celebration of regret, of burned bridges, of discussions about how my leaving affected each survivor, conversations mourned because they never happened when the deceased was alive. Pledges to stop measuring life in absences. My family never seemed concerned about legacy. My father barely managed the present without compounding his anxiety with thoughts of the future, a man who demanded fear rather than respect, and Mom concentrated on mothering five children, even after she married Scott. Necessity limited the scope of her planning. I revise their lack of encouragement when I was a child from intention to ignorance; nothing in their backgrounds equipped them to provide inspiration. If I could go back to that boy and explain his parents' shortcomings, would I steer him toward benevolence rather than enmity? I viewed the price of staying in contact my family as crippling. How would a change in point of view confound my search for identity now? Memory is time travel.

The only time Grayson and Iris visited me here, he paused, surveyed the house, then joked that I'd finally engineered my emotional armor into reality. I should call him and affirm how especially during the pandemic, the design of my concrete box allows me to remain protected, curious and creative.

I respond to Maggie's email, thanking her for the photo of my mother, I muse that memories are like wind on the lake: they can be whimsical, reassuring, or savage, but as they occur to me, I'll record them in the journal and send them to her.

> *Since you left, I've mused that I need to create a list of as many synonyms for the word "silence" as Aleuts have for the word "snow." I'd love for you to see the house in winter when the light from a full moon reflects off the lake and glows on the snow. The night seems to disappear. I may dial back my obsession with privacy and isolation to mere rigor. Maybe you and Samuel can plan a visit for later in the summer.*

I review the two stories about Aidan and chuckle: they resemble press releases. When I wrote my novel, I kept a sticky note on the monitor, reminding myself not to succumb to that ingrained style.

Public relations now…for the young for whom technology was a childhood appendage. Who documented their lives on social media. It may make me sound old and grumpy, but talented people crafting persuasive messages no longer matters. Misinformation, *disinformation*, are the practice. Lying today about something you stated yesterday without shame. With angry conviction. Time…I've aged out of my usefulness.

George visited today. No chores, just checking in. Said he noticed your car was gone and wanted to know how your visit went. I confessed that I'd provoked you and stammered when he asked why. Been reviewing my behavior since you left: if I knew your presence would aggravate me, then why did I ask you to come? Too many superficial reasons came to mind and I dismissed them. I don't want to believe I'm shallow, so obviously there must have been a deep-seated reason. My gift for grasping every point of view, right? But that's the contradiction that's been chewing at me. Not when it came to my family. Your father. That road was a two-way lane of inaccessibility and anyone I perceived as allied with him deserved the same indifference. Through high school, the Air Force, college, and the PR firm, I honed a persona of detached professionalism. Like armor, someone once told me, that I never shed. I believed I'd shed it when I retired and moved to this box, because no one here provokes a need for it. Until you rapped on the patio door that day. Point of view. My first thought that day was fear, that a long-lost child had tracked me down. A threatening tether from my past. Imagine my relief when you turned out to be Aidan's daughter. I confess I never considered your existence. Your sisters' existence. The suspicion that bloomed when you said you'd been talking to my mother. I felt nothing but resistance until we sat in the living room and I hatched the scheme: using you to channel a message to my mother to give up. To stop hoping for a magical reunion, a prodigal return of her son. It wasn't fair to you, Maggie. I'm sorry. I failed, or refused to see, beyond what I understood my mother wanted from you and thus me. I had another memory of your father this morning when I filled the bird feeders, smiling at the one-sided nature of my relationship to the birds that enjoy my efforts. I provide them with seed, with sustenance, and they provide me with the enjoyment of watching them, of noting the beauty of their colors. But that's a fallacy. There's no intention in their behavior. They're dumb animals. Our species has imbued their species with beauty, with meaning, with wonder. Used them to predict seasonal change. All for our own selfish reasons. But my point was feeding the birds. Mom tells the story of when Aidan was first eating solid food, how I'd plead to spoon mashed peas and strained apricots into his mouth, how he opened it in anticipation, like a baby bird. She said I hovered around him like a guard dog, tossing a ball through the slats of his playpen, watching him crawl and retrieve it, and that the first time he ever stood upright was in that playpen to greet me.

I don't remember it. Can't swear it isn't a family myth. But it's distant enough from the battles between us that it seems unnecessary to lie about it. There's always conflict among siblings. It's inevitable. Good parenting can defuse it. My mother and father didn't and you can draw your own conclusions about how I still regard them.

It's clever, I think, to measure stages in my life by the women who figured most prominently during each period. The Mom, Adriane, Maria, Nancy, Solange, Becca, and Carolyn chapters. Too many subchapters to recall. And then the Sandrine chapter. Sandrine saga, or epic? Something with longevity. The final chapter will be the Maggie chapter.

During last night's sunset, I turned to face the house, marveling at how the color pallet painted the expanse of glass in brilliance, surrendering to the analogy of looking backward instead of forward, and I imagined you and Samuel sitting on the patio, not as guests but as residents. I'm going to bequeath you the house. It's only a box and you can fill it with whatever makes you feel comfortable and secure. The notion of you purging the minimalism makes me smile, as does the image of you and Samuel patrolling the beach, Samuel holding the black plastic bag while you drop the trash into it, the two of you gazing up and down the shore, remarking once again how far from Iowa it feels. The two of you sharing a bottle of wine beside the fireplace during a spring storm, lightning illuminating the lake surface like and the distant horizon like a camera flash. Samuel lugging the galvanized bird seed buckets to the yard as the northern cardinals, black-capped chickadees, hooded warblers, house wrens, American goldfinches, blue-gray gnatcatchers, white-breasted nuthatches, tufted titmice, red-headed woodpeckers, rose-breasted grosbeaks, scarlet tanagers, sparrows, wrens, and of course the sparrows, wait for him to refill the feeders.

Or if it pleases you, sell everything and look for your happiness elsewhere. Just remember that I kept moving thinking my life would improve if I could only find just the perfect place to live it, but too often the move was an escape from something, not an escape to something.

I'm unsure how much time I'll spend with Maggie correcting and contradicting the stories she's heard from Laura and my mother, the exaggerations and fictions. That's an itch better left unscratched, which reminds me of what my mother told us as children when we'd pick at the scabs of skinned knees and knuckles: "Leave it alone! The itching means it's healing."

But that was a long time ago.

About the Author

Photo by Robin S. Tryloff Copyright 2022
All right reserved.

In the summer of 1999, John M. McNamara was selected to receive a professional artist residency at the Ox Bow Summer Arts Program for the School of the Art Institute of Chicago in Saugatuck, Michigan. His short fiction has appeared in numerous journals. He is also the author of: *Hunter's War, A Final Reflection, Harmony House, The Dreams of Teddy Schreck, Madonna, The Unabridged Songwriter, Summers on the Nebraska Shore, Failing Billy; Finbar Lovely at the Crossroads*; and *Renner's Reboot*

www.ingramcontent.com/pod-product-compliance
Lightning Source LLC
LaVergne TN
LVHW012045160826
845678LV00014B/2704

* 9 7 9 8 3 6 8 0 1 6 8 1 8 *